Angel

Mary E. Kingsley

D0110719

Little Falls Press

ANGEL
Mary E. Kingsley

Printed in the United States of America.
Little Falls Press
5185 MacArthur Boulevard, NW #721
Washington, D.C. 20016
littlefallspress@gmail.com

For more information about this book visit www.maryekingsley.com

Edition ISBNs
Softcover 978-0-578-09535-6
E-book 978-0-578-09534-9

First Edition 2011.

Cover design by Pete Garceau
Book design by Christopher Fisher
Interior vector art designed by Novi Candrasari

To my parents, Robert and Jeanne Jernigan,
honoring their sixty years of marriage and their legacy of love and wisdom.

Angel

Prologue

There's this picture of all of us sitting on the front porch that I just *know* can help me find the answers I'm looking for—that is if I stare at it long enough. Someone has written the date on the back, *August 1960*. It's one of the only ones I have of my daddy, Calvin Stone Bishop III, who's been gone as long as I can remember—and no, he's not dead. He's just gone.

He was good-looking then, no doubt about it, with his small, fine face, sharp eyes, and his light-colored hair combed just so. He's wearing a plaid short-sleeve shirt and is holding me in his lap, just like he's held my heart in his hands for all of my thirteen years. Trouble is he won't take care of it or give it back to me either. I look and look into those eyes of his to see if I can pick up on anything that would help me understand, anything that warned of the heartache to come.

Mama, whose name is Ruth, is on Daddy's left and kind of leaning in towards him. It looks like she might be taller than he is if she was sitting up straight. She's got on a light sleeveless dress and has her hands clasped together just in front of her knees. She's a slip of a girl, hardly looks any older than I am right now with her freckled nose and ponytail, but I know she is because I wasn't even born until she was nineteen.

Here are some things I know about Mama that the picture doesn't show. Number one, it's in black and white so you can't see that she has orange hair just like mine, down past her shoulders and kind of bushy, especially when it's damp out. I don't know why people always say red hair, because it's not. A stop sign's red and so is a tomato, but our hair is orange.

My grandmother on Daddy's side, Naomi, says Mama can't get all the credit for me having it, that I got it from them too since they're the ones with Irish in their blood. But if Naomi's part Irish she sure doesn't look it to me. Her skin is leathery and brown and her gray hair is speckled through with strands of straight black hair from her younger days.

Number two of the things I know about Mama you can't see in this picture is that she wants to be a doctor. She went back to school when I was little and got her nursing degree and now she's almost quit smoking entirely. She works with cancer patients up at the hospital, but she's been telling me as long as I can remember that she wishes she could have gone to medical school. Naomi's got a thing or two to say about that, too, says it's not right for women to be doctors because they'd have to look at naked men they're not married to. She's honestly serious about that.

The third thing about Mama you can't tell from this picture is that she really does love me. Sometimes she just doesn't know how to show it.

Daddy is way older than Mama. He had a whole life before he met her but I don't know much about that, either, only that he was married before and that his first wife left him before they had any kids. Aunt

Patsy told me she left because she didn't want to have a baby with him, but that's Patsy talking and Naomi always says never mind what she says, she'll say anything because her mind is gone.

Aunt Patsy is Daddy's stepsister. I wouldn't say her mind is *gone*, even if I have to admit she sure can come up with some whoppers. In the picture she's on his right, sitting up real straight and looking strict in her pointy glasses. She's wearing a long-sleeve blouse with a collar that buttons up right at the neck. It doesn't look too comfortable and neither does she, for that matter. Her hair is dark and it looks kind of messy, going all here and there like she could have used some help fixing it.

Right behind us sitting on chairs on the porch are Grandmother Naomi and Grandpa Joe, her second husband and Patsy's father. He's got a great big grin on his face. You can tell he's the kind person with a lot of love in his heart. Naomi looks just like herself, still short and round and mad. She's wearing what she calls a house dress, which is more or less a sack. It's got big flowers all over it and she's pretty well filling up that chair.

Daddy looks so handsome. He's smiling like he's proud to be sitting there with his daughter on his lap and his young wife and sister on either side of him. My little baby hands are together as if I'm clapping. I look all happy, just like a baby should, and it doesn't make a bit of difference that Patsy's just his stepsister because in this picture, we are all a family. But that didn't last.

"Where's Daddy? What's he doing? Why isn't he here?" Wish I had a nickel for every question I've asked about him. He had to work far away, offshore on the oil rigs, they said. I guess the Christmas presents and birthday cards I got from him were supposed to make up for him not being there.

"Well, why can't he get time off to come and visit?"

"He's got a real important job," they'd explain...*as if.*

"Did I cry a lot when I was little?" I'd ask Mama.

"What? Well, every baby cries!"

"I mean, did I cry so much I was just driving everybody crazy all the time?"

"Like you are right now, you mean? I don't know, Angel. I don't remember!"

Naomi is no better, so learning the story of my life is a lot harder than you might imagine.

"Must've been awful crowded around here," I say, "with Joe, Mama, Daddy, Patsy, and *then* me! Why, my being born must've been the straw that broke the camel's back."

"Girl, you need to hush up, rest your head, and forget it. And while you're at it, you can get down on your knees and ask the Lord for forgiveness."

"Forgiveness for what?"

"Ungratefulness, that's what! Here you got a roof over your head and food on the table and all you can do is whine about this and that."

But I don't care what she says. I already know I'm plenty full of sin and I've never been too good at resting my head about anything, especially when it comes to the puzzle of this family. Trying to understand my own life is kind of like trying to remember a dream. You get a piece here and there but you know there's more to it. You know you haven't got hold of the whole thing, but the more you grasp for it the more it seems to slip away. Still, you want it and you want it bad, because you know there's something in it you need, something that would really help you go on.

I may have been young but they never fooled me. I could see that everybody else's daddy had days off from work. I knew they'd teach their kid to ride a bike, they'd cook pancakes on Saturday and take them to get ice cream cones. They'd put them up on their shoulders to watch the Fourth of July parade go by and take them to the carnival— or if they didn't, even if they stayed inside in a dark room all weekend watching football on TV and burping up beer, at least they were *there*.

Did I run Daddy off? That's what I'm thinking.

They named me Angel because I was sent from heaven, they said, but I bet if they had it to do over again they'd surely pick something else. Angels are supposed to bring good news and fix things. They come with bright light, beautiful voices, and wide open wings. But as far as I can tell, after I came along everything went dark, and no one seems to hear me at all. I'm an angel whose wings are tied.

Chapter One

Mama and I live here in Riley, Tennessee, with Naomi. We're down in a valley so there're mountains all around us, everywhere you look. Though Mama does give me a ride in the rain and snow, most days I walk to school, and I feel like I'm walking right through the seasons with those mountains, from warm sunny September and crisp October all the way to white hot June and everything in between. One day they're misty and mysterious and the next sparkling with light.

Sometimes the sight of those mountains makes me feel closed in—trapped, like I'll be a teenager walking to school forever and ever and I'll never get out—like something out of *The Twilight Zone*. But there are other times, especially in the fall when the light falls like magic dust, when my heart lifts up over everything about my life and I'm free.

Riley's not a big town, but we do have two junior high schools and two movie theatres, the Star and the Grand. There's a civic auditorium and a big new high school that's real modern, where your class is in something called a pod, I guess because space travel is the wave of the future.

Other than going to the movies or swimming at the Legion pool in the summer, there's not a whole lot to do around here. Sometimes we walk to Abdul's Grocery on Saturday for penny candy. If you have a quarter you can buy lunch, fifteen cents for a hot dog, a nickel for a Coke and another nickel for a candy bar. When you're a little kid you mainly just run around the neighborhood and the ravine and try to think up something different to do. Then when you get your driver's license the thing to do is drive your car down to First Street on Friday nights and cruise up and down yelling, "Whoooo! Whooooo!" so everybody else will know you're there. I don't know what happens to people when they turn sixteen to make them think this is fun, but I sure hope it doesn't happen to me.

Mama's people live all the way over in Memphis, a whole day's drive from here. We haven't seen them in a long time, I guess because Memphis is clear across the state, but why Mama didn't take me back to be with her family after Daddy left I don't know.

Our house is two stories with wooden sides and a front porch. We used to sit out there on a nice evening, if it wasn't too hot. Naomi would always be doing something in her lap, snapping beans or doing her needlepoint. Mama read, and I would just watch the neighbors go by, but now we have our shows. I like *The Waltons* and *Sonny and Cher*. Mama likes *M*A*S*H* and we'll all sit up late to watch *Marcus Welby, M.D.*, which is Naomi's favorite.

Inside it always smells like something good, a pot roast or pork chops, or a pie baking. Naomi's mostly in the kitchen, humming her gospel tunes while she fixes supper. There might be the whistle of mustard greens cooking down in the pressure pot, or the whooshing of the attic fan on a warm night.

Out back there's a deep yard with a great big old elm tree right in the middle, and a swing hanging from it they say Daddy put up for me.

If he did, it was way before I was big enough to use it, not too long after that porch picture was taken. I know this because even one year after that, a family photo would have looked real different.

For one, Grandpa wouldn't have been in it—he died of a heart attack that summer. Patsy was gone too. By that time her disease had gotten so bad they had to move her to a place where they could take care of her better than we could at home. She's been there all this while and now I'm living in her old room. As for Daddy, his spot would already be empty as well.

If anybody'd even thought to take that other family picture, it would've been me, Mama, and Naomi. It's been that way ever since—until now, which is why I'm telling all of this in the first place, in case you're wondering. Here's how it all started.

It was barely a week ago when we were sitting around the kitchen table having supper. It was just us and our family friend Dennis, who was there cutting some tree limbs out back when it started raining. Naomi had asked him to stay and eat, which she does from time to time when he's over. She likes him all right because he goes to our church and he raves about her cooking.

He's been coming around our house for a while now, mostly to help out but sometimes just for a meal. Mama looks different when he's there. Normally she hardly ever wears make-up. Her skin is white underneath her freckles and she tends to look pale and girlish, but when she came to the table she had on lipstick and wore her hair down instead of in a ponytail. Before, I'd have wondered why anyone would put on lipstick right before supper, but now I'm thirteen and I don't need to wonder anymore.

I like having Dennis over because Naomi's always in a better mood when she's cooking for people and Mama seems happy. He's a friendly looking guy, one of those big, gentle types. When he smiles, his brown eyes look like a little kid with something up his sleeve. He's nice to me too, without asking about the nonexistent boyfriend or saying dumb things like "How you liking school?" His questions aren't what you'd expect.

"Ever had Cheerwine?" he asked me one day, grinning like he had the best secret ever. "Tastes a lot like Coke except it has a kind of cherry flavor."

"Nope," I said. Later that week he came in with a carton of the stuff and seemed pleased as punch with himself over it.

"Found it over there at Bailey's Crossroads," he said. "I swear they got everything in there. They got pickled eggs in a big old jar and they got GooGoo Clusters. Now when's the last time you had a GooGoo Cluster?"

"Never!" I grinned at him. "Not one single solitary time in my whole entire life."

"You're describing a deprived childhood!" he said. "We're just going to have to fix that. It's got nuts and it's covered with chocolate and believe you me, it is *good*. Have you seen the commercial?" I shook my head.

"They have these kids eating them and saying, 'Get your mom to buy you a GooGoo too!'" Then he laughed and I had to laugh too. Dennis is weird but I like him.

So we were sitting there waiting for Naomi to finish the dinner blessing before we could dive into her pot roast. She had her hands clasped together in a little fat ball and her head bowed down to where a loose strand of hair was falling onto her plate. Dennis had been working hard, so he had what I guess was a *man* smell that was sort of all mixed up together with the smell of the food. The kitchen was close and warm from the stove. I peeked at Mama and saw her dabbing her forehead with her napkin while Naomi prayed.

"...And Lord we ask you to just look down on us and have mercy on us in our sinful ways and we thank you for the bounty before us and pray for your forgiveness, and please just help us to understand that we are sinners and you are our Savior and just help us to prepare to spend eternity in your tender care. Amen."

Naomi was almost as bad as the preacher with all that sinner stuff, which if you ask me takes something away from the enjoyment of a meal. It made me sit there and think about my sins, which I'm sure is not good for the digestion. I'd like to take my mind off my terrible nature once in a while if I ever get the chance, which isn't likely around here. Apparently we're all such sinners we need to be reminded of it all the time. That's what the preacher says, anyway. Why, according to him we've got sins coming out our ears—blasphemy and adultery are big ones in his book—taking the Lord's name in vain is another, but you can't forget about thievery, jealousy, gluttony.... If you think you know what all you've done wrong, believe you me there's more.

I had been over at my best friend Sophie's, and we'd been calling this guy Ray's house and hanging up as soon as somebody answered. Now, I know we're not supposed to do that and to tell you the truth I don't know exactly why we were doing it, but it was better than her original idea of going over to ring his doorbell then running off—in the middle of the afternoon! I was able to talk her out of it, which is something I have to do from time to time. Sophie tends to get these big dumb ideas and has to be saved from herself.

The phone prank seemed harmless enough, but I was wondering if things like that would get us sent to hell unless we took Jesus into our hearts, and thinking what a lot of work Jesus has to do forgiving all the bad stuff people do. Some of it was maybe not so bad, like what we did, and some of it was real bad like the guy over there in Mason County who strangled his girlfriend and left her in a ditch. I saw it in the newspaper earlier in the summer and can't get it out of my head no matter how hard I try. I can see going to hell for that one.

So finally we get to our supper and it's for sure not low sodium, low cal. Naomi's got high blood pressure and her doctor says she needs to lose a bunch of weight too, but the butter's making a golden pool in the mashed potatoes and the fresh yeast rolls are steaming. Dennis is talking about his boss at work, some guy with only one whole arm.

"Other one's cut off just above the elbow," he said, "but he still moves it around just like it was regular and points with it and everything."

I was serving up the fried okra, trying to picture this, the guy with a half arm acting like it's no big deal. The phone rang. Mama's hands were full and we were on the other side of the table, so Naomi went to get it. I watched how she slowly pushed her chair back and placed her hands flat on the table to hoist herself up, breathing hard, her upper lip damp with the heat. Seemed like it was taking everything she had.

As soon as she picked the receiver up and said hello, I could see by her face that something was going on. Now, did I know my life was going to change forever from that moment? I can't honestly say that, but there was something about it, something like a hunch except bigger.

She didn't say anything for a second, and when she did speak her voice was too loud.

"Well, I swan! Who'd of thought we'd hear from you today?"

"Who is it?" I asked Mama from across the table.

"How am I supposed to know?" she said. I'd have bet a hundred dollars she had a feeling about it too. She hadn't taken a single bite yet.

"Well, my gracious… how *are* you?" Naomi said. People always ask that and I don't know why they bother, because even if you just got stabbed and the knife is still in your back there's only one thing you're supposed to say: "Just fine, thank you."

"So when's that now?" Naomi turned and showed us her wide back side, as if to help her hear better. I glanced back at Mama and saw she was looking kind of pale, even more so than usual. She was probably like me, wondering if somebody had died. Now even I had quit eating.

"You want to speak to Ruth?" Naomi said. "Well, all right, all right, thanks for letting us know.... Goodbye, now."

Naomi hung up the phone and turned around.

"Well! If that don't beat all I don't know what does!" she said. Her eyes were lit up like she had a fever.

"What?" I said.

"Cal is coming home. Says he'll be here in time for Thanksgiving."

My daddy? Coming home? Thanksgiving? I did a quick calculation, barely three months off from this hot night in August. I felt like pinching myself but looked at Mama instead and saw her close her eyes real slow, like she couldn't look at anybody just then. There was an awkward silence, and Dennis cleared his throat.

"Reckon I better be getting on home," he said as he pushed his chair back and got up.

I expected Naomi to start in about his leaving so soon and not finishing his dinner and didn't he want to stay for her lemon ice box pie, but she didn't.

"Need to take an umbrella?" she asked.

"No thank you, ma'am," he said, keeping his eyes down. Mama looked up at him and watched him go get his jacket off the hook by the door. She didn't speak, but her face said enough.

"Miss Naomi, thank you for supper." He turned and gave us each a little nod, then headed out. We all just sat there and watched him leave.

"Don't be a stranger!" Naomi shouted after him, but the door had already shut before she could say it all the way.

Then there we were sitting together in this peculiar moment—the three of us and the sound of the rain.

"Why'd he go?" I looked at Naomi, then Mama. Neither one of them answered me.

"Well!" Naomi said. "Isn't this the answer to our prayers? Imagine that, just a phone call out of nowhere and Cal is coming back. Praise the Lord!"

"What does this mean?" Mama said. "What did Cal *say?* Is he just passing through, or coming for a visit, or coming home for good? What did he tell you—and where is he?"

"I didn't dare ask anything," Naomi said. "All's I heard was 'coming home,' and my heart just leapt for joy! Just to get to see him is—"

"Why is he doing this now?" Mama said. "Why, after all of this time, all of these years… why now?" Then she turned to me. "Look at you, just about all grown up and about to be a woman, all those years of being a little girl without her daddy around and now, the phone rings and here he comes!" Her hair was all wild and bushed out now from the humidity, and her face was flushed, her eyes bright. She turned back towards my grandmother. "This is not that simple and you know it, Naomi! There are other things to consider! What about—"

"Cal is your husband, Ruth, and don't you forget it!" Naomi wagged her finger at Mama and went on. "I suppose you're wondering about Dennis? So what about him? I'll tell you what—*nothing!* You were never divorced. You said you never wanted to be, that you'd be here for him if he ever decided to come back. You cried and pined and just about made yourself sick over this for years. Well, now here he comes, and by God you better be happy about it!"

"I don't know about this, Naomi, I just don't know!" Mama was practically shouting now. Then Naomi really let it rip, her jaw all jutted forward and her voice shaking.

"You told me Dennis was only a friend! You are cooking up nothing but sin with this here and I'm a-tellin' you to watch your step, little lady!"

Mama shoved her chair back and left the kitchen in a big hurry. Naomi watched her go, scraping her bottom lip with her top teeth. There were beads of sweat on her forehead. Then she turned back to me like nothing had happened. I'm watching all this and trying to put it together in my mind. Seems to me that something's way off but I can't tell what.

Soon as Mama was out of earshot, Naomi grabbed my wrist with her clammy hands, giving it a hard squeeze. There were tears in her eyes.

"Honey, you are finally going to see your daddy," she said. "I have prayed my heart out for this … prayed all of these long, hard years."

My heart raced and I felt my face get hot. So here it was, the very thing I'd been wishing for my whole life, and it had happened right there between the pot roast and potatoes and please pass the rolls. It wasn't what I'd thought it would be like, especially the part about upsetting Mama so bad. Surely something was missing, not that I'd expected clouds parting or a heavenly chorus or anything. Just a little bit of joy or excitement maybe. But there was nothing like that. I just stared down at the table, because I didn't know what to say or think either. This was my dream come true, and I didn't even know what I felt.

Chapter Two

So there you have it. Now everything's different around here. Seems like we can't be our old selves anymore and I don't know if I like it, even if Naomi does forget to be cranky most days. I haven't told a soul what's going on yet, not even Sophie, and I don't even know why. Wish I had somebody to talk to about all this, somebody like God, maybe. Truth is I'm afraid he wouldn't care about hearing complaints from me, being such a sinner and all. But if he did, here's what I might say.

Dear God, I know I should be down on my knees thanking you that we've heard from my daddy and that he says he's coming home. It's what I've always longed for, I know. So, thank you very much. But I'm having this queasy feeling in my stomach because I don't know what it'll be like to see him again. What will I say? What if he doesn't like us? What if he comes home and just decides to leave again? God, I can't lie to you, I'm feeling more mixed up than happy right now. I do promise to try and be grateful. Thank you again, Sir. Amen.

Like I said, I've lived my whole life short on the real information, seeing as nobody's ever wanted to let me in on it. I feel certain that the years of searching and longing and unanswered questions have affected my mind. I get weird things in my head and can't get them out.

Like for instance, sometimes I'll see a shoe lying in the road, just a shoe, and it really gets to me. How does a person lose their shoe in the middle of the road? Are they riding around in their car with their feet hanging out the window and it blows off? I sure don't see people's feet hanging out car windows enough to account for all the shoes I see in the street.

Well, maybe they're crossing to the other side and one shoe just comes off. But if this happened to you, wouldn't you just wait until there were no cars and go back and get it? I mean, I don't know many people around here who have enough shoes to just leave them like that. And how many times do you see somebody walking around wearing *one*? You say, "Hey what happened to your shoe?" and they say, "Oh, it came off in the road a ways back." So how often does that happen? Well, NEVER!

The other things I imagine when I see one shoe are scary, like a dead body in back of a trunk with its feet sticking out. It's like some kind of nightmare and I want to push it out of my mind, but I can't stop it. I see the murderer, who's driving the car and making his getaway. He doesn't know his victim plopped a huge piece of evidence out in the street for everybody to see, never suspecting a mere shoe is going to lead him straight to the electric chair. It's stuff like this that makes me think sometimes my head is going to explode.

Here's another thing that makes me crazy. Naomi says it's a Christian's duty to look your best and go to church on Sunday, but from what I know about Jesus he never did that, not even once. There is that one story about him going to the temple in Jerusalem, but that was Jewish. Why, I don't think they even had church on Sunday way back then, and I've never seen a picture of Jesus in anything but those robes they wore all the time, and sandals. I've never even been allowed to wear sandals to church. So where did Naomi and everybody else in the world get these ideas?

So then a good Christian is supposed to be nice to everybody and love them even if they're sick or poor or different from you. I learned that from Sunday school. If you know the first thing about Jesus, you know that. So what about Old Susan, the lady that lives in a shack across the river? She's not colored, but she's not like anybody else either, stays out of sight most of the time. People say she's Indian, at least partly, but I can't figure out what difference that would make, why that would mean she doesn't get a casserole like everybody else when she comes down with the flu.

Maybe it's because she doesn't go to church. At least the colored ladies have their own church. Old Susan's probably the only woman for miles around that isn't in a Circle. So why aren't they going to see her and trying to get her saved? It seems like they don't want anything to do with her. I've heard her called lots of names, like hag, injun, sorceress, stuff like that. Naomi says she's a heathen.

"What's that?" I asked.

"She ain't saved!" Naomi said.

"Then what about Sophie's mother? You think she's a heathen too, don't you?"

"Well, she's *Jewish*, and they aren't saved either." This makes no sense to me.

"Well, Jesus was Jewish!" I said.

"Hush it! Don't let me hear you ever say anything like that again!"

"Well he WAS!" This makes Naomi boil, but she doesn't yell at me anymore because she knows she's wrong. I think I need to meet a true heathen and see what one is like. I'd like to meet Old Susan.

So if you're going by what Naomi says, looks like there're lots of folks around here who won't be getting into heaven. We have one Catholic Church in Riley. It's called St. Ignatius and it sits way up on a hill. Catholic Hill, we call it. They do Jesus, so what I can't figure out is why they're different from any other church. Naomi considers the Baptists and Methodists and the members of the Fellowship Church to be Christians, even though she might turn her nose up at the way they do some things (like Bingo on Wednesday nights over at Tri-State Bible), but mention the Catholics and you see her jaw set and her mouth go flat.

Years ago I used to play with Mary Beth, who went to St. Ignatius. She even went to school right there on Catholic Hill and had to wear a uniform with a pleated skirt and a little jacket. She told me about the Pope. He's this man that's almost God but not quite, and he lives over in Rome, Italy, which I hear is a city made of gold. He tells everybody what they should do. Apparently, since he's almost God he knows better than anybody else what's right and wrong.

Once, Mary Beth asked me to go to church with her. I was curious and wanted to go, but Naomi said no. She said the Catholics are idol worshippers because they have statues of Mary all over the place and they say prayers to her instead of God and Jesus.

"What's so bad about talking to his mother?" I asked. I like the idea of talking to Mary. About all I know about her is what I see on Christmas cards, her riding on a donkey with her robes draped over a big baby belly, or sitting by the manger looking down at Baby Jesus.

"The Bible says, 'Thou shalt have no other gods before me,'" she said.

"But Mary Beth says that if you go to her first, she'll talk to God for you! It's quicker that way because he's so busy and all."

"They make her too important," Naomi said. "It takes their hearts and minds off of Jesus. That's why Catholics aren't saved."

"You mean *they're* going to hell *too*?" I'm thinking it better be a mighty big place, seeing how many people are going there and staying. But this doesn't bother Naomi one little bit.

"Jesus is the only way," she says.

Well, here are my thoughts on that one. For one, if the rules for getting into heaven are to love Jesus and let him into your heart, it doesn't seem right to get kicked out if you let his mother in with him. And another thing, if there's going to be a father to pray to in heaven, I think it's only fair that there be a mother, too. I'm not sure about this pope, though. How can a man that's way over there in Italy be saying what God's thinking about us here in Riley, Tennessee?

My thoughts just won't leave me alone. I've come to believe it's the unexplained absence of my father that's bent my mind into this agitated teenager who is me, Angel. You'd think the news of his coming home would straighten out such a state of mind, at least a little bit, but I'm here to tell you it hasn't.

Then there's the nightmare, the one that wakes me up in a cold sweat and such a deep darkness I can't imagine there's any way out. It's me lying dead, all curled up on my side like a tossed rag, but I'm hovering somewhere above and looking down at my own body.

I've always had bad dreams, but I've been having this one since last year, when we were supposed to dissect a fetal pig in science class. It was just me and my lab partner Nathan standing there at our station while the teacher was bringing them around. I don't know what I was expecting, but when she put the tray down in front of us and I saw it, I about passed out right there. It was this shriveled little thing all curled up, its tiny legs barely sticking out from its body, just dangling there all lifeless and limp. Its skin was slimy, like a cold sausage, the pickled smell enough to knock you out, but the worst was its face. The eyes were just blind dots, and under the little bitty snout was its slightly open mouth, with an expression that was so pig-like and could have been cute if it was alive, but it was so…so *dead* …and we were supposed to stand there and cut it to pieces to look at the insides.

Nathan said, "Angel, your face is kind of green," which is when I ran out of the room and *threw up* in the hallway—which was very embarrassing.

After that I would not dissect the fetal pig, no matter what, even when the teacher called Mama about it and we discussed it at home. Naomi said she didn't know when I got to be such a sissy.

"Angel, I don't know what else to say," Mama said. "This is not like you." So they sent me to one of the school counselors, Mrs. Rothbottom. She told me if I got a zero on the lab it would affect my excellent grade point average. I told her if they made me use that little knife I was afraid I might decide to cut into myself instead, which I made up on the spot but it sounded good anyway, which is why she wrote me a note saying I could write a report in place of the dissection. I got a little bit famous for this when it got around, though I'd very much like it forgotten seeing as how throwing up in the hallway was such a big part of the story.

So now I have this nightmare and I don't know what it means. I try to forget about it but sometimes it stays with me for days, me seeing myself dead and feeling the darkness all around me. No one knows about all this, not a single solitary soul on this earth. If I'm going insane I'd like to keep it a secret as long as possible because in most ways I probably *seem* like a regular kind of girl, more or less, which is what I want to be—just normal. I try to keep a low profile on the family situation.

School is okay even though I don't have a big social life. That's all right by me because my best friend Sophie is about all I can handle most of the time. The other girls live for phone calls and slumber parties, but we don't go for that stuff too much. Ever since her mama got sick she just likes to hang out with me, mostly in one of our rooms, listening to records and playing games or just talking and hoping nobody will bother us.

Every so often we'll go downtown, on a Saturday, but that takes some planning. You have to wear a cute outfit and carry a purse. Usually Mama drops us off in front of the library and we walk across the street to have lunch at Woolworth's.

"What'll ya have today, girlies?" Alva's the little lady behind the counter that's always there. I'm pretty sure she knows us, but she doesn't let on. She has short, bluish-gray hair and her eyes are sort of watery and squishy-looking. I think a half decent wind coming through the door would knock her over. She grabs her order pad from her apron pocket, whips out the pencil stuck behind her ear and stares at us without smiling. Sophie gets the diet plate because she wants to stay skinny, a "quarter pound o' ground round" with a side of cottage cheese on a peach half. I like the tuna melt with french fries. Then we share a chocolate milkshake.

We can go to the movies if we want, or if there's nothing we care to see we'll go shopping at J. Fred Johnson's or Nettie Lee. They both carry Hang Ten clothes, which is the brand everybody has to have. Sophie wears a small size and is proud of it, though she doesn't say so out loud exactly. She'll just go over to the rack and say, "Let's see, *here're* the fives!" Even though I'm skinny, I'm a nine because I'm "big-boned," Naomi tells me. I hate it when she says that.

Then we just walk around, window shopping up and down First Street. We can see our reflection in the glass store fronts and every now and then I'll glance over to see if I look okay from the side. We sort of hope to see somebody we know—but not really. It's way too weird to have to think of something to say to someone from school when you're downtown. But most of the time we don't, and after a while Mama or Sophie's dad comes to pick us up.

Sophie's good company, but sometimes I'd rather just be by myself, walking around in the woods or sitting out on a summer night listening to the crickets and counting fireflies. I sit up late and read, especially when it's hot and the attic fan is running and there's nothing but me and the breeze and the little light by my bed. One of my favorite books is *Rebecca*, by Daphne Du Maurier, and even though I've read it a bunch of times it still gives me the shivers.

My secret crush is Johnny Dupree, he's the disc jockey at WRIL and I've never seen him but his voice is like warm honey coming through the radio at night. I just know he's handsome. My favorite songs right now are "The Night the Lights Went Out in Georgia" and "Bad, Bad, Leroy Brown." I have read *Love Story* four times and have seen the movie twice, which is my favorite, next to *Jeremiah Johnson* with Robert Redford. I have never ridden on an airplane.

Then there's Mr. Marvelous, my big orange tabby cat. Here's why I named him that. When he first showed up at our house as a stray, Naomi was still being real stubborn about no pets, so I had to feed him in secret until her friend Dottie Ames came by one day and saw him.

"Why, look at that beautiful cat!" she said. "I've never seen such unusual markings, and his hair is exactly Angel's color. He's marvelous!" She was right. If I wore him as a hat you'd never be able to tell whose hair was whose.

My grandmother finally agreed to let him stay on the condition that he lives outside, because she thinks having an animal in the house is unclean. What she doesn't know is that he climbs the hemlock tree by the house and jumps onto the porch roof right under my window. In the winter, he scratches his paw on the pane until I wake up and let him in, but when it's warm I sleep with it open so he can come in whenever he wants. He likes to lie there with me and listen to Johnny Dupree, or on beautiful nights we'll sit on the roof, looking at the sky together and talking. I know he's just a cat, but I honestly don't know what I'd do without him.

Of course, I'm not really sitting out there *talking* to my cat all night. That *would* be looney tunes and I don't think I'm quite that far gone. Although I do sometimes speak out loud to him and he occasionally yowls back softly, we communicate mostly through mental telepathy, this being possible since cats have special powers. I know this is true because whenever I'm having one of those awful nights, Mr. Marvelous knows, and he'll come right through my window and sit on my chest with his feet tucked up under him, staring straight into my eyes. He tells me it's all going to be okay with his big loud purr, sending a low rumble through my body that eases my mind. So besides being my hair twin, he *is* marvelous, "Mr. Marvelous" or "Marvel" for short.

We've been spending a lot of time out on the roof lately. "Why do you think Mama and Daddy fell in love?" Mama had told me about how they met—she was a candy striper at the hospital when he had appendicitis.

"What did they like most about each other?" I'm sure Mama was cute as a button in that pink and white uniform and her long, wavy orange hair, but from knowing her now, I'm not thinking she was the type to flirt just for the sake of it. She's careful, and she keeps close to herself. There had to be something she saw in him. Marvel licks his left paw and swipes it back behind his ear a bunch of times. Then he tucks it back up under himself and it's so cute I just about can't stand it. I think he's telling me you can't always explain such things, but they were both smart people and they thought they should get married and have a child. That would be me.

"So then, what happened? Did they fall out of love?" This is tricky territory because of my suspicion that whatever happened here, it has to do with me. He purrs and I wait, but I don't get an answer, which makes me think maybe I never will.

Chapter Three

As for talking to people, there's not much use in it around here. Nobody seems to care much about what I have to say. All Naomi does is yell about the Lord and whatnot and Mama's just downright frustrating, always being so careful about what she says, always holding back something it seems. The only one I've ever had to talk to is Aunt Patsy, and to tell you the truth, talking with her is mostly listening. She's Grandpa Joe's daughter, but she and my daddy grew up together from the time they were about nine years old, when Grandmother Naomi and Grandpa Joe got married. She's always been "odd" is what they say, even as a girl. Something "off" about her. So now she has to live over there at Crestview, where most of them don't even know what day it is, and she never gets to leave except to come home for Thanksgiving and Christmas Day.

So it's Sunday and we're going to see her just like we do every week on the way back from church. Crestview is over by the shopping center, which not only has Rose's Department Store and the new Hillsview movie theatre but Earl's Pizza, Delilah's Hair and Nails, Sandra's Shape Shop, the One Way Religious Bookstore, and A&P. Bright's Family Cafeteria's not too far. Every so often we'll stop there for lunch afterwards, but not today on account of Reverend Jenkins coming to Sunday dinner.

Our visits are always the same, and this one at least starts out like all the rest. Mama parks our metallic green Mercury Marquis in one of the visitor slots right up close. Naomi huffs and puffs her way out of the car and gets Patsy's plate out of the back. She always brings her something she's baked that week. This time it's that Coca-Cola cake she found in the latest First Presbyterian Church Ladies Auxiliary cookbook. It has Coke in the batter and the icing is chocolate. Absolutely everybody is talking about it.

Just before we walk in, Naomi stops and says, "Now we'll not be saying anything today about Cal's phone call—it'll just go and get her all confused."

Mama's just looking at the pavement and then her nails and doesn't answer. I pretend I don't hear her as I open the door and walk on over to the welcome desk, thinking I can tell Patsy whatever I want to and I'd like to see Naomi try and stop me.

Opal has been working reception at Crestview on Sundays as long as I can remember. She has white hair that sticks out all over her head and wears cat's-eye glasses with rhinestones around the frames.

"It's the baby!" she says real loud when she sees me come in. "I love that baby—come over here and give me a kiss!" I lean over her desk and let her plant her big wet lipstick mark on my cheek.

They know us here at Crestview since we've been coming for about the last dozen years. That's a long time to be in a place like this. Most people die way before then, but Patsy's case is different, they say. She has the kind of craziness that starts a lot younger than most and goes real slow. Naomi says it's good for Patsy that Joe was rich so she can stay in a place like this. Even if the money's tighter for us because of it, she says, it's better than trying to keep her at home.

Grandpa Joe's family owned a lot of land around here which he and his two brothers inherited after their daddy died. Then when some big company folks from New York came along and offered to buy it for their new plant, they were set for life and then some.

Sometimes I wonder if maybe Naomi married Joe just because he was so rich. I know that's an awful thought—God is probably writing that down somewhere as a trespass. But truthfully, I don't see what would be so terrible even if she did. She had not so good luck with her first marriage to Calvin Stone Bishop II, marrying him when she was sixteen and becoming a widow at twenty-one.

Naomi will tell you that her first husband, Calvin Jr., died in the coal mines, which is true enough, though she'll stop short of the whole story. It wasn't the usual sort of accident that happens around here from time to time, such as an explosion or a cave-in that traps the miners. Dottie Ames told me he was stabbed by a guy who apparently had some big reason to be mad at him, which is the part Naomi doesn't want talked about. Calvin Jr. lived awhile after the attack but ended up dead over it, and the guy went to jail for a long time. I don't know what happened after that, it being another taboo subject around here.

Naomi had to look after my daddy by herself for almost five years after that, so when Joe comes along and wants to marry her, I say why not? He was handsome and kind and a recent widower himself, no doubt hoping to find not only a good wife but a mother for his young daughter, Patsy. For love or money or whatever reason there might have been, the match between Naomi and Joe seemed to make good sense all the way around.

"Look at that hair!" Opal always fusses over me. "I swear I ain't *never* seen such hair! Grace, have you ever in your life seen such a purty head a' red hair?"

"It's orange," I say.

Grace, one of the cleaning ladies, is just now walking through the lobby with her mop and bucket. She's a short, plump girl with curly dark hair cut close to her head. Some of the curls are longer than others and hang out a little. She looks up and gives about the biggest smile I have ever seen. Some of her teeth are dark.

"Naw, 'hit's the purtiest ever," Grace says. "Just like an Angel. I reckon that's why they call her that. Ain't that right, Naomi?" She gives my grandmother a wink.

"Yep, she's our Angel all right," Naomi says, but she and Mama keep moving because if either of these gals starts talking to you, you're stuck. We hurry around the corner and once out of her sight I wipe Opal's wet kiss off my face. I expect they'll be giving her a room any day now.

We go down the hall to Patsy's room, number 107, and walk in like some kind of sad parade. Naomi goes first, swaying from side to side with every step. Her gray hair is still curled up nice and tight because her Wednesday "do" generally looks good through Sunday. As always she's wearing a matching polyester slack and shirt set. I think the Reverend Jenkins lets her get away with wearing pants to church because number one he wants people to think he's modern, and number two because if he knows what's good for him he won't cross Naomi on anything.

She has three sets for fall and winter, three more for spring and summer. Today she has on the sky blue set, but come Labor Day she'll switch to the orange, brown and yellow. That is, until December when it'll be a red pantsuit with two different Christmas shirts. One of them has a poinsettia print and the other is a white blouse with green buttons and piping for church.

"Well, hello!" Naomi sort of shouts out to Patsy as we come into the room. Patsy's looking out the window, which is partly opened, staring away past the A&P parking lot and up into the rolling hills. Naomi sets the plate down on the side table beside her chair and reaches over to pull it shut.

"You're letting the air conditioning out... No wonder it's so muggy in here!"

Mama comes in wearing one of her gauzy skirts and a white peasant blouse, her strides long and loose. She's got on a pair of flat, open-toed shoes, which my grandmother doesn't like but will allow if she wears pantyhose. Her long hair is tied into a loose ponytail that's come across her left shoulder and falls halfway down her front. She reaches behind her head with her right hand, pulling it around and out of its tie, all at the same time. With a quick motion it's suddenly up on the back of her head in a bun. She looks at her watch.

I'm right behind them, wearing my ivory summer church dress and flats to match. I've got my hair down now because I'm tired of wearing it in dog ears—that's two ponytails, one on each side of my head. I've worn it like that ever since I can remember, but now I think I need a more sophisticated look.

I have to wear pantyhose too, according to Naomi, which combined with the hair is making a long hot summer morning all the longer. I cannot believe there was a time when I couldn't wait to wear these things. Mama wouldn't let me, said they were too grown up, and Sophie's mom said the same thing. But then we found out they were part of the official Cadet Girl Scout uniform, so Sophie and I signed up for a troop in the seventh grade and our mothers had to give in.

The thrill didn't last. The meetings were mostly about personal hygiene, and by the third one my hose had a run going all the way up my left leg. I couldn't see sticking around talking about shampoo any more just to get another pair, but Sophie stuck it out for the whole year. She ended up making her own deodorant for her science project, which she claimed was inspired by her involvement in the Cadet Girl Scouts and got her an honorable mention at the fair.

"How you doin'?" Mama says sweetly but too loud. You can tell she's not expecting an answer.

"That'll be enough out of YOU today!" Patsy says, then she goes right back to looking out her window. Mama and Naomi don't act like they noticed the outburst. This is because it's fairly typical and makes no difference one way or the other since Patsy probably doesn't even know why she said it. Both of them start fussing around the room, fluffing pillows, straightening up her bed, folding clothes or whatever, just like they always do.

"Ain't no use in y'all bringing that cake," Patsy says, now pointing and wagging her finger at it. "That Rita, she's going to take it."

"So who's Rita?" Naomi always tries to make normal conversation with her because they tell us this will help her mind. "She the one let you have the window open?"

"That nurse who comes in here all the time, the colored one. She'll steal it!"

Nobody says anything to this. Patsy gets suspicious sometimes, especially about the nurses that work there. She always has some big tale to tell about one or the other, like the one she said would come to work in nothing but her underwear, or another one she said was putting poison in her ginger ale. So you get kind of used to stuff like this.

"...But I wouldn't even care if she *did* steal it!" she says, talking like she does when she's mad, taking little stabs with her words.

"Now why would you say that?" Mama asks, but not really paying her much mind.

"Because she knows I'll *hate* it, that's why... especially if it's the one tastes like it's got Coca-Cola in it. Whose idea was that?" This cracks me up and I giggle. Patsy can be so sharp about the funniest little things sometimes, even when she's completely confused about everything else. Naomi makes a "tsk" sound with her mouth.

"Well, she must be new, because I haven't met her," Mama says.

"You ought to, because around here they say she's hell on wheels!" Then Patsy lets out her big whooping laugh like she's enjoying some private joke.

"How so?" Naomi asks, looking up. She's always on the lookout for sin.

"Not telling *you!*" Patsy's raising her voice and starting to get worked up again.

"Tell us," says Mama. "I'm curious."

"Well…she'll sneak people out at night, take 'em down to the River House and get 'em all beered up and….but whoa! I'm NOT TELLING THAT BITCH ANYTHING!" Her head jerks towards Naomi, who's trying to ignore her now. That's what they tell us to do when she gets like this. I try to calm her down a little bit.

"Hey, Aunt Patsy," I say and pat her shoulder until she looks at me.

"Hey, darlin'," she says, her voice changing right away. "How's my girl?" She's always sweet to me, no matter how ugly she gets with the others, calls me her girl and sweetie and such. I think I'm her favorite.

"Tell me about school. You got a boyfriend, honey?" She asks you questions but doesn't stop to hear any answers. "Are you studying hard? What's your boyfriend's name, honey? What do they teach you over there anyhow? They treating you all right? "

"Everything's good," I say. "Everything's just fine." I don't bother telling her that it's still August and school hasn't even started yet. Like I said, Patsy does most of the talking between two people, which is okay by me. She reaches up and touches my hair.

"Look at you—why, you're not hardly a child anymore."

"Aw, Patsy, yes I am," I say but she keeps staring at me. It's like a cloud goes over her for a second, then it passes and she perks up again.

"Awia says it's going to be a cold winter, says the woolly worms is big and there's been some foggy mornings in August. She's never wrong about the weather."

"Is that right?" Naomi says absent-mindedly. Now she's dusting the windowsill with a Kleenex.

"Nobody ever says it's going to be a *mild* winter," Mama says, leaning against the windowsill and taking another glance at her watch.

We hear things about this Awia from time to time, but all Patsy ever says about her is that she's her friend and she can't say more because "they" might hurt her. We don't know who "they" are, but nobody pays any attention anyway. It's an odd thing, but Naomi says it just goes along with her disease—Patsy gets all these ideas in her head and needs to be over there at Crestview where they can help her out. I've asked Naomi a gazillion times why she has to live with all those people who don't even know their names when it seems to me we could help her out just as well at home.

"She's just so nervous," Naomi says. "She can't live with us. The doctors say she needs to be where she can get all of her medicines taken care of and all."

"So what's the medicine for?" I ask.

"Now don't you go fretting about that," she says, which of course is just another way of shushing me. This family does not like questions. Here's what I'm thinking is the truth—they'd be pleased as punch if I didn't speak at all.

"A cold winter doesn't sound so bad to me right now," I say, wishing I could be out of these clothes.

"It'll be cooling off before you know it," Naomi says, kind of muttering to herself while she's wiping up everything she can lay her hands on. "I need to get my collards and beets put in. Maybe I can get out there later today and—"

"Cain't do it today," Patsy says. "The signs is in the heart."

"That's not a thing but nonsense," Naomi says, speaking up now. "I don't go by that old superstitious stuff."

"Go ahead, then," Patsy said. "Hit'll dry up and die, I'm telling you."

"Why's that?" I ask.

"Because it's in a fire sign and the ground won't take it!"

"Glad to see you still enjoy your Farmer's Almanac," Mama says, smiling in Patsy's direction. She always gives her a new one for Christmas because Patsy's an old farm girl from way back. "My granny used to look at it every day too. I remember she always said to plant beans in the twins."

"Yep, when the signs is in the arms." Patsy was nodding.

"What about peas?" I said. "And corn?" I love all that planting by the moon and the signs and stuff.

"Well, you plant peas in the arms or the thighs, long as the points are down. Don't plant any seeds at all in the full moon, 'cept for corn, but don't plant it in the heart or hit'll get black spots on it."

"What do you mean when the points are down?"

"That's when the moon's running low, so the plant'll take root."

"It don't mean a thing," Naomi said.

"You sow four seeds for one good plant," Patsy said. "One for the jaybird, one for the crow, one to rot and one to grow!" Mama and I both laughed. "Awia says to quit a bad habit at the new moon. That's the way to do it, she says."

"Shush, now," Naomi said. "I don't want to hear any more!"

"What's the matter with it?" I said. "I like hearing about all that."

"It's the devil's business, is what it is, all of that with the moon and such," she said. "Now all of you just shush up."

"Why do you have to be so mean?" I say. "You and your old devil! She's not hurting anybody."

"You'd better watch it, young'un!"

"Watch what? What am I doing? I'm not doing *anything*—"

"Angel—cut it," Mama said.

"You're just so suspicious all the time, of everything and everybody—so what is it you're talking about I'm supposed to *watch*?"

"*Angel!*" Mama again.

Watch Naomi being an old fool is what I'm thinking, glaring at her. She won't look at me. I hand Patsy a magazine and start brushing her hair, what's left of it, anyway. She used to have a head of dark, thick waves. Now it's much thinner and mostly gray, but it's still pretty.

"Awia knows everything," she says. "Yes, and what she doesn't know, they tell her."

"Foolishness…" Naomi's over there muttering to herself again.

"Who tells her what?" I ask, trying to see what all I can get her to say. Sometimes she gets going on something and you'll be wondering *what in the world*, but at least she talks. Whatever it is, I hope it bugs the heck out of Naomi.

"The creek people," she says and I'm thinking, *oh boy, here comes a doozy*.

"So who are they?" I ask.

"Them folks that lives down there."

"Down where?"

"The *creek!*" she says. "Where else do you think the *creek* people would be?"

"You talking about Murray Creek?" I ask.

"Yeah, Murray Creek. They must've been down there a thousand years by now."

Mama gives a little laugh, shakes her head and looks out the window. Naomi's got her lower jaw set out against me and Patsy and the rest of the world, I guess.

"So tell me about them," I say, but she's off in her thoughts, looking at her palms and playing with her fingers. "What do they look like?" Now I'm taking her hair and making a braid go down her back.

"Well, they look like Indians, of course," she says with a sigh.

"Indians? You mean like with bows and arrows and painted faces and such?"

She doesn't say anything back. I can tell she's done talking for the time being, so I quit asking her things. Now I've got the braid twisted up in a bun and I'm holding it high up on her head and trying to picture her all dressed up at a fancy party with a handsome date. I wonder if Patsy ever had a date. I've never heard her say anything about a boy-friend or being in love or anything. I let the bun drop down and start taking out the braid. It goes on like this for a while. She's still quiet, so I figure it's a good time to break the news, even if Naomi goes and has a cow over it.

"Guess what, Aunt Patsy. My daddy called and says he's coming home for Thanksgiving."

The next moment is long and strained and I'm brushing the heck out of Patsy's hair waiting for somebody to say something, but about the only thing I can hear is everybody's breathing. Patsy's gone kind of stiff, not relaxing with it like she usually does. She's the one who finally says something, her voice quiet and shaky.

"Awia knows all about Cal, too, yes she does. She knows what he did." I stop brushing.

"What do you mean?" I ask. Now I can hear Mama at the little cor-ner sink washing her hands, and Naomi's rattling the blinds louder than ever wiping them down *again*, so I bend over to look into Patsy's eyes and ask her straight to her face, "What do you mean, what he *did*?"

I think my question startles Patsy for a split second but then her expression changes and she looks back at me with such hard eyes it's downright spooky. She grabs my hand and squeezes it tighter than I ever thought she could.

"She knows everything," Patsy says. We hold our gaze for a mo-ment longer, and my heart is pounding in my chest while I'm thinking *how I can get her to say more*, but of course Naomi has to chime in.

"I don't know who or what you're talking about, Patsy, but it seems to me like it's about time for you to be getting on down to lunch, and we've got the reverend coming over for dinner."

"Let's go," Mama says. "We don't have time for this. I've got work tomorrow."

"We don't have time for *what*?" I ask as they charge out the door, without answering me, of course.

Chapter Four

$\mathcal{M}$ama walks out ahead of us to pull the car around while Naomi takes a seat on a bench by the door. I'm waiting with her. What happened in there has got me in a state. I know better than to say anything, but I do anyway.

"What did Patsy mean when she was talking about Daddy?"

"Now didn't I *tell* you not to say anything about that?" Naomi says. "All you did was go get her worked up over nothing. Now, thanks to your mule-headedness, they'll have to give her something extra to calm her down. I've a mind to give you a good whipping!"

Years of experience have taught me there are times when I really need to zip my lips, and this is one of them. It's been a long while since I actually got the switch, but the memory of it's enough to make me careful. When I was younger, mostly when I'd let Satan take my tongue, as Naomi would say, she'd tear off down the block to the old willow tree on the corner and cut one off, just for me. I was good at disappearing before she got back, but once in a while, I got it.

One time she whipped me for lying when I'd said Jesus told me to pick all the jonquils out of the yard and bring them to Mama. I really thought he had. It was such a beautiful sight, all those pretty yellow heads bobbing in the wind. I was certain I heard a heavenly message on that sweet breeze, saying a bunch of those was just what Mama needed. Before I knew it I'd plucked every one. There weren't any left for Naomi's church circle meeting that week, so she let me have it but good. The sting in my ankles was bad, but not as bad as the pain in my heart for being called a liar.

There are big dirt clods next to the sidewalk where we're standing and I start kicking them for some reason.

"Quit it!" Naomi takes the folded church program out of her purse to fan herself, mumbling into the hot air, "can't believe a word that child says anyway."

"Why not?" I say, taking my flats off and slapping them together. The dust is flying. "And why do you call her 'child'? She's old!"

"Git your shoes back on—and look what you've done to 'em! What a mess!" Naomi fans faster and turns away. She's fed up with me by now, so I give up expecting any kind of answer and settle for leaving my shoes off anyway. But there's one thing she *has* let on in spite of herself. That "nothing" she says Patsy's so worked up about sure must be something.

As we get close to the house Naomi starts humming. I can tell she's switched her thoughts to company coming. She sure does like the Reverend Jenkins. Everyone knows her hair appointment is on Wednesday afternoons because Bible study is Thursday mornings, and she's always the first to his home with a hot meal when he's under the weather. When he was so sick last winter and not getting any better after weeks and weeks, it was Naomi who finally took him back to the doctor. Sure enough, he had pneumonia and went to the hospital.

Then of course she was the one to organize the meal sign-up for the whole month after he was home. It was a big job. She had to be on the phone all the time, lining people up and making sure there was an appealing variety. When she bakes, she'll make extra and take it to him. She drives him around when his car is in the shop and even does some grocery shopping for him every now and then. Sometimes I have to ask myself who she's more taken with, Jesus or Jenkins?

Now, I have no problems with Jesus, but as for the reverend and all he spouts, I'm not so sure. Naomi says I have to go to church, though if the truth be known I would rather not. I just don't understand why we should go sit in this big hot room listening to this fellow tell us what a bunch of sinners we are. Half the congregation's snoozing, anyway. I can't go to sleep because Naomi would pinch me, but I've learned how to go away in my mind so as not to hear what he's saying.

It doesn't make me feel any better about myself to have him up there hollering about being damned. And hearing that God loves me like a father? That's not particularly reassuring in my case. It just doesn't all fit together if you ask me.

So God, how come it is that you love us all so much but you'd send us to the eternal fires if we don't act right? If I had children, I don't think I could ever watch them burn no matter how bad they were and I'm not even God. Imagining a prayer like this, I could swear I feel myself moving closer to the flames, just for even thinking it. But that doesn't stop my terrible mind from going on.

And if Jesus forgives everything, why can't he forgive us if we don't really believe that in all of creation, he's the only way to heaven?

This one has always bugged me, especially on account of Sophie's mother. Looks like I have a problem if I want Jesus in my heart even if I can't believe that. The preacher says you can't have it both ways, you can't "pick and choose" what to believe, so I guess I'm in a real pickle.

I'd also like to ask you, God, why'd you let all those babies in that Bible story get killed, the one where Herod that bad king heard about baby Jesus and went and killed all the little boys just to make sure he got him? Then there's that other baby-killing story, the one where you sent the bad angel around to everybody's house to snatch them. Now what's a kid supposed to think after hearing that one?

Well, I can tell you from firsthand knowledge that between hearing this story and the preacher shouting all the time to "FEAR THE LORD!" any churchgoing kid's going to be shivering in his sheets at night when the light goes out.

One more question. *Dear God, with all due respect, I would like to know why it's all guys running everything up there? There's you, then there's your son Jesus, then there's this fellow the Holy Spirit. I don't know exactly if I've ever heard him called "He" but I sure haven't heard him called "She." The whole thing seems a little one-sided to me.*

I asked Naomi one time if she'd ever wanted to be a preacher since she likes church so much and she just laughed, said a woman can't be a preacher because the Bible says women have to keep quiet in church, and I said, "WHAT? Why on earth?" Then Naomi said you don't question what the good book says, the Bible says what it means and means what it says and you must never doubt its truth.

So I guess it's no wonder that I lay awake in my bed at night wondering what's going to happen to me, being such a terrible person and not thinking the way I should. Maybe my messed up family is my punishment for being the way I am. I must be one of those bad angels, cursed by my own thoughts. It's a wonder God even lets me live another day considering what all goes on in my mind.

For Sunday dinner today we're having pork chops, mashed potatoes, green beans, baked apples, buttermilk biscuits, and bread pudding for dessert. You might guess by looking at him that this is Jenkins's favorite meal. He'd probably do well to try Naomi's diet for awhile, but there's no way she's going to cook like that for him and I'm glad. The meal is the best part about his visit. But before we get to eat he has to give the blessing, naturally, because talking to God is part of his day job. That's the worst part.

"*O Lord...*" he starts, and it's on and on from there, and I'm bowing my head and holding my hands in prayer, way down close to my plate, thinking "*O Lord,*" how I don't like this man, and how many different ways my soul must be lost.

"So Angel, you going to be ready to start back to school in a week?" he asks once his plate's all served up.

"Yes, sir." I glance up at his round, shiny face and give a quick smile, then look back down into my green beans as soon as I can.

"So what grade will you be in?"

"Eighth," I say, again looking up and back down again. I'm now noticing the steam rising up off my pork chop and wondering when to start eating. Then he picks up his fork and I know it's okay, I can eat now and probably won't have to say much more the whole meal. Mama's not big on dinner conversation when Jenkins is here either, so it's usually pretty much between him and Naomi.

"We're all just so sorry about your loss, Reverend," Naomi says in her most syrupy, sympathy card kind of voice. Jenkins' mother, who was at least a hundred and fifty years old, just died way up in Kentucky somewhere and he was gone the whole week seeing to everything. Naomi kept an eye on his house for him.

"Why, thank you," he says, his head cocked a little to one side. "She had certainly lived a long, blessed life and when Jesus called, she was ready. Praise the Lord!"

"Amen!" Naomi hollers, then pauses like she's waiting for Mama and me to shout back. We don't, so she goes on. "How was the service?"

"It was a beautiful memorial of a wonderful life," he says, taking a bite of potatoes. "...a glorious celebration of her going home. Would you please pass me a biscuit?"

"Obliged," said Naomi, handing him the warm bread basket, covered with a blue and white checked napkin. "Now tell me who all came," she says. "All of your brothers and sisters make it back?"

"Oh, yes, all nine of us were there, plus about fifteen of the grandchildren and even a few of the great-grandchildren." Jenkins butters his biscuit and takes a bite. "Hmmm ... delicious!" he says. "I preached the sermon right there at the gravesite. She was a woman with a strong faith and I know she was ready to be with God. He kept her here a good long time to be a witness to the unsaved souls whose paths crossed hers."

In my mind I saw a shriveled little old lady lying in a bed in some nursing home way up there in the Kentucky mountains, raising up a tiny clawed hand whenever anybody entered her room. "Repent! Repent!" she'd croak in a raspy voice, and whoever had come her way would fall on their knees and receive God, right there by her bedside.

"So what did you do after the service?" Naomi says reaching for a bowl. "...And have some more beans while you're at it."

"Why, thank you!" he said, serving up his plate again. "We all went over to my sister's house and ate. Seemed like the whole county had brought food over. With friends and family there must have been fifty of us or more. It was a fine afternoon, a very fine afternoon. Then the next day we went back up to Mama's house and divided everything up, all of her furniture and belongings. There's somebody wants to buy her house right away, and my siblings want to take up the offer while it's out there."

"So what are you bringing home?"

"Well," he says, "somehow I got most of the big pieces of furniture. There's an old bedroom set and an armoire, a couch and a loveseat, some end tables. I got practically a whole houseful and nowhere to put it. My own house is too small for it all."

"How come none of your brothers and sisters wanted it?"

Naomi's questions are about wearing me out. *Can you let the man eat?*

"They're all married and have a whole lot more stuff than me already. For some reason they thought that with me being a bachelor I'd have more room for it. I tried to tell them otherwise, but they wouldn't hear of it. Now I have to figure out where to keep it until I can figure out how to get it into my little house."

"Why, maybe we can help you out with that! We'll just have to give that some thought, won't we? Y'all eat the rest of these pork chops, now. Ruth, you having another?" She pushes the plate towards Mama, who looks up at her and then at the reverend, probably wondering like me what in the world Naomi's got in mind.

"No, thank you," she says. "I've got plenty." Then there's this pause. Jenkins finally gets to take another bite and no one is talking and what I want to ask the reverend just slips out before I can think about it, or talk myself out of it.

"So you knew my daddy," I say. It's not even a question.

I hear Naomi clear her throat and Mama's fork clank on the plate as she puts it down and takes a sip of her iced tea. Jenkins looks startled.

"Your daddy?" His eyes dart away from me. "Why…no, I'm sorry, I'm afraid I didn't."

Nobody says anything for a good while after that. It's a lie and we all know it.

Chapter Five

So now it's Friday afternoon a few days later and I'm waiting for Sophie to get ready, sitting in her living room with her Mama, Genevieve. We're going to the football game over at school. They always have one right before the year starts so we'll get to feeling school spirit right off the bat. I don't care a thing about football and neither does Sophie. She just cares about Ray, who she thinks is going to be over there. This is not something I want to do, mainly because it's hot as Hades out, but it's better than walking back and forth in front of his house "just in case he comes out." That's what she wanted to do.

"So, Sophie, what would we do if he *did* come out?"

"We'd have to hide quick! Wouldn't want him to think I was chasing after him or anything."

Fortunately for Sophie, she will listen to reason from time to time and I was able to convince her, once again, that this was not the best plan. So we came to an agreement—I'll go with her to the game this afternoon and help her try and spot him if she'll go down to the ravine with me tomorrow.

Some might say that Sophie and I are an unlikely pair. For one, she's beautiful and I'm just okay. She has long straight brown hair, big brown eyes, and skin that looks like coffee cream. This is not to say I'm one of those mangy girls that latch onto the beautiful ones to pull themselves up. I'm not really sure what I am. I think I've decided there just isn't a category for me. I have to admire Sophie because she could be surrounded and adored by all the others who look just like her, or a lot like her anyway, but she chooses me, the girl with orange hair and freckles, the girl without a group.

It's also quite nice to be petite, which Sophie is and I am not. I'm tall as a bean pole, Naomi says. And if it's dark and skinny you want, well I've got the skinny down. But I've just had to accept that my complexion will never, ever be that nice caramel color Sophie's gets in the summer. I have tried everything from baby oil to reflectors and every cream, rub, and solution out there, but sun-bathing gets me nothing other than pain and more freckles. In case you're wondering if you could ever have so many freckles that they run together and make a tan, believe you me it doesn't work. I'm thinking, though, that there may be hope. They have a cream now that you just rub all over you and it gives you a beautiful tan without having to lie in the sun! I've seen it in Greer's Drugstore and am thinking about trying it.

So anyway, I'm waiting for Sophie to come out. Martha, the help, is banging around in the kitchen getting supper ready. She's been coming over here most afternoons since Genevieve's been back in her treatment and is so weak. Martha's like part of everybody's family. She used to work for us way back when Naomi was down with shingles, just like she goes wherever another hand is needed with everything from new babies, broken legs, hernias, or Dottie Ames's big parties. I bet she knows something about Daddy. She steps out to speak.

"You girls want to eat something before you go?" Martha's built for hard work, thick set and strong, with lively greenish eyes and cheeks that always look flushed and rosy, like she's just been out in the wind. She wears her hair back in a loose bun—it's rusty colored and unruly. Naomi says she's got the Irish in her too.

"I think we're just going to eat over there. We'll get a hot dog."

"Can't believe you'd turn down my meatloaf for a hot dog!"

She's right. I'd probably rather stay here and hang out in the kitchen with Martha than go over to that dumb old football game, but I'm stuck.

"Next time," I say.

"Well at least have a Co-cola," Genevieve said. "Go on in there and get you one."

"No thank you. I'll just wait until we get there."

"Can't imagine why you wouldn't want a Co-cola."

"It's all right, really," I say, feeling awkward and wishing Sophie would hurry up.

The news is on TV, but the sound is off. Genevieve and I are both staring at it anyway. It's something about Vietnam, always Vietnam. I have prayed every night since as long as I can remember for it to be over so we won't have to be looking at those pictures any more, the people with blood all over them running away from guns and fire and soldiers. They say we're out now and it's going to be finished, but it sure doesn't seem like we've won anything.

I used to imagine that maybe my daddy was over there on some top secret mission. That's why nobody could talk about it. It was a good story because it explained everything, why he disappeared from our lives so totally and never came home. Then sometimes I'd think *maybe it would be better if he'd gone over there and gotten killed.* He could be a hero and I wouldn't have to be so worn out with so much wondering.

Genevieve suddenly brings me back.

"Oh! Let me show you what I got today! Martha took me to the doctor, and afterwards we had the best time...didn't we, Martha? Didn't we have fun?"

"Yes we did, Miss Evie, we sure did!" She's got to yell over the running water for us to hear.

"I went and spent some money...for no reason. Does that seem silly to you?"

"Well, no," I said. "I think you should do whatever you want to do, I mean, if it makes you feel better."

"Don't you want to see what I got?"

"Sure," I said.

"So reach over there by the door, honey, and get that bag. I'm feeling a little worn out." I hop up and do what she says. It was a big bag from Roses, the department store that has everything in the world.

"All right now, reach in there and pull you out something."

The first thing was a white teddy bear with a blue and red shirt, obviously left over from the 4th of July.

"Aw, he's cute!" I said.

"Go on, see what's next." It was a t-shirt that had *Priceless* written across the front in glitter. Then there was a bottle of scented toilet water, some fuzzy purple socks, a book of LifeSavers like the ones we always give each other for Christmas, and a refrigerator magnet that said, *"Don't let the turkeys get you down."*

"This is neat stuff." I looked up and saw that her face had changed. She was staring at the bag and not smiling anymore.

"Not really," she said. "Now that I look at it." She sighed. "I just wanted to go shopping—for anything—and since I can't do much, and there was this big clearance table right inside the door...well I just thought you and Sophie might find some of those things enjoyable."

"We do! I mean, I do. They *are*. They're...fun!"

"I thought I could do some things after my doctor's appointment but I was feeling so weak."

"Oh, should I—"

"You know what's ahead for me, Angel," she says.

"Yes ma'am, I've been hearing. From Sophie, I mean." I didn't want her to think people were talking about it, even though they were. "I'm real sorry." I didn't know what else to say.

"No need to be sorry," she says. "It's not like any of us is *not* dying. Everybody is one day closer to leaving here then they were yesterday. It's just that from the looks of things right now, I'll be going on sooner than most." Her voice trails off as she looks over to the window. I never thought of it that way before and now that I do, here comes that bad feeling over me, like a dark cloud that's going to swallow me up. I'm feeling scared and it's getting hard to breathe. Genevieve doesn't seem to expect me to say anything, thank goodness, so I don't.

Sophie is fixing her hair down the hall with that blow dryer she got for her birthday. She saw it in Greer's around Christmas last year and just had to have it. Her mom never would let her go out with wet hair. Over the years we played many a game of Candy Land and Go Fish while she sat with a pink bonnet on her head, waiting for that long ribbed hose full of hot air to get her dry enough. I remember the smell of steamy hair and hot plastic, but not any more now that Sophie's gone modern.

I'm listening to the sound of the blow dryer and thinking it must be sucking all the air out of this house. Even if it's getting on to fall, it'll be hot here in east Tennessee for a while to come. Every year I spend a lot of time fantasizing about living in New England, where it gets chilly right after Labor Day and you get to wear knee socks and sweaters that match the leaves from the first day of school.

I'd like to live there, or at least live somewhere else. This town sometimes makes me feel like I have to gasp for breath, and I'm not talking about the weather now. It's something else that I can't quite put my finger on, but I feel it in places like Greer's where the smell is the

same year in and year out. I have sucked in that smell since I was a little
girl and let it out again with every gum ball, popsicle and pencil eraser
I've ever bought in there.

But it's not just a smell. I get the same feeling down on the street
corner a half-block from my house on a summer afternoon with the
sun baking down on the concrete and the whole world still and aching
like it wants to break out, or break free, or something. Or sometimes
when I'm with Sophie and we can't think of what we want to do, or
she's excited about something and I'm not, or it's late afternoon and
the light in the kitchen is low and sad and the day's going before it
should. It's in such moments that I wonder if there is air enough to
keep me going and I think it must be different in some other place. It
just has to be.

"There are regrets, of course," Genevieve says. "I'll be leaving a
teenage daughter. I probably won't get to see her going off to the se-
nior prom, or graduating from high school. I won't get to help her plan
her wedding or see my grandchildren. This really makes me sad."

Then she drifts away again. I'm pretty much speechless, so I just
stare. Her face is kind of pasty-looking and has lots of teeny little lines
all in it. They aren't wrinkles like an old person's, just hundreds of
tiny shrivels, almost like her skin is going faster than she is. She seems
weak, and the way her short, mousy colored hair is matted down on
her head makes me think of a baby duck that shouldn't be out in the
world alone. I just sit there, until the silence gets to be too much and I
feel dizzy and need to say something just to break up the stillness. "So
when do they think it will be?"

"What?" she asks, as if she can't believe I would ask such a thing.
Now I'm stuck here and can't think of any way to get out of it.

"I mean, um, when are they thinking it might happen?"

"When do they think what will happen, dear?" she asks, as if to
taunt me. I have no idea what to say and feel like I might pass out. I

look down at the floor and consider dropping my head between my knees like they say in the health book, but I don't want to do anything so dramatic. I just want to disappear.

"Oh," she says, more kindly this time. "No one knows that, dear. There could be an earthquake tomorrow that kills all of us at the same time, or you and Sophie could leave here and get hit trying to cross the road. Anything could happen. I just wake up every morning amazed that I'm here another day and determined to make it count... and I will never, ever, even to my last breath, give up on the possibility of a miracle." Suddenly she's smiling again and she leans over to say in a loud whisper, "Want to know where Martha took me on the way home?"

"Where?"

"Burger King! I had a Whopper with cheese and French fries! Ate the whole damn thing!" She seems so tickled with herself over this I have to smile.

Now here comes Sophie tearing down the hall. I finally get one good breath.

"Let's go, Angel, or we'll miss the kick-off!" I jump up.

"I'll be seeing you," I say. "...I guess." As soon as I say it I realize how it must have sounded, and my face burns with shame as I follow Sophie out the door. Hearing Genevieve laugh behind us doesn't make me feel one bit better. I wonder if being sick like that makes people unpredictable.

"You girls be good now!" Martha calls from the kitchen.

"Yes ma'am!"

"We will!"

"Hey, Sophie?" I say.

"What?" She's walking fast across her yard about three steps ahead of me.

"Be careful crossing the street."

Chapter Six

I don't know why I was surprised the next day when Sophie wouldn't come out. She said she was having cramps. This was a double insult. Number one, she's always changing the plans that are my idea. We were supposed to follow the creek all the way out to Sunshine Bakery and buy a Honey Bun, and I was looking forward to it. Number two, it's just another way for her to rub it in that I've never bled yet.

I'd been feeling bad about maybe being the only eighth grade girl at Ralph Coleman Junior High in this situation. It has probably never occurred in the whole history of the school, if anybody kept track. But I didn't really care about it one way or another, at least most of the time. I was just tired of Sophie talking about it is all.

I have to accept the fact that it's always something with Sophie. If it's not the curse messing up our plans, then it's her asthma. I don't understand asthma, except that it attacks, and when it attacks you can hardly breathe and that's really scary. Sophie's doesn't get that bad very often, but she has to be careful. That's why she doesn't walk to school with me, because it might "act up." It means she doesn't want to do something is what I think.

Once when we were up at Camp Windy Pines and she was in the bunk over me, she had a bad attack and was making the worst noise trying to get a breath and I thought she was dying. They called her mom and daddy to come get her and I cried the whole rest of the week, thinking she was dead, but when I got home she was just her same old self.

"Are you okay?" I asked when I saw her, but she acted like no big deal.

"'Course I'm okay!" she said. "What are you talking about?"

That's about the way it goes with Sophie.

I went on down to the ravine where we always start our creek walk and sat down on the bank to think, not caring that it was damp and I'd probably get dirt and grass stains on my shorts. It didn't seem to matter. Things were strange at home and the air was downright sticky with everything that wasn't being said. This thing about Daddy coming home was so big you'd think that would be all we could talk about in the two weeks since he called. Truth is, nobody had talked about it at all. Naomi was mad at Mama about Dennis, of course, so she'd been tight-lipped. And Mama was mad at Naomi for telling her what to do, but it seemed like more than that to me.

"Do you think he'll really come?" I asked her one night, sitting at the kitchen table doing my homework. She was reading one of her doctor books.

"Sure sounds like he means to." She let her fist fall from her forehead and looked straight at me before her blue eyes darted off to the side. Mama hardly ever wears make up. Her skin is white beneath her freckles, just like mine, without any signs of her age that I can see. It can be confusing sometimes, to look at her and see this *girl* mom. You'd think it'd be like growing up with a friend, but it doesn't feel that way.

"Doesn't that make you happy?" I asked.

"For you, to have your daddy back…if it's what you want." She looked down and messed with the page corner of her book. Her hands were shaking a little bit, like they did sometimes, and her hair was falling on either side of her face. She was wearing her favorite brown and green plaid flannel shirt, the one she liked to put on with her jeans after work.

"That's not what I meant," I said, trying to catch her eyes. Mama sighed and gazed up like she always did, like she was checking in with the Almighty before she answered, or for whatever reason it was that she couldn't quite look at me.

"It's complicated."

"But don't you want us to be a real family again?" I said.

"So what do you think we are now, a bunch of chickens in a hen-house?" She gave me a weak smile and tried to laugh.

"Mama, stop teasing! You know what I'm saying."

"Of course I do," she said. "You want your daddy. What girl wouldn't? But you've got to understand that if he does come home, it's like somebody bringing you a pig in a poke."

"A what?"

"It's an old expression," she said. "If the pig's wrapped up in a poke, you don't really know what you're getting." Then she got up from the table and headed for the door like she'd heard something calling, which I knew was a cigarette.

"Mama, don't! You've been doing so good!"

"Leave me alone, Angel."

Don't ask me any questions, Angel… don't trouble me with your heartache… don't make me look at you….

"Why don't you just disappear, Angel?" I say, but of course she's already out the door and doesn't hear me. This is what I'm talking about.

So where does that leave me? I guess in the middle somewhere, all full of wanting, just like I've always been, wanting so much I'd forgotten what it was like not to have it pulling at my heart. It had been my companion so long, this invisible thing, that maybe I wasn't even sure exactly what it was that I wanted anymore—except for answers, and I was for sure looking for some of those.

If I put my mind to it, I figured, today would be a good day to find out something new. It was a beginning, the first day of September, and the world was wide open for possibilities. So where to start? Dottie Ames? If I went and tried to get her to talk to me about all of this it wouldn't be the first time, but I didn't have high hopes that I'd get any further. She was probably too much in cahoots with Naomi to ever let on much. Even back in June when she asked me to come over to the church and help her set up for Vacation Bible School, I had a whole morning with her without learning hardly a thing. She was good at keeping the conversation going her way, until I just flat out told her that I needed somebody to tell me more about my daddy.

"These are things you'll understand when you're a little older," she said.

"When will that be?" I asked. "I've been waiting a long time already and I don't know how much good it's doing to wait until I get smarter, or whatever."

"It's not about being smarter," she said. "It's about trusting the Lord that you'll know everything you're supposed to know, when you're supposed to know it. Can you understand that?" I didn't answer. I was stapling cut out magazine pictures onto a bulletin board under the caption, "I THANK JESUS FOR…" So far, I had a picture of a girl eating corn on the cob, a field of sunflowers, a glass of milk, a dog, some mountains, a policeman, and a stack of pancakes. I was looking for something a little more unexpected.

"Well then, can you tell me something about my mama when she was younger?"

"I can tell you she was a girl of her own mind. She sure knew how to upset her mama."

"You mean by marrying Daddy? I know that much."

"You know plenty for now—and I don't think we need that big picture of a spider. It might frighten the children."

"Why? Didn't God create spiders right along with everything else?" Dottie looked at me for a minute, as if she was considering more than what I'd just said.

"Tell you what," she finally said. "Later on, if you've still got questions, I'll be glad to talk to you."

"Later on? So when in the heck is *that*?" Dottie cringed at my almost-bad word, but she couldn't get mad at me and she knew it.

"It's…it's just not now, not yet. You're going to have to grow up a little bit. That's all."

I turned back to the bulletin board and put the spider picture smack in the middle.

So I'm sitting there on the bank wondering if I've grown up enough for Dottie yet when I heard voices up behind me. I knew it was the boys, and sure enough, when I turned to look up, there were Hank and Myron racing down the hill. *Uh-oh.* This wasn't what I needed. They could really mess up my day if I wasn't careful.

I trusted they'd try to avoid colliding into me but I stood up just in case I had to get out of the way quick. You couldn't ever count on these two for sensible behavior. It was just this kind of thing that had earned Hank the unofficial award for the most visits to the emergency room before high school. He was always needing stitches or breaking a bone or something. If it wasn't too serious, meaning if he was conscious and could walk, his mama would send him out to the curb to wait on Doc Ames's nurse, who'd hop in her car and come take him to emergency, then she'd go on over to get him later when he got patched up. Everybody knew the drill.

Myron's injuries may have been less in number, but he sure outdid Hank two years ago trying to swing across the ravine on a vine. He ended up in a body cast for three months and still has a limp, which is why Hank beat him down the hill now, though not without coming into a slide at the bottom and rolling the rest of the way into the creek.

"No fair!" Myron hollered. "You got a head start!"

Hank pulled himself up, panting and dripping, and looked up at me with his eyes blinking real fast. This was his nervous tic. He'd done it as long as I'd known him.

"How'd you know we was going to be here?" he asked. He had gotten so tall and lanky. I could tell how thin he was under the soggy clothes hugging his body. The ends of his hair were wet and hanging in his face. I had to laugh.

"I didn't," I said. "I was just sitting here." I didn't tell them about my plan, knowing full well they'd want to come along. Hank and Myron were my playmates from way back. We'd roamed the neighborhood together since we were little, riding bikes and catching bugs all day and playing Kick the Can in a million summer twilights.

"Okay, let's go walk the drain." Hank started back up the hill to the street.

"No thanks," I said. When I was younger I'd go with them, crawl down through the gutter into the big round pipe that leads to the creek. It felt a lot more adventurous than just walking down the hill, but I wouldn't do it since Mugsy died. He was Hank's boxer, and we'd send him down first so he could chase out all the rats before we went in.

"Oh, come *on!*" Myron said in his whiniest voice. "What's the matter? Scared it's gonna mess up your hair?"

"Right," I said. My mind was searching the options for successfully getting away from them. It wasn't going to be easy at this point. They were desperate for an audience and tended to attach themselves like creek leeches if you weren't careful.

"Look what I found." Hank reached in his pocket and pulled out a beautiful crystal.

"Let me see that," I said, but he jerked it away and gave me a sly, sideways grin.

"What will you give me?"

"Oh, shut up! Looks to me just like the ones they've got up at Big Joe's Trading Post." That's the gift shop out on the highway with the big Indian out front, the one standing up about forty feet tall and not wearing a thing except a headband with a giant painted wooden feather, and a belt around his waist with a flap hanging in the front. Given the size of the statue, I'd bet anybody a hundred dollars there was never a person could look up at that flap without wondering what's underneath.

"I found it, I swear! This one and a bunch of others, and a whole lot more cool stuff too. You gotta see."

"Where?" I asked.

"In the drain," he said, grinning real big. He knew he had me. Sometimes I thought he was cute, but mostly not.

"All right," I said. "I'll come into your stupid drain, but only to make sure you're not lying."

I started back up the hill with them, remembering the excitement I used to feel at this sort of thing and realizing that it was gone, all gone. I was hot and bored, not just with this day but with my whole life. This was not what I'd had in mind when I started out this morning.

We got back up to the street and I watched while the boys lifted the grate off the gutter.

"I'm not going in there first," I said. "You get to scare the rats out."

"Sissy!" Myron dropped his legs over the edge and let himself down the hole. He wasn't moving fast enough to suit Hank.

"Hurry up, fatso!"

He slipped himself down as soon as Myron had cleared the space. Then it was my turn. I sat on the curb and looked down into that dark hole, gulped in a deep breath, and did my old trick of holding it all the way until I passed through the gutter opening into the drain below.

Once down there you could walk, but it wasn't near high enough to stand up straight. You had to stoop way down and make your way towards the light, which was where the drain ended and spilled out into the creek. It was wet, dank, and slimy, full of germs and molds and God knows what-all venomous creatures waiting to attack. The boys were making plenty of noise just ahead of me, so at least any self-respecting rat would be long gone by now.

The pipe was held together at the seams by these thick concrete things that were only about half the height of the drain, high enough to be well above the waterline even in a downpour, so the tops of them were like little shelves about every twenty feet or so. Down near the end where there was more light, the boys had used these spaces to arrange their collection of findings.

"So how you like our museum?" Myron said.

I couldn't believe what I saw, beautiful old pots and stones and arrowheads, pieces of woven cloth, strips of what looked like animal hide. There was a stone bowl with another long, hand-sized rock that was smooth and rounded on the end, like it had once been used for pounding things into powder.

"This thing smells like garlic," I said. "Somebody's been using this."

"Naw, nobody's used that for thousands of years. Me and Myron found it in this old cave. We're the first white men to ever discover it.

You know this here land used to be crawling with Indians, like that old Indian witch woman. Bet you a buck she's one of them."

"Man, she is sooo weird!" Myron said. "She sits over there and puts spells on people."

"Show me the cave," I said. "I want to see it."

"No way," he said. "That's our secret. We swore it in blood not to show anybody else.

"Well, what'd you do that for? Nobody even cares. Besides, you might get blood poisoning doing that." I looked out the end of the pipe into the sunshine thinking I might just head on down the creek by myself, if only I could get rid of these two. I'd have to be careful how I did this, being already in great danger of being stuck with them the whole rest of this long hot day. They'd stepped away from me and were walking back deep into the drain to discuss something. They whispered for a couple of minutes and came back.

"We've got a deal for you," Hank said. "Interested?"

"Well go ahead, might as well tell me." I sighed. By this time I was real sorry I had let myself get sucked into this.

"If you'll go over and see the old Indian woman—and we mean *walk into her yard and knock on her door*—we'll show you the cave. We'll let it count even if you run away once she answers."

"I'm not doing that!" I said.

"Hey, ain't she one of your relatives?" Myron said.

"What are you *talking* about?" I said.

"Just seems I heard that somewhere."

"No, she is *not* one of my relatives, for Pete's sake, and I don't know where you come up with such stupid stuff. Just forget it. I'm going." I started walking out.

"Wait up!" Myron said. "Give us just a sec." They disappeared up the drain again. It didn't take them a minute to come back this time, but I was already leaving anyway.

"Hold on," Hank said. "Fair is fair. We'll show you the cave if you'll show us…well, you know, let us see some pussy."

"What!" My face was suddenly on fire. I couldn't say anything else for trying to catch my breath.

"Oh, good grief!" Myron said. "We're not going to *do* anything. We just want to see. Just pull down your pants and show us. We promise that's all we want."

They both stepped toward me and each took an arm. I wasn't sure what was happening. The way they were gripping, it didn't feel like a game of spin-the-statue or tag-you're-it. I tried to snatch myself away but they held fast.

"Let go of me!"

I tried to ram my elbows into their ribs, but they just kept holding onto me and laughing, like they were having the best old time watching me squirm. I guess that's when I panicked, because I swung a kick right between Hank's legs. I didn't hold back. I didn't miss, either. He let go, all right, and kind of doubled up on the ground with his face on his knees.

"What'd you do that for?" he squeaked when he could talk again.

"I'm telling!" Myron said.

"Telling what?" I said, backing away towards the opening. "You going to tell what you were trying to do to me? Go right ahead! Just how STUPID do you think I am? Don't you ever, EVER say anything like that to me or try to touch me again or I will snatch those puny little dicks right off of you and feed them to the damn snapping turtles right here in this creek!"

Then I ran out of there as fast as I could, ran out of the pipe and out into the sunshine and on up the hill to the street.

"Gosh, Angel, CALM DOWN!" I heard Myron yelling from below. We was just kiddin'! Wasn't we, Hank?"

"Yeah…" he said, sounding like he'd barely caught his breath. "We didn't mean it!"

When I got to the top I kept running all the way back to my house and plopped myself down at the kitchen table. Once my heart stopped pounding, I got to feeling so mad I thought I might just bust right there. How could they do that to me? Who do they think they are and who do they think I am? How can they think of all the fun stuff we used to do when we were kids, and now think of me as...well, like that?

I wanted revenge. I wanted them to hurt. At least I showed Hank, but I wanted to go punch out their stupid little horny eyes and kick 'em again, see them both doubled over. I wanted to tell somebody what had happened to me, but I didn't know who. Something told me Sophie was not the one.

Then that black feeling started, pressing down on me like a lead balloon and choking me out, and I knew I had to do something or talk to somebody or I was going to go all-out, flipping-my-wig nuts. Mama and Naomi had driven over to Knob Hill that morning to get some vegetables from Miss Kitty, the lady from church who sells them right out of her garden, so they wouldn't be back until later.

I was trying to think what to do. I thought maybe eating something might help, so I got up and looked in the pantry. There was nothing there but the usual flour, sugar, oil, Corn Flakes, Pop Tarts, and the like. I checked the fridge. There was cherry jam, eggs, milk, cheese, a bowl of Naomi's potato salad, tuna fish, lettuce in the drawer, and a jello salad still in the mold. It had fruit cocktail in it. I figured that must be for Sunday dinner the next day.

I pushed everything around until I saw a foil package at the back. It had been there for months, since Christmas, just like it was every year until somebody finally decided to throw it out. It was the fruitcake Dottie Ames always gave us and nobody ever touched, much less ate. I realized I wasn't even hungry, just aching for something and didn't even know what.

I slammed the refrigerator door shut and sat back down with this funny feeling like I was the only person left in the world. Even though

I knew everybody else was going on about their business, I just had that *feeling*. They say Jesus is going to come back one day and whoosh all the believers up to heaven, all at once, and everybody else will be left back here wondering what happened. That would be bad, but not as bad as that *Twilight Zone* episode where this guy got left by himself on this other planet because he was late getting back to the ship.

I was starting to feel so alone myself I was afraid of what might happen if I didn't do something quick. So I started to sing a song I remembered from when I was little.

> *The water is wide*
> *I can't get o'er*
> *And neither have I*
> *Wi—ings to fly*
> *So build me a boat*
> *That will carry two*
> *And both shall row*
> *My love and I*

I like to sing, even if that old biddy that leads the junior choir told me just to mouth the words and not sing with the rest of them, which is why I quit. I like the sound of my voice. It seemed to be coming from somewhere else and helped calm down my thoughts.

Seems like there's different kinds of being alone. People say folks are alone when they don't have a husband or wife around. They talk about my mama being alone as if Naomi and I don't count. Then there's Naomi alone in her widowhood, and me alone in my room sometimes and Sophie alone as a child whose mother is dying and her daddy who'll be alone when she does die, except for Sophie being there, but everybody will say he's raising her by himself. If you think about it, when you're lying there in bed in the dark, no matter how many people are in your house or in your room, or even in bed with you, aren't you alone in your own body? Somewhere along the line, it's just you and it, whatever *it* is.

Then there's the kind of alone where there's nobody else around you in your life, like that Old Susan. I wondered if she wanted it that way or if she had any choice about it at all, and why the boys had dared me to go harass her just because they think she's strange, just because she's out there all by herself. And then how in the world did they get from that to wanting me to *show them—pussy*? Come to think of it, Old Susan's been around a long time. Maybe she knows something about Daddy.

All of a sudden I felt kind of drawn to her, and it occurred to me to go and pay her a real, regular visit, just like Naomi and the ladies from her circle would go see a new widow, or take food to somebody that was sick. Her house wasn't that far from the Sunshine Bakery, just across the bridge and down the gravel road a bit. Everybody knew where it was, but I didn't know anybody who had ever been there. I could still walk the creek and go get my Honey Bun, all on the way to her house. Thinking about the Honey Buns made me feel a whole lot better.

First thing, though, was figuring out what I could take her. Naomi always took something on a visit, preferably something homemade. I had made cakes and cookies and stuff before, but I didn't have time to do it right then. What could I take from here, something that wouldn't be missed?

Then I thought of the perfect thing. *Even if we don't like it, maybe Old Susan will.* So I tossed the fruitcake in a brown paper sack and was on my way.

Chapter Seven

Our street runs along the top of a ridge that slopes down to Murray Creek. Walking along this valley, you can look up and see which house you're behind. That's how I kept track of where I was.

The creek was high because we'd had lots of rain. I started out trying to keep dry on the rocks, but in two seconds my shoes were soaked, so pretty soon I just started walking in the water, feeling the ooze squishing its way into the holes of my old Keds. I didn't reckon Old Susan would care one way or the other.

I looked around. The woods are dense down there in the ravine. The trees still had all their leaves and were low and thick like what I imagine a jungle to be like, or maybe a swamp, but since I've never seen either I don't really know. I'll bet that's what Vietnam looks like. It's different up on the hill, for sure, where there's barely any grass on the lawns from kids stomping and tearing around with their bikes and everything.

There's also lots of trash down there, tires and old shoes and ripped-up jeans caught up in low-hanging tree branches. Like with the shoe in the road, I wondered who in the world lost their jeans and what awful thing might have happened in order for them to end up in the creek. It made me think about what had happened with the boys and it gave my stomach a lurch.

The sun was getting higher. I took off my long-sleeve shirt, trying to decide whether or not I really wanted to keep going. We used to live for this kind of thing, walking along the creek to get a Honey Bun or just running around down in the ravine. Now it all seemed flat and dull, just dumb ideas little kids would think up.

It was pretty weird, how just as I was thinking about all this I came up on the stony slope where me and Sophie used to come play. We made it our fort. It didn't really look like anything. Unless you knew what it was, you'd pass it right by, nothing but a rocky place in the hill-side surrounded by oak and maple and sweetgum trees, curving in just enough for two kids to think they had a secret hideout.

It was that fall in the fifth grade, when it was sunny and warm and dry just about every single day until Thanksgiving. For a while this was practically all we thought about. I'd run in the house after school, throw my books down, change clothes, and get over to Sophie's as fast as I could. She always had to practice piano for ten minutes before she could leave, but as soon as she was done we'd be out the door lickety split, every day carrying the same things with us—a red plaid wool blanket, the Peter Pan lunch box with our snack, and a small straw bag that held a deck of cards and the books we were reading. My favorite that year was *A Wrinkle in Time* and Sophie's was *My Friend Flicka*. We'd check them out of the school library over and over again until Miss McNulty the librarian told us we had to give somebody else a turn.

So we'd go down there and play cards or read, sometimes play pretend—like kidnapped Indian princesses, or archeologists, or just work on the fort. We stretched branches between two big boulders on either side to make a roof and piled leaves on top for the covering, even if they didn't stay very well. It needed repair just about every time we went there. The different rooms were marked off with sticks and we changed it around all the time. We used rocks for furniture and spent hours collecting moss for the perfect green carpet. We'd "dust" with dried leaves and pretend to cook dinner with acorns.

It was like magic then, playing in our secret place, watching the leaves turn colors as the weeks went by. It got cooler, but it was still dry and sunny until after Thanksgiving. That was when everything changed.

The weather turned rainy and cold. The Jackson twins invited Sophie to their slumber party but not me. I didn't know whether to be hurt or relieved. Those girls were in the sixth grade and really popular, and they were already wearing bras. That night I spent the time alone in my room, reading Madeline l'Engle and pressing my palms together with my elbows out, full of hope and dread about things to come.

We never went back down to the fort after that. Winter came on in and we never even talked about it anymore, even when spring came, like it had just vanished. But it hadn't, it was us two little girls who'd vanished. This had been here all along.

I stepped in and looked around. A couple of the branches were still stretched across the boulders, and now I had to duck to walk underneath them. I sat down on one of the rock chairs, the one that had been mine, thinking about how I hated Hank and Myron and was mad at Sophie for breaking her promise and sick of Mama and Naomi's hiding things from me and tired of wondering what in the world about Daddy and sad that whatever was good in my life had passed and the future just made me feel afraid. It was such a downright nasty day, so muggy and all, I almost decided to give up, head back up the hill and go home. What in the world was I doing down there all by myself, wallowing through the muck just to see the town's most famous crazy person?

I leaned down to pick up an acorn, a nice smooth one—and saw something that made my heart stand still. There under the other rock chair, not three feet from me—lying quiet but surely getting ready to strike—was a huge snake. I shivered at the length of it sprawled out there, maybe six feet long but all curled up just waiting for someone, something to kill. I watched for a minute and might have decided it was dead if it hadn't moved just a little bit. I thought I might just go ahead and die right then and there, save it the trouble of biting me, until I realized it wasn't the least bit interested in me. It acted like it didn't care that I was there, like its mind was somewhere else.

I knew it must be one of those water moccasins, so poisonous they'll kill you within one minute of a bite. I saw that on TV. They'll chase you, too. I couldn't figure why it was just sitting there like that— and then I saw it, the skin up and down its long body starting to turn milky white. I was in a trance watching it. Here I was, face to face with a venomous reptile, and all I could do was sit there and gawk.

I thought about Eve, the very first woman. Maybe that snake she met was in the middle of shedding when she came across it. Maybe she stood there watching it and thinking, *I'd like to do that. I'd like to just let go of this thing that's wrapped around me, all of this that the world sees as me, and just let it drop off. I'd like to see what's underneath.*

I know we're supposed to think Eve ruined everything, but I think she just did what she had to do. Maybe she was just so tired of everything being the same day after day with her and Adam. Maybe hanging out in that garden the whole time wasn't as great as everybody makes it out to be, running around buck naked all the time. Then the snake tells her about that apple and she's open, she's ready for change, she's onto something new.

The snake started to move. Then I saw it glide forward, right on out of its skin and out towards the creek, leaving that thin, papery shell lying right there where it came off. It still didn't seem to be the least concerned with me but I grabbed my knees into my chest anyway and waited until it was good and gone.

My heart was racing, but it was time for me to get going, one way or the other. I went back over to the bank and looked around, surprised to see how far I'd actually come. The snake had shaken me out of my mood. It had shed its skin and I'd let go of something too.

So instead of turning back I struck out into the field that stretched between the highway and the creek, leaving the shelter of the woods and walking towards the asphalt world of Hardee's hamburgers, Valley View Chevrolet, Southern State Discount Department Store, Big Joe's Trading Post, and my first stop, the Sunshine Bakery. The field was muddy, but it didn't matter since I was already covered in the stuff anyway.

For the first time that day, I was glad to be alone. Sophie would have fainted dead away into the water at the first sight of that snake. Then I'd have had to do mouth to mouth resuscitation on her and I'd have never heard the end of it.

When I walked into the shop the woman who was always there looked up. Her face was full and smooth, her hair pulled back tight with a hair net over it. Together with her overall roundness and white uniform she looked like a moon lady. Her name was embroidered on the left. *Tammy*.

"Where's your friend today?" she asked.

"I don't know," I muttered, too tired to explain.

"So you're out there messing around in that creek all by yourself?"

"Reckon," I said.

"A gal your size ain't supposed to be doing stuff like that." I handed her ten cents for a Honey Bun, only I didn't have to say anything. She knew what I wanted and had already put it on the counter. Then she turned to the cooler behind her and pulled out an orange Nehi.

"It's on me," she said. "You look like you need it."

"Thanks!" I meant it. I went over to the small table by the window where we usually sat and let out a big sigh, wondering what is was about this whole day that was somehow off.

Tammy disappeared into the back. The Honey Bun was stale, but the Nehi was cold and good. She had been right. It was just what I needed to keep me moving. I picked up my sack of fruit cake, put my bottle up on the counter, and left the Sunshine Bakery, heading out in the direction of the river bridge.

It was past noon by now, and steamy hot. I felt peculiar. Maybe it was just nerves, but I started thinking about what I was going to say to Old Susan when I got there. No matter how hard I tried, whatever I imagined saying just sounded stupid. Maybe she would take it the wrong way. Maybe she'd think I was just curious, or coming to make fun of her or something. By the time I got across that rickety old bridge I was beginning to lose my nerve, pretty sure she wasn't going to tell me any more than anybody else. But I was pretty well into this thing by now, and thinking to see it through.

I was headed up the gravel road, actually beginning to enjoy myself a little more now that I was in the shade, when I saw somebody coming the other way. I knew it was her, a short, stocky woman with long dark hair wearing a long purple muu-muu. She reminded me of that lady who sings with The Mamas and the Papas. All of a sudden I felt shy, but I knew I couldn't just turn and go the other way now. It would look like I was running from her, so I decided I'd just act like I was out for a stroll and happened to pass her by, like there wasn't a thing unusual about a mud-covered girl wandering around by herself on the far side of the river bridge.

We moved closer and closer to each other. I didn't know when to speak or what to say, but when she got close enough for me to see her rugged brown skin and sharp dark eyes looking straight into mine, she smiled real big. Then she spoke.

"Adawehi!"

That made me forget everything I had thought about saying.

"Um…I'm Angel," I said, not knowing what else to offer.

"Why, I know who you are!" She just kept looking at me and smiling. Her face looked familiar to me somehow, but I couldn't place it.

"Why, look at you! Hardly a young'un any more! How's your granny?"

"You know her?" I asked.

"Naomi and I go way back," she said. I'd never heard my grandmother say a word about knowing Old Susan personally. "Well, you sure are a sight!" She laughed as she looked down at my wet, filthy legs and feet. "Heee! Look at you, like something rose up out the mud!"

"I've been walking up the creek," I said. "We like to do that, or we used to anyways, and me and Sophie were going to do it today but she wouldn't come out so I thought I might just come on over here and…" I heard myself rambling on. It was embarrassing. "Anyways, I brought you something."

"Why, thank'ee!" she said. She seemed genuinely pleased about it, which made me feel better. "Won't you come up t'the house?"

"I'd like that."

"Well, come on, then," she said as she turned to take me back towards her place.

"Don't let me stop you from going wherever it was you were headed," I said. "I can come back another time."

"What? Naw, I was just coming out to meet you."

"But how'd you know I was coming?"

"Figured you might be," was all she said.

I was puzzling over this as we walked down the road, neither of us saying anything. We only went a short way before taking a foot-path through the trees that led to a clearing. There was a small white clapboard house surrounded by what looked like several little gardens, some marked off by split rail fences, others by low stone walls or old stacked railroad ties.

There were different kinds of flowers blooming all around, most of which I didn't know, but I did recognize the bunches of yellow flowers with the dark centers growing on either side of her front door—Black-Eyed Susan. There were a couple of chickens running around the yard and at least two goats that I could see. The woods were all around, and in the distance a view of the mountains rising up above the river valley. It all had a nice feeling.

"Welcome! Hit ain't much but it's home!" She laughed, then looked up at me. I saw way into her face. It was wrinkled for sure, like Naomi's, and had seen its share of sun and wind, but it was a kind face, maybe holding more kindness than I'd ever seen in a person, maybe enough for the whole world.

"Oh, here you go." I handed her the brown sack. I wasn't proud of the gift, but it was too late to back out now.

"We'll have tea," she said. "You can stay?" I nodded, trying not to show all the things I felt, like excited, curious and a little bit scared. She led me around back of the house and sure enough, there was a big open fire pit with a pot hanging over it. She took it off its hook and walked over to a well to fill it up.

"There's some wood stacked over there." She pointed with a tilt of her head. "If you'd put a couple of logs on the fire I'd appreciate it."

I ran to collect a few pieces and placed them carefully, glad to have something to do. She came back and hung the pot, now full of water, and stoked the coals. The flames were soon leaping up over the logs. Then she pointed to a little table that was sitting by a big old cedar tree.

"Have a seat over there a minute," she said. "I'll be right back." I sat and waited, looking all around. I could see nothing but the woods on one side and a view of the mountains in the other direction. If I didn't know I was just across the river bridge I never would have guessed. It seemed far away, like I'd slipped into some curious new world, dreamy and safe.

She went into the shed and came back out with her hands full. Then she took two clay mugs from a hook beside the door and placed something in them. It seemed she might be more accustomed to visitors than I'd thought. I wondered what kind of tea she was making as I watched her go over to the fire and ladle the boiling water into the cups.

"Drink this." She set the mug on the table, sat down across from me and smiled, still holding the paper sack. Then she reached inside and pulled out the foil package.

Oh, why didn't I think to take the red ribbon off of it? It looked more than ever like a leftover Christmas gift, but when she saw it she just started laughing.

"Why it's Dottie's fruitcake!" I was mortified. It was so obvious what I'd done, but she didn't seem to think anything of it.

"Will you have some?" she asked.

"Yes, I'll have a little, thank you." Served me right, having to actually *eat* some of it.

She opened up the foil. The cake was already cut up into neat, sticky pieces, so she handed me a slice.

I decided right then she was probably not a witch. Yes, she had a boiling pot over a fire, but as far as I could tell there wasn't anything but water in it. I didn't see any shrunken heads or bones lying around and nothing that looked like a freshly dug grave. I didn't know what else to look for in trying to spot a witch so I figured the tea was probably safe.

She took a slice of cake for herself and bit into it. Then she looked up at me as if waiting for something, so I took a bite myself. I chewed and tried to swallow, but it was the most awful tasting thing I think I've

ever put in my mouth. She just sat there watching me without any expression on her face at all until I couldn't stand it anymore and gulped
almost the entire mug of tea trying to wash it down. I tried to avoid
her eyes but finally looked into them, and we both burst out laughing
like it was the funniest thing in the whole wide world.

"Ain't it the worst stuff you ever tasted?"

"Gosh, I'm sorry," I said. "What's in that?"

"Well, it's got Doc Ames's homemade bourbon in it for one thing.
She gives it out all over the place at Christmas and I'll swear I don't
think there's a single person that eats it."

"You know Dottie Ames too?" I asked.

"Who doesn't know that old bird? She went to school with
your granny and me, and I see her when she comes up here for her
arthritis remedy."

"But her husband's a doctor. Why doesn't she just go to him for
her arthritis?"

"'Cause there're just some things a doctor don't know how to fix,
but they can't never admit it. She has to come up here on the quiet.
Now mind you, it don't need to get around that Dottie Ames comes
to see Old Susan Blackfoot! What d'you think old Doc would do if he
found out his very own wife was taking her aches and pains to someone who's barely even been to school?"

"I guess he'd have a conniption fit," I said, "... whatever that is."
She laughed out loud and whacked the table, which made me laugh too.

"Conniption fit!" she said. "I like that!" Then she got up and went
into her little house again but soon came out carrying a beautiful loaf
of fresh brown bread and a crock full of butter that looked like it had
just been churned. She cut and buttered a slice for me and it tasted like
heaven. I hadn't even realized I was hungry. Then she got me some
more tea. I wondered again what it was.

"It's chaste berry," she said with that way she had of seeming to know what was in my mind already. "It's a good tonic for a woman, and you're a woman now."

"What do you mean?" I asked.

"Never mind." She laughed. "Just mark my word. By the way, is your mama liking her work up at the hospital?"

"I guess so. She never really says one way or another."

"She still interested in being a doctor?"

"How'd you know about that!"

"Been around here a long time, like I been telling you. There's not much folks don't know about each other in a place like this. So, does she?"

"She doesn't ever mention it," I said. "But I know she thinks about it, and she reads. I've seen all the books piled up in her room. There's some big test for medical school, and I guess she studies for it, thinking she'll take it someday. Are you some kind of doctor too?"

Then she told me about how she grew all of these things around her house for medicines, how her mother and grandmother taught her all about healing herbs and plants and how to use them like the Indians did way back before there were regular doctors.

"My daddy was Irish," she said, "but my Mama's grandmother was full-blooded Cherokee."

"I'm part Irish too!" I said.

"Yep. A good many are around here. Bunch of 'em came and settled here right along with the Indians, married 'em up all over these hills, as did the Germans and Scotch and all. Daddy'd never allow much to do with the Cherokee ways. He was agin' it, said it wasn't Christian. I had a sister who was a lot older than me, left home young, went and got married, and Daddy didn't live too much longer after that. When he was gone, Mama took me and my baby brother back to her people down in Georgia where I learned about the old ways -and I knew that was how I wanted to live.

So Old Susan lived alone with her animals and her gardens. She made a living with a small mail order herbal business, had customers all over the place. She grew the plants, cured and dried them, pounded them into powder and whatnot, then packed them up and shipped them to wherever they were going.

"So what brings you way over here on this particular afternoon?" she asked.

"Well…" I said, trying to think of a way to bring it up about Daddy.

"Don't matter anyhow," she said. "Folks generally end up over here when they're ready. So how's Patsy?"

"You know Patsy?" I said, by this time hardly even surprised.

"Well, haven't seen her in years."

"She lives over at Crestview because something's wrong with her mind, they say."

"They treating her all right?" she asked.

"I guess." Old Susan looked at me and nodded, like somebody does when they're trying to figure out who you look like. I saw my chance.

"So if you know everybody, then you knew my daddy." I tried to sound casual, but my voice was a little shaky.

"Yep, I knew him."

"So what do you know *about* him?"

"Well, I know he hasn't been around in quite a while, and I'm guessing you've got lots of questions about that." Another answer that was no answer. "But I've got a feeling about that, yes I do!" She paused here and took another bite of bread, then a sip of tea. "I've just got this feeling that something's going to be happening more sooner than later here, and you'll be knowing everything you always wanted to know and more. That's what I'm thinking."

"Well, you're right about the sooner part—he says he's coming home." Old Susan looked straight at me without blinking an eye.

"So what's that feel like?"

"I always thought it would be the best thing that could ever happen," I said.

"So why isn't it?"

"I don't know. It might be different if I felt like I knew the whole story, like where he's been all this time and why he's practically ignored me my whole life and why he left in the first place. But nobody's ever wanted to talk about it, and everything seems all wrong now. I can't tell what's going on with Mama because I never can, and Naomi's all mad at her and she's mad at Naomi, and I just don't know anything anymore."

"Well, sometimes things just ain't as simple as we think they're going to be."

"There's more to it," I said. "I just know it."

"Sometimes it's okay not to know it all, at least not right away. For pity's sake give yourself some credit for being young. You ain't supposed to have it all figured out!"

"But I'm *thirteen!*"

Old Susan slapped her hands to her knees, looked up to the sky and let out a great big belly laugh. "Believe me, you've got time," she said. "Meanwhile, I've got you some advice—if you want to hear it, that is."

"All right," I said. Advice wasn't exactly what I wanted, but if it was all she was giving I'd take it.

"Be careful what you wish for," she said, "and pay attention."

"Pay attention to what?" I asked.

"You'll know."

That was it? One thing I now knew about Old Susan was that she's not going to tell you what you expect to hear, or what you think you want.

"Yes'm." It was the only thing I knew to say.

I stayed a good while that afternoon. We sat at that table and I talked and talked, almost like I never do. For once I wasn't being told to be quiet. She just sat there listening and not saying much so I kept on going, all the while having the feeling that she already knew everything.

"I saw a snake when I was walking the creek," I said, feeling like I needed to tell it to somebody. "It was shedding its skin and I stood there and watched it."

"It's a sign," she said.

"A sign of what? What's that mean?"

"You'll know soon enough."

"Well, I got really mad at the boys before I left today," I said, not believing I was opening up this can of worms. "Do you think it has something to do with that?"

"Which boys?" she said. "You talking about those two live up there on the ridge?"

"How'd you know?" I said.

"I figured you just about growed up with 'em," she said. "You was all born about the same time."

"They've always been like my brothers," I said. "Until today." I paused.

"So you gonna tell me, or what?"

"Okay, well, they had this cool stuff they'd found, these old things that looked like artifacts, said they found them in a cave and they'd show it to me if I'd show ... well, they wanted me to...." I looked down, feeling ashamed to tell, ashamed even remembering it.

"Why those little fuckers!" she burst out. "I've a mind to...you didn't do it, did you?"

"No ma'am!" I said, so glad I could say that.

"Good," she said. "Don't ever let them or nobody *ever* force something like that on you. Y'hear?"

"Yes'm I hear," I said.

"Now tell me what all they had, the things they said they'd gotten in some cave."

"Well, there were pots and stuff and then what looked like tools or something." She seemed real interested.

"Did you see anything like a grinder, this long smooth rock inside a bowl?"

"I saw something like that, sort of like the one sitting on the counter in the pharmacy at Greer's."

"Were there some crystals?"

"Yes! And beads and a leather bracelet and a carving knife." She nodded her head like she knew exactly what I was talking about, but she didn't ask anything else. She just looked thoughtful and kept nodding her head.

"We'll get back to this," she said, then got up abruptly. "Come and see my place."

Old Susan showed me her gardens and told me about some of the plants. I met her chickens and her two goats, Maribelle and Jazz, and got to peek inside her two-room house. But when I saw the late summer light coming sideways through the trees, I knew I had to head for home. Mama would be looking for me.

"Now remember what I told you!" she called to me as I was walking away. I nodded and waved.

"Pay attention," I said out loud to myself as I made my way back down the road to cross the bridge. She'd said I'd know to what, which I didn't. Not yet, anyway.

I decided I wouldn't go back by the creek. The road was much faster—you just had to watch out with all the cars zipping past. So I was walking along minding my own business when some guy slowed down and yelled out something stupid I couldn't understand and didn't want to.

This had happened before, when I was with Sophie, but I was surprised that it happened to me—I'd always thought she was the one they were yelling at. I walked as fast as I could and got home just as the cicadas started bringing in the twilight.

"Look at you!" Mama said when I walked through the back door. "Where've you been with all that mud!" She did the head to toe thing with her eyes.

"Murray Creek," I said. Naomi looked up at me from snapping beans.

"Lord Jesus," she said. "Don't tell me you've been down in that ravine with those shorts on!" I didn't answer, headed quick as I could up the stairs to take a bath, but she hollered after me.

"You shouldn't be out loose like that! It ain't right!" I hurried to get away from the rest of it, but as I reached the top of the stairs it was only Mama's voice behind me.

"Sophie called."

I went into the bathroom and started pulling off the soaked clothes, the navy tank top, the white bra, the tight denim cut-offs now plastered to my body with mud and grit. The underpants came off with them. Then I saw something, and it wasn't mud. It was red as could be and spread all over the white underpants and even on the inside of my thighs. It was trickling down the backs of my knees and down my calves... blood! Must have cut myself on something. But there were no cuts or scratches that I could see.

So this was it. This thing that was never going to happen had happened today, this day of all days right before eighth grade when I had waited forever it seemed. I felt proud and relieved, like I'd just earned the Girl Scout badge everybody else already had. I also felt a little sad, wondering if this meant I'd never again have another day in the mud like this one.

What now? Go running to Mama? I hoped she was prepared, that she hadn't forgotten this was supposed to happen. Then I thought maybe I should call Sophie first, since she'd been the one always reminding me what a freak I was by not having it yet.

I decided I wouldn't do either one right away. I would wait. Number one, my mother would probably tell me I couldn't take a bath and I really wanted to. Number two, I didn't feel ready to listen to Sophie going on and on about it, not just yet. There was something about it, that moment, something I wanted just for me, just for a little bit.

I touched the red stains on the inside of my thighs and followed the red trail down to my ankles. I thought of the snake I'd seen that afternoon, how I'd watched it shed its old skin and slide off in its new self. I remembered what Old Susan had said about it being a sign of something. I figured this might be it. *Pay attention.* Then I got in the tub and took a long hot soak, wondering what Sophie would say to my doing such a thing against all advice, wondering if I would even tell her.

Chapter Eight

The next morning I wake up with my heart about beating out of my chest like I'd just run a mile. It's the dream again. I've been having it as often as not lately, only there's more to it now. As always, I'm seeing myself lying there all curled up and dead, and it's nothing but black and still and cold all around—but then I see the drain we crawl through to the ravine, but instead of just a drain, the whole ground opens up and there's this huge black hole that goes down and down forever, and I know that if my body gets sucked down into the darkness it's the most horrible thing there could ever be and I am doomed to hell—or worse, if there could be such a thing.

Sometimes I lie there awake half the night just thinking about dying. I think about it in all kinds of ways, like how old I might be, or how it might happen and who might show up at my funeral. I even think about what songs they might sing—maybe *Morning Has Broken*, because Cat Stevens made a record of it. Would anybody cry? But all of that's not nearly as scary as the dream. That's the worst. I think I'd almost rather die than have it. I'm not even sure I'd mind it so much, being dead, that is—I just wouldn't want it to hurt.

It's the day before Labor Day, and that's when Dottie Ames always puts on what she calls her Dog Day Tea for the ladies, so named because it's the end of summer but still hot as heck. They get all gussied up in their dresses and hats and go over to her house where she'll have her garden looking perfect and her dining room set up with all kinds of fancy food and a punch bowl full of something she says she only serves on this day. I don't know what's in it, but Mama and Naomi always come home from Dog Day Tea in a real good mood.

What's different about this year is that I'm invited. Sophie is too. It's supposed to make us feel grown up, but we're both complaining about it. We don't want to stand around in pantyhose listening to this and that and answering all those questions adults always ask, but Naomi said I have to go, it's an honor to be invited, and she won't let me go bare-legged on account of dog days either. My suspicion is that Sophie really does want to go because she loves people making a fuss over her, which they're bound to do because of her winning ways. I'd like parties better if I could just be a fly on the wall and watch everybody instead of always having to answer questions about my hair.

I guess I'm not real lady material. I'll never be like Dottie, not ever, not even when I'm old. She wouldn't be caught dead without her stockings on and her hair fixed, not even just to pop into the A&P for a loaf of bread. But every June she gives a lawn party where she goes western, with a red plaid shirt tucked into blue jeans, a bright blue bandana tied around her neck, a straw hat, and pointed boots. She puts on red lipstick and lets her hair down, too. People get a huge kick out of seeing her cut loose a little. I wonder what she wears when she goes to see Old Susan, and if anybody else ever sees her going over there.

I know Dottie well because she and Naomi are friends from way back and she's been around as long as I can remember, calling up and dropping by and bringing stuff or whatever. She's what you'd call the mother hen type. She prides herself in knowing what's best for everybody and most of the time she's right. You might think she'd be real snooty, being the doctor's wife and having such a fine house and all, but she's not. She treats everybody like her own and takes care of whoever needs anything.

It was on account of Dottie that we found Martha when we needed her. I was nine years old when Naomi got the shingles and couldn't do a thing. Mama had finished school by then and had just gone to work as a nurse, so there was nobody home to take care of me after school and nobody to do the cooking and cleaning.

Dottie told her husband Martin, or Doc Ames as we call him, that we needed help. Since he knows everybody and everything about them, he said he'd keep a look out. Well, he did more than that because they say he put up a *HELP WANTED* sign at his office, right there in the little window where you sign in with the nurse and everybody who came in could see it.

So that's how we got Martha, a farm girl from way back up in the hills who knew how to work, Doc said, and then everybody else got her too. Dottie alone keeps her busy enough with all these parties of hers.

When we pull up at the Ames house I see Sophie and her mom going up to the front door. Genevieve is using a cane to help her walk.

"Law me," Naomi said. "Look at that." Mama watches them both a second before she turns off the car.

"Yeah, her last bone scan wasn't good." She knows stuff like this from working up at the hospital. We all just sit there a minute without moving. "I'm not sure she should even be driving."

"I'd like to know who's going to tell her that," Naomi said.

"Well, one thing's for sure. It's not going to be a problem for too much longer."

"What's that supposed to mean?" I said.

"It means Genevieve isn't going to be getting any better," Mama said. "You might as well know it."

"I *know* that," I said. "She even says it herself. It's just that—"

"It's just that it's about time she found the Lord!" Naomi said.

"That's not what I was going to say."

"Are we going to this thing or not?" Mama asked.

"I reckon." Naomi opens the car door. It takes her forever to get out, so I just walk on in ahead of them and start looking for Sophie.

This is by far the fanciest party I have ever been to in my life. First of all, the mile-high ceilings in Dottie's house make you feel like you've walked into the White House or something. Then she's got this huge long dining room table set with all kinds of sandwiches, pastries, nuts, and candies. There are these little square cakes covered with icing and tiny flowers on top. When you bite into them you find several layers with icing in between. They are so sweet and delicious I can't quit eating them. The triangle pimento cheese sandwiches are fine too and so is the chocolate bridge mix, though I definitely do not like the bourbon balls.

I see L.B. coming in and out of the kitchen with various trays of things. He's related to Martha somehow, a cousin or something or other. You can tell because they have the same ruddy-looking face and hair that probably used to be like mine but now it's sort of silvery orange. Dottie's got him working the party too. He was a regular mess, in and out of jail and never holding onto any job until she got hold of him and somehow discovered he was good at a lot of things, including flower arranging. I'm sure he did the centerpiece with the yellow and white chrysanthemums mixed in with some dried stuff and seed pods and such. It's what I'd call exotic.

Dottie's dining room opens to the living room, where there's a double glass door leading out to the garden. She's got it all opened up today, so the ladies are moving in and out carrying their little round plates and glass punch cups. It's a sight to see, with all of them in their breezy summer dresses and hats. There's a lot of laughter and cackling going on—sweating, too. You see them dabbing their foreheads and upper lips with their napkins, working hard to talk and breathe at the same time. Here is what I'm hearing.

"Law, it's hot!"

"Feels like the devil's kitchen!"

"Can't hardly eat anything when it's like this. Think I'll have me some more of that punch."

"They said it's going to rain."

"Lord knows we need it!"

"Look at that flower arrangement! Did L.B. do that?"

"Ain't he something? Now who would've thought?"

Sophie and I are standing at the end of the table by the hot hors d'oeuvres. Genevieve is sitting on the loveseat in the living room and Mama has fixed a plate for her and taken it in there. Naomi is standing at the other end serving the punch. I have just discovered the cheese and asparagus wrapped in a crescent roll when a tall colored man comes up and hands us each a glass of ginger ale.

"They really think they're going to keep us out of that punch, don't they?" Sophie says. My mouth is full so I can't answer, and that's right when Mrs. Price, Hank's mother, walks over and starts talking to us.

"Look at you two beautiful young ladies!" she says. "How are y'all doing! I'll bet you can't wait for school to start next week." She's very tall and slender and is wearing a slim fitting flowery dress. Her lipstick is a perfect pink.

"Yes ma'am," I say as soon as I can clear my mouth.

"Well, I know Hank's ready, even if he'd never admit it. Only so much running around like a wild animal you can do before it starts getting old. At least we haven't had any stitches this summer!" She laughs. Then Mrs. Goldman, Myron's mother, comes over to join her in oogling over us. She's shorter and kind of fat, but I'm thinking those two must be attached at the hip, just like their nasty boys.

"Well, look who's here!" she says. Her voice is loud. "Since you're all about grown now we don't see you around like we used to."

I burn at the thought of what Hank and Myron did to me the other day, almost like it shows or something, like somehow I did something wrong. I try to smile just to be polite.

"Yes ma'am," I say, since it seems to be the only thing I can come up with, then turn my head back to the food table and pray somebody else will come over so I can slip off. Sophie's doing better with it.

"Is Hank going out for any sports this year?" she says. God bless her, she sure knows how to fawn over the adults. I know she'll go far in life.

"We're encouraging him to wait until spring baseball," Mrs. Price says. "Hopefully that will give him plenty of time for his studies in the fall." My eyes about roll out of my head. His *studies*? Hank's been pestering me to let him copy my homework since elementary school, and I've been telling him to do his own for just as long.

Sophie turns to Helen Goldman. "And how about Myron?" she asks, just like she was born for polite conversation. Maybe she'll get to be president or something, if girls can even do that.

"Well, he can't do anything rough for a while after that accident, so he's joining the swim team. We think it'll be very good for him." She's turning her head sideways and nodding like she's looking for somebody to agree with her.

"That's great," Sophie says. "I'm thinking about running for class president."

"Oh, my! Well, good luck with that!" Janey Price says. "And what about you, Angel? I hope you're going to try out for majorette again this year. I'm sure you'll make it, especially with all that beautiful red hair."

I'm just about choking on a sandwich I think is cream cheese and olives, but I'm not exactly sure. It's weird. I take a swig of my ginger ale to wash it down and collect myself enough to think of something to say. Number one, my hair is orange. Number two, I know Sophie has no intention of running for class office, she's just being a smart ass. And number three, I don't appreciate Hank's mother bringing up my unfortunate attempt at being a twirler on the drill team last year. I dropped the baton three times during the tryout and lost the spot to Kathy Bledsoe. The humiliation still hasn't worn off. How my hair was supposed to help makes no sense to me.

"I'm thinking about cheerleading," I say.

"Oh?" Both ladies seem confused and give each other a look.

"You are *not!*" Sophie whacks me on the shoulder, and then I grin.

"Just kidding," I say. Mrs. Price smiles and pats my arm before she turns and goes to the other end of the table for more punch.

"You girls be good now," Helen says, and follows her. Sophie doesn't skip a beat.

"Come with me," she says right into my ear, "and bring your glass."

"What?" I say, but as usual I go along, not because I particularly want to do whatever she says but because that's just the way it is between us. She leads me through the swinging door into the kitchen. Martha is standing there stirring up something.

"Well, now, there's a couple of good-looking gals. Ain't y'all a sight for sore eyes!"

"Hey, Martha," I say. Then L.B. comes flying through the door carrying an empty tray.

"Now what're you young'uns up to back here?" he says.

"Nothing. It's just sort of boring out there," Sophie says. "Need any help?"

"Thought you'd never ask. Here, put some more sandwiches on this tray while I go back out there and get the fruit bowl. It needs filling up too."

"Sandwiches are in the ice box," Martha says. L.B. is out the door again, and Sophie already has her head in the fridge looking around.

"Don't see them."

"Oh, for Pete's sake, Sophie." I step in front of her and find the Tupperware container with a label that has *Tea Sandwiches* written in red magic marker. This is just like Dottie. I also see the gallon container marked *Punch*.

"Come on and help me now," I say. "You're the one that got us into this."

Martha laughs. "Ever' time I see y'all, looks like you've grown another inch," she says, spooning the "devil" part into the deviled eggs. I've always wondered why they're called that. "What're we going to do when you're bigger than all of us?"

"Well, Sophie gets it from her father," I said. "He's six foot something, isn't he Sophie?" She seems distracted but she nods.

"Yeah, something like that." We're working on putting all the little Wonder Bread triangles in a cute design on the platter. There aren't any crusts to get in the way.

"Let's put them in a star," Sophie says.

"No, then we can't get enough of them on there. Let's do this." I show her how to make sandwich flowers by putting them in layers. Besides the strange cream cheese combination, there's pimento cheese, egg salad, cucumber with mayonnaise, and ham salad.

"I wonder how tall my daddy is," I say, hoping Martha might offer something, but the door swings wide and L.B. comes back in with the empty fruit bowl.

"What's this? It don't have to be all fancy, now!" he says. "Just get them on there and somebody take them out." We finish what we were doing and I carry the tray to the dining room. On my way back in I pass L.B. with a full bowl of fruit and Martha with the platter of deviled eggs. Sophie is standing by herself in the kitchen holding our two punch cups.

"Come in here with me!" she says. "Hurry up!"

I followed her again. She seemed to know where we were going, to a little powder room just off the butler's pantry by the kitchen.

"Sophie! What—"

"Just shush and get in here!" She pulled me in and shut the door again. It's a tiny room with a strong flowery smell that makes me sneeze.

"Ah-choo!"

"Stop it!"

"Most people would say *bless you*," I said. "Must be that guest soap." It was sitting on the sink, shaped like a light blue flower. I picked it up to look at it and it made me sneeze again.

"*ANGEL!*"

"Sorry. By the way, are we hiding from somebody?"

"We're just waiting, and we don't want anybody to know we're in here." She was whispering now.

"Oh." Struggling not to sneeze again, I put the toilet seat down and sat with my nose pressed between my hands. We heard somebody come into the kitchen, move around awhile, and leave again.

"That was L.B.," she said.

"Sophie, why are we—"

"SSSHHH! Now here comes Martha!" We heard more of the same.

"I'm waiting until they're both gone again," she said, and turned off the light. Then she cracked the door just the tiniest bit so she could peek out and watch. We waited. I was still holding off a sneeze.

"Perfect!" she said.

"What's perfect?"

"The coast is clear! Hold on, I'm going to go get us some punch."

She eased out the door, leaving it slightly ajar so I could see her tiptoe across the kitchen, open up the refrigerator, get out the jug and fill our glasses! I was sure somebody was going to walk in and catch her and knew for certain I was never going to be allowed to do anything anymore, not even breathe, but she was back before I could sneeze again. She handed me my punch and locked the door behind her.

"Cheers!" Sophie lifted her glass and downed the whole thing in no time. I took a sip. It tasted awful, so I spit it right out in the sink, thinking I'd surely discovered the secret to the fruitcake *and* the bourbon balls.

"Uggghhh!" I said. "That's disgusting! Here, take mine," and darn if she didn't down that one as well.

"Whoa, slow down," I said. "How can you drink that stuff?"

"Yeah… pretty bad," she said wiping her mouth with her arm and taking a deep breath. I'll take the next one slower."

"Sophie, we can't stay in here. Sooner or later one of those ladies is going to have to pee and then we're caught."

"You're right! Let's get out of here."

She opened the door slowly and peeked around. I was right behind her as she darted out and ran across the kitchen to the door opposite the dining room into a hallway. We quickly found an empty bedroom and plopped ourselves onto the ivory chenille bedspread, backs down, looking up through the lacy curtains into the hazy, hot, late summer sky visible through the window.

"Whew!" Sophie said.

We were both quiet for a minute, breathing hard. I figured it was a good time to tell her all my news, beginning with the part that was easy to talk about.

"Guess what," I said. "I started yesterday."

"Started what?"

"You know, *started!*" Then she got it.

"Ooh! Wow! That's neat," she said, still looking up as if studying the ceiling. "Well, welcome to the club. It's about time!"

So that was all she was going to say about it? I have to admit I was downright disappointed. After all she'd hounded me about this thing, I expected her to turn into Miss Know-It-All on the subject, but she hardly even reacted. Didn't I deserve some kind of a fuss? I sure hadn't gotten it from Mama. She just handed me a box of pads and a belt, and told me the rules about no swimming, bike riding, or baths. She never said anything about cartwheels.

So Sophie and I were just lying there saying nothing and I was beginning to think she'd gone to sleep, but she finally spoke up.

"What are we going to do, Angel?"

"About what?"

"About everything."

"What everything?" I said, though of course I knew what must've been going on in her head, seeing her mom walk in with the cane and hearing what Mama had said. She always acted like she didn't want to talk about it and then at times like this when I thought maybe she did, I didn't know what to say. But I could listen.

"So what's on your mind?" I said.

"Ray."

"*Ray?*"

"Yep, can't quit thinking about him no matter what I do. Angel, sometimes I just lie there and I swear I can feel his hands all over me... and I mean ALL over me!"

I didn't know what to say to that. I honestly had nothing to add, no special knowledge or experience to draw on, so I just started in on what was on *my* mind for a change.

"Well, there's something I can't quit thinking about either."

"Who is it?" Now I had her.

"It's not what you think."

"So what is it?"

"It's not a what. It's my daddy."

"What about him? You never talk about him."

"Nobody talks about him. That's just it—I don't know anything about him, and I still don't know why he left or where he is and nobody will tell me anything, and then just the other day..." I stop, thinking my voice might start shaking.

"Maybe he's a secret agent," Sophie says. "Wouldn't that be neat!"

The lump that has started in my throat gets caught and I hear myself start laughing. It shakes the bed and then she starts too.

"I've actually thought of that!" I said. Then I'm laughing hard and we're both so tickled, I roll over on my side and laugh some more and it feels so good just to let loose like that and not care one bit about it. This goes on awhile, each breath more hilarious than the last, and the bed's vibrating now almost like one of those ones in a motel room that takes the quarters. But then we gradually stop and we're breathing hard. We both sigh real long and loud, and there's my sadness again.

"He called," I said. "He says he's coming back, for Thanksgiving."

"Wow! Angel, that's so...you must be so..."

"So what?"

"So...oh, I don't know, *thrilled!* Isn't it what you always wanted? Isn't this your dream come true?"

"Yeah."

"Well, I'm going to go out there and get more of this punch. Want some?"

Sophie's attention span can be short when it comes to things that aren't about her, but I was actually relieved at the change of subject. She sat up on the edge of the bed and looked around. I could tell something was bad off with her.

"Oh my God, this room is MOVING!"

"Uh, Sophie, don't you think—"

"I'll tell you what I think, I think I want more punch!"

She headed out, a little sideways, but made it into the hallway and back through the kitchen door. I charged around just in time to stop her from opening the refrigerator.

"Stop it, Sophie. You're going to get us in so much trouble we'll never get out!"

"Okay, then I'll just go get it out of the punchbowl," and she turned towards the swinging door.

"Oh no, you don't!" I grabbed her arm just as Martha charged back in.

"Wondering where you girls were," she said.

"Yeah, we're going back out there now," I said, cool as a cucumber, knowing that was the worst place to go but we had to get out of the kitchen before Sophie gave herself away. So I walked her right out and was headed through the dining room to a side door, keeping my eyes straight ahead so as to ignore anyone looking at us. It was going okay.

"Be nonchalant," I whispered.

"Non *what*? HEY! You passed up the punch bowl!" Then, turning towards a bunch of women hanging around the table, she blurted right out loud, "I wouldn't eat those bourbon balls if I was y'all! They taste like—"

"Hey Mrs. Haney, how you doing?" I waved at her, the director of junior choir,who I hadn't seen since I told Mama I wasn't going anymore. She and several others looked up as if to say *what in the world*, but I just smiled and kept us moving, aiming for the porch along the side of the house. There was an old swing there where we could sit and get some air for a few minutes. I think we'd have gotten away with it completely, that is if Doc hadn't been sitting out there in his rocking chair. I was used to seeing him in his white doctor coat whenever I went for a checkup, but he was wearing a cotton plaid, short-sleeve shirt, loose and summery.

"Well, hello there, girls! Come have a seat. What an honor to have you join me this afternoon! How's the ladies' tea party going?"

"Oh, uh…hello, Doctor Ames," I said. "It's going fine. We just need some air."

"Yeah…s'mair," said Sophie, nodding her head too much. He looked up at her. His eyes were brown and sort of watery but I could tell he saw enough.

"Looks like you might need a drink of water, too," he said as he stood up and helped Sophie into the swing. "Angel, why don't you go into the kitchen and get that for her? A nice tall glass."

"Sure thing," I said and darted back into the kitchen, thinking we were going to get it now. Best thing to do was get the darn water. L.B. was in there trying to wash up punch cups, because they'd already run through every one of them.

"Miss Angel, your granny's looking for you," he said. "Where've you two been?"

"Oh, um…Sophie's out on the porch with Doc. She's not feeling so good."

"I'll go tell your mama," he said.

"No, that's okay!" I tried to stop him but he was gone, so I went on back out to the porch with the water, only to find that Sophie was a regular mess, holding her face in her hands and crying like a baby. Doc was sitting beside her with his hand on her shoulder, not saying anything, just letting her sob.

"Sophie? What is it?" I said. Doc looked up at me now.

"She'll be all right," he said. "I just think she's a bit overwhelmed, but she'll be okay. Have you been in the punch too?"

"No sir," I said.

"You're a good friend, Angel."

That was nice for him to say. He must know all about me, I figured, all about us, and Daddy, and the whole thing. Heck, he knows everything about everybody. Boy, would I ever like to pick his brain! Then Mama shows up.

"Hello, Martin…Angel? What is it? She looked at Sophie, who was drying up a little now.

"I feel sick," she said.

Mama placed her hand underneath Sophie's chin and tilted her face up.

"I guess you do," she said. Her eyes met mine for just a second. "We'll take you on home, Sophie. Naomi can come later with your mom whenever she's ready. Okay?"

"That'd be great, Miss Ruth," she said. "I'd appreziate it."

Later on I hear Mama and Naomi going at it down in the kitchen. I figure it's about me anyway, so I just walk on in.

"So there she is!" Naomi says. "I want to know how on earth you let that child get in such a state over there. I just pray to God Martin doesn't tell Dottie what y'all was doing! If my knees wasn't so bad I'd be off down to the old willow tree!"

"Oh, for heaven's sake," Mama said. "Just what was she supposed to do? Why should Angel be responsible for Sophie's bull-headed ideas? Be glad she had the good sense not to do it herself." Never mind that the reason I didn't was mainly because I didn't like the taste. I was grateful for her taking my side.

"I wouldn't be so sure about that!" Naomi said. "*Do not enter the path of the wicked, and do not walk in the way of evildoers.*" She was looking right at me but talking like I wasn't even there.

"Leave her alone," Mama says.

"*For the wages of sin is death—*"

"Jesus Christ, Naomi, will you stop it with all that?"

"*Thou shalt not take the name of the Lord thy God in vain!*"

"I'm not taking his name in vain," she said. "I'm pleading with him to shut you up!" Naomi stared at her for a second, her eyes big as saucers, probably because she couldn't believe Mama's nerve, but she kept right on.

"Your disrespect is *shameful*, that's what it is—you letting Satan have your tongue!"

She had to stop and get hold of herself, her face red and her chest heaving up and down, almost like she was having a drunken fit. I jumped in and tried to change the direction of the conversation.

"Is Sophie going to be in trouble?" I asked.

"Nobody knows about it but us," Mama said, "and of course, Doc. I'm guessing the child could use a break."

"Shameful," Naomi said, calmer now but still shaking her head.

"How bad is it with Genevieve?"

"It's not good," Mama said. "That's about all anybody can say right now. You never know about these things, but it's not good."

It gets me thinking about dying again. I guess no matter what, we're all walking in that direction every day, but I wonder what it's like once you're getting closer. Even if a person's not expecting it, is there something that tells them to listen more to what's going on around them, and take a longer look at things? Is there something inside them that knows?

Chapter Nine

Today is the first day of school, the day after Labor Day, and Sophie is none the worse for the wear. We're standing in the girls' bathroom. I'm waiting for her to finish picking at her face so we can go eat.

We got in the same language arts class this year, which is the period right before lunch. Mr. Sams is the teacher. Everybody thinks he's a queer and tries too hard, but I think he's okay. He announced that in addition to our weekly spelling and grammar lessons this fall, we'll be reading two Shakespeare plays, and every Friday we're going to move all the desks into a circle and have "Rap with Will," an informal discussion about the week's reading. There was groaning and snickering in the room, but he went on.

"This unit will culminate at the end of November with the revival of an event from the early years at Coleman Junior High, which we here in the language arts department hope to reinstate as an annual tradition—the eighth grade Shakespeare Bee!"

A *Shakespeare* Bee? Mr. Sams was the faculty sponsor for the school newspaper and had a column about interesting things from the history of the school, but I thought maybe he was taking things a little too far with this idea. I checked out my classmates. Some were looking around, saying, "*Huh?*" and others were just cracking up, laughing right out loud to the point I thought the spit wads were going to start flying.

"Wait a minute! Wait a minute!" he said. "Now hear me out. You'll be partnered with one other person, each pair making a team. You can work with your partner to prepare or not, but be informed that *both* members of the winning team will be awarded the grand prize."

"What prize?" someone called out.

"Well, it's just become official," he said, grinning wide like he knew he had us. "Sometime during the Christmas break, I will take the two prizewinners to Knoxville to attend a matinee at the historic Tennessee Theatre, followed by dinner at Smith's Steakhouse."

Smith's Steakhouse! NOW he was talking! That place was famous. I'd seen the ad on TV that showed a girl and her parents sitting around a beautiful table eating their steaks. You can see *happy* just written all over them. I don't know if it was the thought of a steak, baked potato, and salad with blue cheese dressing or the notion that I might be the girl with a real family in a restaurant that made me think I wanted to go there so bad.

"You may pair up on your own if you wish," Mr. Sams said. "Take a moment to discuss it and raise your hand if you have your team. Otherwise I'll assign you."

The room started buzzing and Sophie, sitting right behind me, was already tapping my shoulder and leaning close to my ear.

"Be my partner, Angel…please!"

There was no way out of it. Of course I would, because she was my best friend and had asked me first, but this wasn't my best shot at getting to Knoxville. Sophie wasn't exactly the scholar. I'd have to crack the whip with her for us to have any kind of chance.

"Okay," I whispered to her, looking around the room and realizing there were much worse possibilities. Her hand shot up like a rocket.

"Me and Angel Bishop!" she said.

"All right. Anyone else?"

Then everybody was grabbing partners and shouting out their names left and right. In no time at all they were all set up except for Maureen Callahan, that girl who's always scowling and looks like she never brushes her hair. Then the bell rang.

"It seems we have an odd number," he said as we were all picking up our books to leave. "We'll figure it out tomorrow."

So that was ten minutes ago, and I'm still waiting on Sophie.

"Smith's Steakhouse, here we come!" she says, inspecting her nose for the hundredth time.

"We have to win first," I say. The excitement of it all is fading in the bathroom.

"Ugh! My face is *so* broken out!"

"It'd be fine if you'd quit messing with it."

"No, LOOK!" she cries and starts picking all over again.

So I'm standing here doing nothing. I look at myself in the mirror and study my face, trying to figure out what in the world I'm supposed to do with the information that's in front of me. My nose isn't bad, or at least it's not too big. My eyes are blue, just like Mama's and then there's that little scar over my eyebrow from when I was six and rode my bike into a low tree branch. Other than that, I really don't have much to say about my face except that it's covered with freckles and sometimes looks too shiny. But I tell you what, I'd rather go eat lunch than stand here in the girl's bathroom and stare at it.

Then there's the thing I try not to pay much attention to and hope nobody ever notices. It's a small red birthmark, tucked up under the left side of my chin so that I'd have to be looking up or you'd have to be much shorter than me to really see it. It's such a curiosity, sometimes I stand in front of the mirror at home and stretch my neck up to study it. It's splotchy red, a port wine stain they call it, and shaped something like a heart. It's okay though, since I guess nobody else in the world has one exactly like it.

There are rules for beauty at Ralph S. Coleman Junior. High School: You need to have very shiny lips. They have the right kind of lip gloss at Greer's, but it can get expensive since you have to put it on every five minutes or die. You also need a thick layering of cover-up all over your face, which you use whether or not you have any pimples, because one could pop out at any moment while you're in class and go undetected until the next bathroom inspection. I don't wear it myself because it makes me hot. I'll figure out what to do about pimples once I get them, but so far I've been lucky. Braces seem to be a necessary evil and are acceptable if the wearer complains enough, making sure everyone around her knows she hates them. There's a reward for this in the end, because no matter who you are or how big of a nobody, when your braces come off you are automatically entitled to a day of fame.

Glasses are the kiss of beauty death, so if you need them your chances of true popularity are drastically reduced. Everybody wants contacts but hardly anybody gets them in junior high. Still, there are those who try the complaining tactic, "I can't stand my glasses," or better yet, they walk around blind.

Thanks to my cousin Kit in Memphis, I had some preparation for being a teenager. Number one, I knew a long time ago that Bonnie Belle's *Ten O' Six* is the best thing for pimples, but if you get one do NOT pinch it, especially if it's within the triangle around your nose because you might get brain damage. Number two, use orange juice cans for rollers to tame unruly hair. If you're thinking it's impossible to sleep that way, you're right—but it works. Also, comb in lemon juice on sunny days to get blond streaks and take a tablespoon of castor oil if you want to get skinny real fast, but not the night before you have to be somewhere the next morning. There's lots more where that came from. Kit is a wealth of information on every topic.

Sophie has it all. Her hair looks like the lady's on the Clairol box, I swear. She does not wear glasses, has beautiful brown eyes, and her braces came off in seventh grade. She'll get maybe two pimples a year and pick them to death, but I suppose she has to have something to hate about her looks so she can complain.

Now we're finally on our way to lunch. The weather's good, so we're taking ours outside. We have to walk across the field to get to our favorite spot.

"So what's a Shakespeare bee?" Sophie asks.

"Well, I wouldn't know, but I *guess* it's the same as a spelling bee except you're answering questions about Shakespeare instead of spelling words." My sarcasm is lost on her.

"But I hate Shakespeare!" she says. "They talk funny and I don't know what's going on in the story." I sigh. This is what I figured. Smith's Steakhouse is a long shot.

"You'll catch on," I say. I'm wanting to tell Sophie about Old Susan. Somehow I never got around to mentioning to anybody that I was over there, wanting to keep it to myself for some reason. But here we are settling down underneath our tree and getting out our sandwiches, and I'm ready now.

"Have you ever met that old lady over there across the creek, the one we used to call *witch woman*?"

"Now how would I have met her?" she says. "She lives over there all by herself and never comes around anybody. Besides, she's an Indian."

"What does that have to do with anything?"

"Didn't they used to scalp white people?"

"For crying out loud, Sophie, I'm sure Old Susan's never scalped anybody! Besides, don't you know that white people killed plenty of Indians too?"

"Well, all I know is that she's strange," she says. "And I bet she's crazy and she smells bad. Maybe she really is a witch."

"You just said you'd never met her, so how in the world can you say she smells bad! That's just *mean*, Sophie. And all that witch stuff is nothing but gossip. Honestly, you should know better."

"Oh, so I guess *you* never gossip, especially about Kathy Bledsoe and the majorettes."

"They're snobs and they deserve it! You're talking about an old lady that lives by herself with no friends or family and the whole town making fun of her."

"So what? Who cares? Why are you all of a sudden so curious about her anyways? And why do you call her Old Susan?"

"Maybe I'll tell you," I say, waiting for her to press further. I'm thinking I might give her the whole story since we have the time and I'm aching to talk about it, but just then a black Plymouth Duster drives by and she gets distracted.

"I think Ray was in that car!"

"Well if it's him then he's in trouble because you're not supposed to leave the school grounds during lunch," I said, still hoping she'd ask me something.

"No really, I think it *was!*"

"Well so what? I swear, Sophie! You aren't interested in a thing anybody else has to say unless it's about you! You know, you just might learn something if you gave yourself a chance."

"So who are you, Miss Know-It-All, taking up for some dirty old Indian lady! Guess what? You're right. I don't care about her, or you, or anything right now. Maybe if you just wore my shoes for a mile you'd see it differently."

"The saying is 'walk a mile in my shoes,' Sophie. And besides, I can't wear your shoes because you're two sizes smaller than me!" Then we both sort of laugh, and she throws a Cheeto at me and I throw it back.

"Stop it, Angel. You're not funny." Her eyes go dull, like a thin veil has fallen in front of her face. I hate it when she get likes that.

She picks up her sandwich, takes a single bite and then, holding it, rests her hand on her knee and looks straight at me.

"What do you think happens when you die?" she asked.

Any question in the world I could wish Sophie wouldn't ask me, that would be the one—and here it is. I look in her direction and shrug.

"You go to heaven, I guess." My voice doesn't sound like me. It's too chirpy or something and I know it sounds fake.

"Yeah, but we're Jewish and we don't do that thing where you get saved, and you know how they say you have to be saved to get into heaven and if you don't you have to go to hell forever?"

"Yeah, I know," I say. I'm having a hard time looking at her.

"So what do *you* think, Angel?"

I can feel my heart thumping and the air going in and out of my lungs. The breeze feels cool on my forehead, like there's a little bit of sweat there. The sunlight's coming through the trees to where we're sitting and making like little dancing spirits all over the place and I remember that September is one of my favorite months.

"I think it's stupid," I say.

Well, of all things, you wouldn't believe this. Or if you knew Sophie, maybe you would. In language arts today, the very day *after* Mr. Sams told us about the Shakespeare Bee, guess whose schedule changed so that he got moved into our class? RAY! So then, naturally, he got teamed up with Maureen Callahan because she was the only one without a partner. Sophie, of course, had an all-out fit.

"It's just not fair!" she said. "Why should that girl get to be with my boyfriend!"

"Your *boyfriend*? Sophie! Have you ever even spoken to him?"

"Well, no… not yet, but I'm sure it's only a matter of time. Angel… we shouldn't have been so quick to pick each other!" *She actually said this!* "I'm thinking about talking to Maureen and seeing if she wants to trade."

"Do what you want, Sophie," I said, "but number one, did you ever think about consulting me on whether I want to be Maureen's partner? And number two, that is so pitiful and obvious it's pathetic. Everybody knows boys don't like girls who're desperate."

She didn't like my saying it so plain, but she knew it was true. Not that I'm Miss Experience or anything, but it doesn't take a genius to figure that one out. Besides, I don't think you want to go mixing up education and romance. It gets too confusing between your heart and your brain.

"I guess you're right," she says. "Also, it might not be good for the relationship—you know, the pressure of it all. There's only one thing to do. We have to practice, practice, practice and *win* this thing so Ray and Maureen don't get to have this big fancy out-of-town date! Honestly, I think I would just about die of jealousy."

So that's it. Now all she can talk about is when we're going to study Shakespeare, but I'm not complaining. Smith's Steakhouse is calling!

It's Wednesday, the day Naomi usually drives me over to Crestview on her way to get her hair done at Delilah's, which is right there in that strip mall back of the home. It takes about an hour and a half for her wash, rinse, set, and dry, which is fine by Patsy and me. I really like going over there by myself and spending time with her without Mama and Naomi. We'll play a game of Parcheesi or something, or if Patsy's feeling tired I'll read to her from her *Ladies Home Journal*.

Her favorite is "Can This Marriage Be Saved?" That's the monthly article where they take a husband and wife who're ready to throw in the towel and interview both of them so you get both sides of the story. We love to talk about whose fault it is, his or hers.

I have friends over there, too. There's Clarice, who is what you might call a character. She sits in the dining room and shouts out bad words, sometimes *really* bad words. I know this is true because one Wednesday when Naomi was late I was sitting with Patsy at dinner helping her with her noodle soup, which isn't that easy to eat when the noodles keep sliding off the spoon. Suddenly out of the clear blue, I hear, "SHIT!" yelled out real loud. I slammed my hand over my mouth, about to die laughing, and looked up to see the nurse head straight over to Clarice and tell her she was going to have to watch her language if she wanted to stay in the dining room.

"UP YOURS!" she said, real loud again, though none of the other residents seemed to even notice, probably didn't even hear it. By this time I was getting so tickled I couldn't hide it and got the evil eye from that nurse as she wheeled Clarice off back to her room, screaming, "ALL YOU FUCKERS JUST GO ON TO HELL, Y'HEAR?"

I started going in to say hello to Clarice after that, but she has never once used bad words when I'm in the room with her. She says things like, "How kind of you to pay me a visit," and calls me "charming" and "delightful" and old-fashioned things like that. She's really just a proper little lady, but something takes hold of her in the dining room. I'll bet she just gets in a bad mood there because it stinks of things like overcooked cabbage and spilled milk.

Usually I'll go look in on Miss Ida too, the one in the room next to Patsy who can't talk much on account of her breathing, but I like to go in and say hi. She's got tanks sitting beside her bed with these clear tubes that run out of them and into her nose. It's terrible looking at first but you get used to it pretty quick. Then there's Frank in the

kitchen. I always talk to him if I go down to get Patsy a cup of Oval-
tine. He's from New York and has the funniest accent you ever heard.
Here's how it goes with him.

"How ya doin!" he almost yells at me.

"Not bad," I say.

"Have a cookie, doll," he says, and then we get to talking. He always has a story to tell, and if there's not a new one he might tell me
about the time when Mr. Bixler's daughter tried to get him to go on a
date with her, or when Janie Odom's bird got loose in the building. I
don't know if they're even true or not, but it hardly matters.

So Naomi's taking me over there now even though I know she doesn't
want me to go, considering how Patsy spoke about my daddy the other
week. I think she's afraid of what I might learn, but it'd be way too obvious for her to try and stop me because the hair appointment is never
to be missed and there's no reason for me not to ride with her. That's
not to say she didn't try.

"You need to stay here and get your homework done."

"I already did it."

"How could you have already done it when you just got home?"

"I did it in study hall. Besides, school's just started and they've
hardly had time to give us any yet."

So then I have to ignore her grumbling about my being lazy and
why couldn't I do something around the house for a change, knowing
that any kind of back talk would likely get me stuck at home doing
some dumb chore, so I just keep my mouth shut and get in the car
like I usually do on Wednesday afternoons. Last week I didn't get to
go because we had orientation at school, so I'm about jumping out of
my skin to get back over there and have Patsy and whatever she wants
to say all to myself.

On the way, neither of us is talking, so I'm thinking a change of subject would take some of the tension off.

"You know Old Susan Blackfoot...?" I say.

"I reckon."

"So how come everybody just ignores her?"

"She's not a Christian," Naomi says, as if that's all I need to know.

"So why don't you try to get her saved? Maybe she'd come to church if anybody ever asked her."

"She's a heathen and there's not much anybody can do about it. Even if you got her into church it wouldn't do any good, so why bother? You can lead a horse to water but you can't make it drink." I honestly can't believe Naomi sometimes, especially since she's my own flesh and blood, and normally this is where I'd just shut down my ears and wait out the ride, but I was after something.

"Do you know her at all?" I ask, baiting her to tell me she knew her from school, but she doesn't bite.

"Haven't hardly seen her in years," she says.

"Do you know anybody that knows her?" I'm wondering if she has any idea that Dottie Ames is a regular over there.

"She keeps to herself," Naomi says. "I reckon if she wanted to be with people she'd come around more."

When I got over to Patsy's, this tall colored woman was there helping her with her bath. Her skin looked like one of those natives you see in *National Geographic*, so black it was almost purple.

"Well, who we got here?" she said when I walked in. She had a big voice and a big wide grin.

"Why, it's Angel," Patsy said. "Come on in, honey. How you doing? Tell me about school. You got a boyfriend, honey?"

"Hey, Aunt Patsy." She was wrapped in her big fuzzy robe and getting her hair combed. Aunt Patsy's pretty, or you can tell she used to be and still could be if she wasn't so tiny and slumped over. She has nice even features and a perfect little nose that fits just right on her face.

"Look here, Rita's got me all washed up."

"Pleased to meet you," I said, and offered my hand out. Rita grabbed it and shook like I was some old backyard pump, all the while looking straight at me with two of the most twinkly eyes I ever saw.

"Look at this child!" she said. "What a beautiful young lady! Where'd you get that red hair? Why Patsy, I believe she looks just like you!"

"It's orange," I said, wondering how in the world she'd seen a resemblance between Patsy and the likes of me. "And we're not blood related. She's my daddy's stepsister."

"Why, that don't matter! Folks don't favor each other only because of blood," she said. "We take on features from those we love." Rita laughed, a booming sound I swear rattled the blinds. Then she picked up the wet towels and left.

Patsy looked small all bundled up in her robe. I was sure she'd shrunk since I saw her last.

"Something about that Rita," she said.

"She's nice."

"She's from Africa, you know."

"No, Patsy, I don't think—"

"YES, she IS! She was a queen, had her a whole tribe of people to look after and wore this big thing on her head with feathers and beads and stuff, but then she came here."

"Because she wanted to work at Crestview?"

"She's looking out for me. She's not going to let them hurt me."

"Let who hurt you, Patsy?"

"They come in my room at night to devil me. They get right up close and say things terrible things right in my ear. They're trying to get me, but she won't let them."

"What do they say to you?"

"I don't know honey… it's in a different language."

"Well, I'm awful glad Rita's watching out for you," I say, wondering where in the world her mind has gone today.

"Read to me, Angel." I didn't want to. I wanted to talk, to ask, to *find out something.*

"How about we just visit for a while first?" I say. "Tell me about when you were a little girl, about you and my daddy growing up together."

She put her head back in the chair and closed her eyes, like she was going to drop off to sleep, but then she started.

"It was on a farm," she said. "There was a pond there, and some ducks, and a tree with a swing on it and my Daddy would push me up way high, a *way* up high till I thought my feet were going to touch the clouds—"

"But Aunt Patsy—"

"And we had this old dog named Sky, don't know why we called him that, but Sky would sit under the tree and bark at me while I was swinging, and Daddy would say, 'What's the matter, Sky, you want to swing too?' and I'd just laugh and laugh to think of it."

"I know all about Sky," I said.

"And then there was the night that big storm came and Daddy came and got me out of bed and carried me down to the basement. The wind was a-blowin' and the branches were a-knockin' and Sky was down there with us—"

"And he was a-barkin," I said, thinking to hurry this story along a little bit. I'd been listening to it and loving it since I was a little girl. I used to beg her to tell it to me, but it was other stories I wanted to hear now.

"Yes he was, he was a-barkin'! And then there was this big crash and great big THUD and I grabbed my daddy and held onto him for dear life because I thought the whole house was coming down, and all of a sudden, you know what?"

"What?" I asked. It'd been the same as long as I could remember, me going along like I didn't know what she was going to say next.

"Sky stopped his barkin'! Just like that! Next morning we went out there and that old tree had come plumb down! Darn near hit the house!"

"But Patsy, that was before you came to live with Naomi and Daddy, when you were *real* little."

"That was me and *my* daddy."

"I want to hear stories about my daddy! Cal! You know, your step-brother?"

"Nope."

"Yes you do! You said it the other day, said your friend Awia knows what Cal did, so I want to know too. What did he do?"

"Awia knows everything,"

"What *is* it! PLEASE tell me! I really, *really* need to know!" She was looking straight ahead, her head and neck now rigid, like she'd left me in her mind and gone somewhere else. I wondered if she'd forgotten I was there.

"Aunt Patsy?" I grabbed her shoulder and tried to get her to look at me. "Aunt Patsy!"

I was starting to wonder if she'd had a stroke or something and was about to run get Rita when she did look at me straight on and spoke in a loud wobbly voice.

"Don't you worry now, I know where it is. And believe you me I know what to do."

"Where *what* is, Patsy?"

"I took it—and I hid it!"

"You hid something?" I asked.

"He told me I was beautiful," she said, and lowered her eyes.

"Who said you were beautiful? Who're you talking about? Tell me!" Now this was getting *real* interesting. Had Patsy had a sweetheart? I thought I might bust a gut if she stopped there, but then I saw her mouth quiver and the tears roll down her cheeks. This was going too far.

"Oh, I'm sorry! Never mind, it doesn't matter—it really doesn't," I said, even though it really did. I jumped up to give her neck a hug and kissed her on the top of the head. She smelled like baby powder. I rested my cheek there while swaying her ever so gently back and forth, hoping to calm her down.

Of all the people in my messed up family, Patsy wasn't the one to pester about things, and I knew it. It hadn't ever gotten me anywhere before, so why would it now? But what else had she been keeping up her sleeve? I had a hard time believing she was as crazy as everybody seemed to think, but maybe she really didn't remember, and besides, it was true that sometimes she just made stuff up.

It didn't matter. She was my biggest fan in the whole wide world, and in her eyes I could do no wrong. I swear I could go in there and tell her I'd just murdered somebody and she'd say they must have deserved it.

"How about the latest installment of our favorite column?" Time to change the subject and perk her up. -

"I'm sleepy, Angel," she said.

"You want me to go?"

"No, just let me take a little snooze, then I'll be all right."

"Sure, Patsy. I'll just be right here," I said, sweet as pie, thinking what I really wanted to do was run right out into that parking lot and scream.

Chapter Ten

It's been over a month now since we got the call from Daddy. As if we didn't have enough going on around here, now Mama is having some sort of a spell. Something's really gotten into her. The mama I've always known generally doesn't have too much to say beyond what's necessary, usually keeps to herself and minds her own business. But things aren't sitting lightly with her these days. She's quick to let her mind be known. Naomi says it's her nerves, like some kind of a breakdown, but if you ask me I'd say it's more like she's breaking through.

Here's what happened in church the other day. We were sitting there like we always do, trying to make it to the end. I was passing the time drawing flowers on one of those little envelopes they put at the end of the pew until Naomi reached her hand over and made me stop, so I looked up and tried to listen. The reverend was going on and on, his voice up real loud, then down so low you almost had to lean forward to hear him. Then he'd come up again practically yelling, so loud it'd wake you up in case you'd dozed off. That morning he was talking about marriage. This struck me as somewhat coincidental considering our family's current events.

"... and God speaks to us of the sanctity of marriage in many places throughout the Bible. I read from Romans," he said. "'By law, a married woman is bound to her husband as long as he is alive so then if she marries another man while her husband is still alive, she is called an adulteress.'"

I was hoping that Mama, sitting on the other side of me, would be daydreaming. It'd been a rough day already, since she'd made Naomi mad by keeping us waiting in the car then showing up at the last minute wearing her flowered Mexican skirt with Dr. Scholl's sandals and navy blue knee socks. Naomi was furious but had to put up with it, otherwise we'd have been late and she hates that worse than anything, so she had to settle for crabbing at her the whole way like she was a kid.

"Can't believe you'd show up in God's house like that! You look like one of them young folks on the TV that's always standing in big bunches and yelling at the police!" Mama stayed quiet and ignored her the whole way to the church, but I could tell by the way she was fidgeting more than usual in the pew that all this had gotten to her.

"God is clear in His message concerning marriage. I read now from First Corinthians: 'A wife must not separate from her husband. But if she does, she must remain unmarried or else be reconciled to her husband. And a husband must not divorce his wife.'"

Mama had her long pony tail in her hand now and was holding the end of it in the other palm as if inspecting her split ends. I could see her if I cut my eyes sideways but I didn't want to turn and look at her directly. She took in a deep breath, then let it out hard. I was hoping this might be ending soon, but old Jenkins just kept on going.

"As God took a rib out of Adam's side to create woman, so He intended that she remain with him as his helpmate," he said. "This is His will. To dishonor the vows of marriage is a sin against the LORD!"

I guess something inside her snapped, because my mama just up and left. And she didn't leave like somebody going to the ladies room, either. She was getting out. Something was stuck in her craw real bad. I didn't have to wonder what it was or how come Jenkins had decided to speak on this topic, today of all days. One look at Naomi's face told me about all I needed to know. I followed and found her standing out front, her face lifted to the sunshine. She was holding a cigarette in her hand, but it wasn't lit.

"Mama, you okay?"

"Why is he talking about this today?" she said. "I just can't listen to it anymore." Then she lowered her head and looked straight at me as if asking for a response. My heart took a leap in my chest and I held my breath. She was letting me in.

"What does *he* know about marriage? Or my life...*our* life! Angel, I'm so sorry. You didn't deserve this, none of it. You didn't deserve to grow up without a daddy and now all of this...this confusion. I should just let you be happy right now. You shouldn't have to know what I'm feeling or thinking."

"No, Mama," I said. "I mean...I *want* to know. It's not exactly what you think with me, either. It's..." I longed to open my heart to her, even if I wasn't sure how to say it all, but Dottie Ames had to pop her head out the church door just then and yank away my chance.

"Just checking to see if you're all right."

"I'm fine." Mama said. "It's amazing what a little fresh air will do."

"Want to come on back in?" Dottie said. "I'm sure Naomi must be wondering what's going on."

"No thank you," Mama said. "I won't be going back in there. Angel and I will just wait out here for her, but I appreciate it." Dottie had the whole story from Naomi, no doubt, so of course she knew what was bothering Mama.

"Now, Ruth," she said, "take your problems to God. Come back in here and bow your head and seek him in your time of trouble."

"I will be seeking God elsewhere from now on," she said. My heart practically burst with pride. This was by far the bravest thing I had ever seen my mother do.

"I see," Dottie said, but instead of turning away she just stood there for a second and looked at us. It was like there were two Dotties and she was trying to decide which one to be. There was the one that would have been shocked and prayed for Mama's soul, and the one that knew exactly what she was talking about, the one that crossed the river to see a heathen Indian woman for her aches and pains and what other reasons I could only guess.

"Well, I reckon you've got to suit yourself," she said before going back inside. If she was trying to seem like church lady Dottie for our sake, it didn't fool me.

Now anybody could predict that wouldn't be the last of it, and it wasn't. By the end of the coffee hour, I'm sure Mama had been added to the prayer chain and the whole incident had been described to Duane Cook of the pastoral care committee, but we were long gone by then.

We'd left in a big hurry. Naomi came on out the side even before Reverend Jenkins had a chance to position himself at the front door to shake hands with everybody. This was a first. She had never before, to my knowledge, left church without speaking to the preacher on the way out.

When we saw her coming we headed toward the car. Mama was lagging behind, so I turned around just in time to see her plunk that unlit cigarette into the trash can at the edge of the parking lot. Then she got in the back seat with her arms crossed, which left Naomi to drive. This hardly ever happened. I sat up front to be an extra pair of eyes. Didn't take me long to see that we weren't headed towards Crestview.

"Where're we going?"

"Home," Naomi said.

"We're not going to see Patsy?"

"She's not been feeling good. They called and said it'd be better if she just rested today." As much as I wanted to believe Naomi was just making up an excuse not to go to Crestview, I had the nagging feeling she might be telling the truth. Every time we'd seen Patsy lately it seemed like she was weaker and less talkative. She couldn't remember conversations from one day to the next, and I had yet to get her to say anything more about Daddy.

The radio was on WRIL, which on Sunday morning was usually the *Preacher of the Week* broadcasting a sermon, but instead they were playing "Time in a Bottle" because Jim Croce had just died in a plane crash and they were doing a tribute show. Naomi flipped it off like it was the worst thing she ever heard.

I turned to look at Mama in the back seat, but she was gazing out the window and her face was shut. I felt sad knowing that every time I heard "Bad, Bad Leroy Brown" now I'd have to think of him dying in that terrible way, and sad too, that I couldn't see Patsy today. But there was nothing else to be said about it. We were going home. I had to fight to keep back tears, and suddenly didn't even want to go to Crestview, afraid I'd see more of what I already knew. Maybe it wouldn't be so bad just to go home and hang out with Marvel for awhile.

That afternoon after dinner, Mama was out in the yard pulling out her petunias and I was up in my room doing homework. The window was open so Marvel could come and go as he pleased. I heard the phone ring, then after a few minutes I heard the screen door slam and saw Naomi walk across the yard to talk to Mama. I could hear everything from up there.

"That was Duane Cook," Naomi said. "He'd like to come by and pay a little visit, if it's convenient."

"Well, it's not convenient," Mama said. "Or necessary."

"Now Ruth, you can't just tell him not to come over like that. When a church elder calls and says he wants to come visit, you say yes whether you want him to or not. You can't just turn him down."

"Why not?" Mama said.

"Because it looks like you're being disrespectful, that's why. Surely we can be hospitable and let him just come on over for a piece of pie."

"That'd be fine, if pie was what he was coming over for. But it's not, Naomi. He's coming over to find out why I walked out of church this morning, knowing full well what the situation is here at the house because you apparently told your friend Jenkins all about it and all about me and Dennis. Now they've taken it on as their project to save poor old Ruth, who's headed down the road to adultery and thereby taking a shortcut into the fires of eternal damnation!" Mama's voice was getting louder and louder as she went on, almost like Jenkins in the pulpit. I'd never heard her do that before.

"*Let not sin reign in your mortal body, that you should obey in its lust!*" Naomi yelled back, then turned toward the house, her fists clenched and muttering something to herself.

I crept down the stairs and stood just behind the wall so I could hear what was going on in the kitchen, hoping she was going to call Duane Cook back and tell him something. I was not disappointed. She picked up the phone and started dialing.

"Duane? Naomi Bishop here. I'm afraid Ruth is not herself this afternoon, we'd best put this off until a better time....I know, Duane, but it's not going to do a lick of good today. I'm telling you, she's not well....Duane, you are preaching to the choir here. I know all of that. But your coming over here this afternoon ain't going to change any of it. We'll do it another time....I *know*, Duane! Listen here, I don't think you're hearing me right. I *said* it's not a good day, and I *meant* it.... Yes, and I'll call *you*, not the other way around!" She banged down the phone.

"Damnation!" she said, and I had to cover my mouth with my hand and double over not to make a sound over there on the other side of the wall. I didn't know exactly who she was cursing, Duane or Mama, but it struck me so funny I about died.

Well, let me tell you, it gets even better after that. That evening after we finished our tomato soup and grilled cheese sandwiches, one of our favorite Sunday night suppers, we were sitting down to watch "The Wonderful World of Disney." The theme song was playing and Tinker Bell was just sprinkling the castle with fairy dust when we heard a knock.

"Now who in the world?" Mama said as she got up to go see. We heard the door open and a very familiar, way-too-cheerful voice.

"Well, good evening, Miss Ruth! May I come in?" Then we heard *slam!* ...and Mama came back in the room and sat down, just like that. My eyes about popped out of my head and all I could do was stare at her, but Naomi was all over it.

"What did you just do?" I could see the blood vessels in her neck bulging out. "Wasn't that the reverend?"

"It was," Mama said, looking straight ahead at the TV, "and I shut the door on him."

"Why in the world....?" Naomi jumped up and went for the front as fast as she could. I followed her. When she opened it, he was still standing there and smiling like a fool.

"Miss Naomi!" he said. "Good evening! May I come in?" Did he know my mother had just shut the door in his face?

"Good evening, Reverend. Just step right on in here and have you a seat. Now what can I get you? We've got some cherry pie left over from dinner today. Can I get you some coffee to go with it?"

As we walked back into the sitting room I noticed he was carrying a Bible. Mama wasn't in there anymore.

"Why, thank you," he said. "I would like that very much. Coffee and pie, yes that would hit the spot." He sat himself down in the chair Mama sits in, the one she was sitting in just a minute before, and made himself real comfortable while Naomi was in the kitchen. Then he looked up and noticed me standing there.

"Hello, Angel," he said. "How are you today?"

"Fine." At first I couldn't help my eyes from going just about everywhere but his face but then I got the courage to look at him. "Your sermon was very interesting this morning," I said. He looked a little startled but was rescued from having to answer me because Naomi was back.

"We're so glad you came by to visit," she said.

"Actually, I came to see your daughter-in-law," he said. "Is she here?"

"She's not feeling too good right now." She put the coffee and pie down on the table beside him. "I think she must've gone upstairs."

"Well, that's unfortunate. I was hoping to see her in case she had any questions I might be able to help her with." Then he leaned forward with his elbows on his knees. He had his Bible in one hand and was tapping it with the index finger of the other.

"Why, thank you, Reverend, but if I have questions I think I can find my own answers." It was Mama, leaning in the doorway now with her arms crossed in front of her. "I don't need any advice from you, and I'd appreciate it if you'd go on about your business now and leave us to our Sunday evening. We like to watch 'Disney' together and we're missing it because you're here. So if you don't mind, we'd like it very much if you'd leave."

"Ruth Ellen!" Naomi said. "Well, I never!" She looked back at Jenkins as if *he* had an explanation.

"Why, I can understand that," he said. "I'll just be on my way then, but I'd be much obliged if you'd just let me pray with you for a moment and ask the Lord for forgiveness in your time of doubt. You can't ever be too careful, Ruth. That old Satan is always just around the corner waiting for a chance to come into an empty heart."

"I don't want to pray with you."

"I see," he said, nodding his head. Naomi's head jerked back toward Mama, but she went right on.

"And as for my doubt, what I doubt is that you have any more clout with God than anybody else. And as for my heart, it's not empty at all, but I figure it'd be better empty than filled up with all of this I've been trying to swallow all these years. And what is it you're saying I need forgiving for? Do I need forgiveness for raising my child by myself because her daddy's not here? Do I need forgiveness for waiting and hoping and wondering, and then when it's all said and done and I've about gone and decided to move on with my life, that I can be somebody without him, then here he comes back like all those years don't even matter, like everything's all right now just because he decides to get his butt back in town? So you're saying I need forgiveness for that? How in the *world* can you come in here pretending you don't know what I'm up against? And where in the Bible does it say I can't have a friend?"

The reverend had his eyes closed at this point and was muttering to himself, praying under his breath, I imagine.

"Ruth! That'll be *enough!*" said Naomi, her eyes like daggers. Then turning to Jenkins, her hands shaking, "Thank you, Reverend, thank you so much for coming. We'll get this all straightened out. As you can see, Ruth isn't herself right now, and we'll let you know when's a good time for you to come back. Here, let me see you out." She grabbed him by the elbow and led him to the door.

"I think I'm probably more myself than I've ever been in my whole life!" Mama yelled after him. We heard some muffled words, then the door shutting again. Naomi came back into the room.

"What in the world is *wrong* with you, girl?" she said. "How could you be so rude and disrespectful to a man of God? I have never been so mortified!" She sat down hard on the sofa and let her face fall into her hands.

"What's wrong with me is what I've been told all my life," she said. "Now it's time for me and my life to change. And as for being rude, I think I could ask what's wrong with *him*. And guess what? As much as he's a man of God, then I am a woman of God and deserve the same respect! How dare he force himself into my home and tell me to watch out for Satan. Well, I can handle Satan. What's to be feared is him and all those others claiming to know God better than anybody else!"

"I'll not have that kind of talk in my house! I'll not have it!" Naomi was holding both her fists up and shaking them in the air like a woman gone wild.

"And I'll not have anybody telling me what to say or what not to say!" Mama yelled back. "I don't care whose house it is, I'll be speaking my mind!" Then she stomped up the stairs.

"Oh Lord... oh *Lord!*" Naomi said. "I have never in my life...." She walked into the kitchen and plopped herself down at the table, putting her face in her hands again. I wondered if she was praying. After a minute she looked up and took a deep breath.

"Angel, I don't know what to do," she said. "I...I've got a headache. I've just got to go to bed, that's what."

So she did, and that left me there to watch the "The Wonderful World of Disney" all by myself, not paying a bit of attention, either.

Now Mama and Naomi aren't speaking. Mama gets up and leaves for work real early, just after I come down to the kitchen. She'll pour her coffee and be out the door before Naomi even shows up. Then in the evenings while Naomi and I are eating supper she'll stay up in her room reading her doctor books and doing whatever else, I don't know.

Dottie Ames has apparently been concerned about this situation. She'll be over having iced tea with Naomi when I get home from school. As soon as I walk in the door I can hear their voices change from serious to pretend.

"Why hello, Angel, how was school today?" Like I've been saying, Dottie doesn't fool me. This one day, though, she had some real news and they barely even noticed my coming in.

"Martha's having a time of it, sitting up there at the hospital with Clyde," she said. "He's bad. Marvin had to take his leg off the other day on account of his diabetes, and when he woke up and realized it was gone he got so upset they had to plumb knock him out. It's hard on Martha," she said, shaking her head while gazing down into her glass. I got my own tea and sat down to hear more of the story. Being Doc's wife, Dottie often has inside information on his more interesting cases.

"Well, when Clyde came out of it he started crying and carrying on, said he couldn't be buried one-legged, he wasn't going to go meet Jesus maimed."

"What in the world was he thinking to do about it?" Naomi asked. "Get his leg back?"

"That's it! Begged her to go find it for him!" she said. "Said it was his dying wish, and would she please go and try to get it back. Have you *ever!*"

"Law!" Naomi said. "What'd she tell him?"

"Good thing Mildred was working the floor that morning," Dottie said, "because she knew the little fellow working downstairs that day and talked to him about it. He told her to send Martha down to the incinerator quick, and if it wasn't too late already, see if they'd go in there and get it back before they burnt it up. Can you imagine!"

"God, can they *do* that?" I asked.

"Angel, I have told you time and again, do not take the Lord's name in vain."

"It's not in vain. There's a reason for it. That's the grossest thing I ever heard!" Somehow I felt like I could get away with being more sassy when Dottie was around.

"You know my meaning, young lady!"

"Well anyway, what's she supposed to do with it when she gets it—the leg, I mean." I wanted to get Dottie back to her story.

"From what I hear, some kid working the graveyard shift went in there and found it! Had it all wrapped up, so she took it right over to the funeral home and asked them to save it for her until the rest of him got there." She smacked the table with her hand. "Said she'd bury it with him!"

Naomi gasped. "Well, I never!" She'd forgotten my sin.

"I don't know why he thinks he's going to need his leg in heaven," Dottie said. "That good-for-nothing barely used it while he was here. He spent most of his life in the La-Z-Boy while Martha worked her fingers to the bone."

"So how's your body supposed to get to heaven once it's buried?" I asked.

Naomi reared her head back and gawked at me like I'd grown two heads.

"I raised you up knowing the Good Book better than that! It's the Resurrection of the Body, promised to us in the Bible! Don't you know?" Then, turning to Dottie, "This is what I'm fearing, this is what's been heavy on my heart, that she's got so much of her mother in her the devil's going to have his day with her and she'll be lost!"

"Naomi, don't be speaking that way in front of the child!" Now Dottie did look shocked.

She turned and put her hand on my arm. It felt cool and smooth. Then her voice changed and she said, "Never you mind your grandmother, Angel, honey. Things are a little bit confusing right now."

I looked at both their faces. Dottie's was kind and soft and her eyes were reaching to me the same as she was. Naomi's was hard, but it was plain as day that she was afraid.

I went to my room and turned on Johnny Dupree. "So that was Helen Reddy singing...Delta Daawwn." He said it real slow like he wanted to taste the words, like they were pieces of chocolate melting inside his mouth. I had a picture of him in my mind. He's real tall and slender, his hair is blond and wavy and his eyes are ocean blue. I imagined our first meeting, him looking at me like I'm someone he's been searching for his whole life, those eyes looking not at me but *into* me and he doesn't even have to speak because his gaze says it all. But he's so kind, and he knows I'm too young right now, so he touches my cheek gently, which causes an electric shock to course through my body, then he walks away because he knows he has to wait for me and his heart is broken. "Coming up first after the break, we'll have Paul McCartney and *Wings* singing... 'My Love,'" he croons. I'm thinking maybe it's a sign.

I was wondering, was this how the devil might have his day with me, giving me thoughts of me and Johnny Dupree? What did Naomi mean by that, exactly? Marvel came in to help me figure this out, but only if he could sit on my lap and get a good neck scratch. So if Satan had come to Eve in the form of a snake, well then he'd come to me by the creek. Funny thing was, if that snake was the devil, he didn't seem as awful as all that. Mama'd said she wasn't nearly so scared of him as she was of people who thought they knew God better than everybody else. Now *that's* something to think about.

Next thing I know I'm looking down on myself again, all curled up on my side, and there's the big hole, that big blackness—only this time it's black water and I'm *sinking* further and further down into pure nothingness until it changes, and there's this wave washing over me and I'm so lost in this feeling of awful sadness I don't know what to do. I'm under water and struggling to come up, knowing that if I don't break the surface I'll die.

Then I'm bolt upright in my bed, my heart beating like a war drum. For a second I didn't know where I was. It was twilight. I'd fallen asleep in the afternoon. The radio was on and Cher was singing "Half Breed" and Mama was coming up the stairs and going into her room. I couldn't lie there anymore by myself, not another second, so I got up and knocked on her door.

"Mama?" I said. "Mama? Are you in there?"

"I'm here."

"Can I come in?" My chest was still heaving up and down. I felt like if I couldn't talk to her right then I didn't know what in the world I was going to do next, who I was going to go to, feeling that suffocating thing again. I had never asked much of my mother, but here I stood practically desperate, waiting on word of my fate. Either she would talk to me or no, she wouldn't, leaving me alone in this valley of the shadow.

"Mama?" I said. "*I need to talk to you!*"

She opened the door. I rushed in and fell on her bed and started just bawling away like some kind of lunatic taking the shortcut to Crestview.

"What are you doing? What are you doing in here all this time? What's going to happen to us?" My shoulders were shaking real hard, like something big was trying to make its way out of me.

She sat down on the bed beside me and started rubbing my back, which felt good, like it was helping my tears come out.

"Angel, what in the world?"

"What's going to happen to me?"

"What do you mean, what's going to happen? Nothing *bad* is going to happen to you, Angel. What is it you're afraid of?"

"I don't know… I can't…I can't describe it." I was sobbing so much it was hard to talk. I'd wanted to tell her about the dream and here was my chance, but I didn't want to go back to it, didn't want its horrible darkness right now. I wanted to just be with Mama for once. I took a deep breath. Finally, I could speak.

"Just…just a lot going on, is all…I guess."

"I understand *that*," she said. Neither one of us said anything for a couple of minutes. I pulled myself together a little more.

"Mama, I was glad you told Reverend Jenkins what you did the other night. He deserved it." She perked up and laughed like I hadn't seen her do in weeks.

"I guess maybe I got a little carried away, but once I got going I couldn't stop myself. It just felt so good to say it all out like that, what I was really thinking."

"Do you worry about the devil?"

"Why? What about him?"

"Well, Naomi says he's going to have his day with me." Mama laughed again.

"Don't worry!" she said. "He's no match for you."

This hurt. She didn't know—but how *could* she know—what it was like, lying awake at night with all this in my head. But at least I could be with her, at least she wasn't telling me to leave her alone.

"Have you been studying your medical school books all this time?" I said.

"Some, but that's not all I've been doing. Can I show you something?"

I nodded. She knelt down beside the bed and pulled out a white shopping bag. In it were several balls of beautiful yarn, all different colors; red and purple, brown, yellow, blue and green. She put them down beside me then knelt again, this time bringing out a pair of knitting needles attached to what looked like a blanket in progress.

"You've been *knitting*?"

"Yeah," she said, looking at me now. "I guess it calms me down."

I almost laughed at the thought of it. Here I'd pictured her all hot and bothered, when all the while she was just up here going *knit, purl… knit purl,* like some old woman. I ran my hand over the soft knitted yarn.

"Angel, I just want you to know that I understand what you must be feeling right now."

"Oh, Mama!" I wanted so bad for it to be true, that she did know how it felt, that I wasn't just crazy or ungrateful, that maybe she was letting me in a little bit.

"Is Daddy really coming home? I don't even know if I want it anymore! We've been okay, you, me, and Naomi, but… it's like I didn't even realize it all this time. I was too busy feeling sorry for myself growing up without a daddy. But that's not nearly as bad as having your mama dying, or being all alone, or lying in a home with crazy people. I feel like I don't know anything anymore. I just want it to be…I don't know, I just want to feel peaceful inside, you know?"

I'd never thought of it exactly that way. Seems like everybody wants this thing or that thing, or they want it some way they can't have it, when really all they want is that quiet in their hearts that says everything is okay.

Mama took a long time to answer. "I know," was all she said. She looked out the window and took in a big breath, like she might fly out of it on the same breeze that had brought her in to be close with me just now. "But you know what? Doing this has made me feel better." She took out more stuff, a knitted scarf, a pair of socks, a cap, all things she had done while sitting up here avoiding Naomi.

"Here, let me show you how to do a stitch." She started working the needles, real slow so I could catch on. I watched her in the lamplight, how she handled the needles and the yarn and how her hair and face were glowing, and the moment had this sweetness about it that I know I'd been craving for so long. Whatever had happened before or was going to happen in the future, at least I had this. If only I could hold onto it forever.

Then Mama looked up and said, "You know, my Granny Belle used to have a weaving loom. I wonder if it's still around."

Chapter Eleven

"It's behind the loose board!"

"*What's* behind *what* loose board, Aunt Patsy?" I ask. There's no denying it now. She's getting worse.

"You'll never get any sense out of her," said Naomi. "Patsy's slipping."

"She is not! She's just tired is all, tired of *you!*" I say.

"You watch your mouth, girl!"

"Well, how would you like it if every time something came out of your mouth somebody said you were crazy?" I don't care if Patsy's mind turns to mashed potatoes, I'll never let Naomi get away with counting her out like that.

"Calm down now, Angel," Mama said. "I know it's hard."

"The child needs a whipping, that's what she needs." Naomi is glaring at me like she's daring me to sass her again. I glare back.

"It's *behind* the loose *board!*" Patsy says, this time with tears popping into her eyes and starting down her cheeks. I can't stand it anymore in there with all of them, can't watch Patsy's frustration and hear Naomi say Patsy's slipping and seeing Patsy act like she *is*, so I walk out, and not knowing where else to go, I duck into Miss Ida's room.

She's lying on her back looking straight up at the ceiling, not propped up in bed as usual.

"Afternoon, Miss Ida." She doesn't move her head but cuts her eyes sideways so I know she hears me. "It's me, Angel."

Then she speaks, but so softly I have to lean over to get what she's saying.

"What is it?" I ask.

"Take me," it sounds like.

"Take you where? You need to go somewhere? I'll go get Rita for you."

"No," she says in a stronger voice. "I said *take me*. You're an angel, come to see me…" Her oxygen tanks hiss as she struggles to take another breath. "So I'm asking you to take me now… I'm ready to go, I've …been here long enough."

"You mean take you on up to heaven?" I laugh, as if I think she's making a joke even though I don't think she is. "Miss Ida! I'm not that kind of angel. Besides, you don't want to go yet, you've still got us and all your friends here. We'd miss you too much. Don't go, Miss Ida. You've got all kinds of reasons to stay. Now tell me what I can get for you. Isn't there something would make you more comfortable? How about some juice or something?"

She rocks her head from side to side on the pillow.

"No, no, no," she says, talking in barely a whisper now.

I fish around in my sweater pocket, looking for what, I don't know. There's a ratty Kleenex, a mint somebody gave me during math class, and the acorn I'd picked up at the fort and been carrying around. It feels good, so cool, smooth, and round.

"Here you go." I place it in the palm of her hand and close her fingers over it, ever so gently. "This is for good luck, Miss Ida. Make a wish before sundown and maybe it will come true." She gives me a little nod and a faint smile before I leave the room, quick as I can. I feel a little bad about the wish thing, because I just made it up.

I have never known anyone that died before, except Grandpa Joe and I was too young to know anything then. Then there was President Kennedy but that was different, even though his death felt like family, the way Mama took it and all. She loved JFK. She loved him as president and I think she might have loved him even more after he was dead.

I'll never forget the day he died. I'd been outside playing and came busting through the front door to find her sitting in front of the TV crying.

"They shot the president." She looked up at the screen. Then she sobbed, hiding her face in her hands all full of tissue. I was too little to understand any of it, but I cried too because I knew something awful bad had happened, and spent the next few days sitting with her, watching it all on the screen, the big black hearse going so slow down the street and those horses plodding along, Jackie and the kids all dressed up and standing there like little dolls.

Caroline is not much older than I am. Ever since then I've wanted to meet her. One time when I was eight years old I did write her a letter but never sent it because I didn't know her address. This is what it said—*Dear Caroline Kennedy, I just want to say that I know what it's like living without a daddy. Maybe you could come see me sometime. Yours truly, Angel Bishop.*

All I can say is, thank goodness I didn't have that address because I would be embarrassed to death today knowing I'd sent a letter like that. Why in the world would Caroline Kennedy want to come to east Tennessee?

As for Miss Ida, I have stood by her bed many an afternoon holding her hand and talking to her about the bluebirds out her window or

why she didn't like what they had for lunch or sometimes just helping
her remember where she is, but I never even once thought about the
day when there wouldn't be that hand to hold. I ran out of her room
and just about smacked into Rita coming the other way.

"Whoa, Angel! What's your big hurry?"

"Miss Ida! She's saying she wants to die—and she wants me to
take her to heaven, just because my name is Angel."

"Why, ain't that something!"

"It's something awful if you ask me."

"What? That she's asking you to be her Angel of Death?"

My mind is swirling into that big, black hole. "Help her *die*? How's
that helping somebody? Don't we call that murder?"

"Well, now, I'm not talking about that. I'm talking about her seeing you as the angel come to help her to the other side. There comes
a time when death is a blessing. Haven't you ever heard the story of
Aunt Misery?"

"Who would have a name like Misery?

"Well, there's an old tale about her." She took my arm and led
me past Patsy's room all the way down to the little cubby at the end
of the hall that's the nurse's station. There wasn't much in it but
a small refrigerator and a long, black formica countertop with a
chrome edge. Sitting on it was about a quarter of the apple pie we'd
taken Patsy that Sunday.

"Set yourself right down here while I get these ready." Rita pointed to a green vinyl chair with foam rubber coming out of a hole in the
cushion. "You're wondering what I'm doing with your aunt's pie," she
said as she was getting out all these little paper pill cups.

"Well, I'm just thinking how we didn't really believe her when she
said you'd take her cola cake."

"Everything y'all bring her just sits there. She acts like its poison
or something. I've tried to get her to eat it, whatever it is, week after
week, but she won't touch the stuff. So I take it out and give it to the

folks who enjoy it. They so many old people over here don't get any visitors or nothing, you take them a piece of home-baked pie or cake and it makes their day." As she talked she was filling each cup, one by one, with each patient's pills.

"She also says you sneak patients out at night and take them drinking," I said.

Rita reared her head back and let out a big cackle. "Law me!" she said. "Now *that's* a good one! Hee-hee! Miss Patsy's gone and outdone herself now."

"…and that you were queen of an African tribe before you came to work at Crestview."

"Now I wonder how she knew that about me?" she said like she was serious, then she let loose again and we were both laughing.

"Well, I have a tale for you too," she said, "though I don't know how I can top Miss Patsy on the stories."

"Go ahead," I said. "I'm all ears."

"So Aunt Misery was this old lady that lived way over there on the other side of the mountain, thought she could trick death into not taking her away when her time came. She trapped him up in a tree so's he couldn't take anybody. Seemed all right for a while until folks started complaining. First the preacher got mad, said people weren't coming to church anymore because they didn't have to worry about where they was going after they died. Then the undertaker came and said he had a wife and family to feed and if nobody was dying then he didn't have any business! Well, Aunt Misery just ignored them, didn't care what they said, that is until her old friend Sarah came calling. Sarah was old and sick and ready to be done with this life.

"'Let him go,'" she begs her friend. "'Let old death out of that tree so he can take me!'"

"Aunt Misery's heart softened and she said she would, but first she made death promise he would never, ever come back to get *her!* Death was so desperate to get out of there that he agreed, and that's why they say that as long as death keeps his promise, there will always be misery in this world! So what do you think of that?"

"I don't know." I shrugged, messing with one of her little white pill cups. "I mean, it's a good story, I guess. So you're saying death isn't such a bad thing?"

"Well, law, honey, there just comes a time when the body has run itself out, and ain't nothing ever going to change that! And when a body is old and crippled up like that and has had a good long life like Miss Ida, well then no, it's not such a bad thing at all."

"What about when you're not old and crippled?" I said, thinking of Genevieve. "What if you get sick anyway?"

"Well now, there's nobody living that can answer the reasons behind such things as that. I know that ain't a very good answer, but I don't know anybody that's got a better one."

"Where's Ida's family?"

"They don't live around here," she said, "so she don't see them much. Day in and day out, we're about all she's got—you, me, and the others. It's like that with lots of the folks in here."

I got to wondering about Rita, who she was and how she ended up here at Crestview, but I didn't know how much I could ask without seeming nosy.

"So where do you live?" I asked.

"So where do you *think* I live?" she said. Then I felt bad, because of course she lived in Riverside with all of the other colored people.

"I mean...um, do you know Nathan Owens?" He was the one colored kid out of about a dozen in my whole grade that I'd gotten to know a little bit over all the years in school, my lab partner in the fetal pig incident.

"Sure I know him, and his mama and daddy too. Nice boy."

"Yeah." I watched her sorting all those pills and marveled at how she could keep them all straight, get the right ones in the right cups for everybody. "So I've always wondered, what kind of medicine has Aunt Patsy been having to take all these years?"

She looked at me over her glasses and lifted her eyebrows in a way that made me even more curious.

"You asking me what she *has* to take, or what they're just giving her?"

"What do you mean?"

She sighed and held up one of the jars on her countertop. "Well, this one here is for the nerves."

"The nerves?"

"Yeah, you know…just feeling jittery and stuff, like you feel scared but you don't really know what it is you're feeling scared *of*."

"Oh," I said. That sounded kind of familiar. "So what would happen if she didn't take it?"

"She'd be more alert, wouldn't sleep so much," Rita said.

"But what else? I mean, what does it do to help her?"

"Takes her mind off of things, I reckon. Miss Patsy, she seems to have a lot of torment for such a little old gal."

"Torment?"

"You know, fits and bad dreams and such. She cries out in her sleep and gets all out a-whack and you cain't tell what it is that sets her off. You've seen it. Most likely been that way a long time. I'd love to get inside that head of hers and see what rattles it so."

The phone rang down the hall. "I gotta get that," Rita said. "Opal's gone to lunch. You wait here, honey. I'll be right back."

I was left sitting alone in that tiny little room, looking at those pills and thinking about whose torment was whose. Rita came back into the room just as Naomi was calling to me from down the hall.

"Angel, where in the world are you? We're leaving whether you're in the car or not!"

"Listen to your granny hollering like that with all these old people trying to nap! She do you like that at home?"

"I gotta go," I said. My mind was racing.

"All right," she said. "You take care of yourself, now."

I walked back down the hall, stopping at Miss Ida's room just to peek in the door for a second. She lay still on her bed, her chest rising and falling to the sound of the tanks as they hissed away the slow minutes of her waiting.

Chapter Twelve

Sophie is really stepping on my last nerve. I mean, I know her mother is dying and all, but I have problems too. I'd like somebody to listen to me for a change and she's my best friend, so naturally I'd expect her to be the one, but all she wants to talk about is Ray and how cute he is and how much she likes him. She's having a fit about Maureen Callahan getting to work with him on the Shakespeare Bee.

"So do you think he goes over to her house on the weekends?" she asked.

"Well, what're you asking me for? *I* don't know!" I said. "I kind of doubt it, though. I wouldn't want to go there, would you?"

It's a great big old house, just about busting at the seams with the forty kids they have. Actually, I think the number is only fourteen, but whatever it is, they've got shutters off the hinges, a sagging porch, broken railings, and stuff all over the darn place. The screen door looks like somebody shot a cannonball through it. Then there're the dogs, these two big old boxers that growl at you from a block away. I always cross over to the other side of the street when I go by there because if you walk right in front of the house they'll run after you, or at least that's what I've heard.

"I guess you're right," Sophie said. "Well then, I wonder if she goes over to his house. It's probably real nice and quiet over there."

I couldn't picture it. Maureen and all those other Callahan kids were like some tribe that lived all around us but not really with us. They were everywhere, there being at least one for every grade, but you never saw them actually being with anybody but each other. It was strange. I'd known Maureen all the way through school and seen her riding her bike or walking downtown, but we'd never even had what you would call a conversation. When I thought about it I didn't know why, except maybe it's because she seems mad all the time, like something in her face says *don't talk to me*. So I never have, and the thought of her going over to Ray's house to study just doesn't add up.

In class we already read *Romeo and Juliet* and now we're reading *Macbeth*. Every day we go around the room, taking turns reading out loud. Mr. Sams helps us with the pronunciation and tries to get us to read it like we mean it. One day Ray had to read out loud that scene where Romeo watches Juliet at her window. He sounded like a robot.

"See how she leans her cheek upon that hand... O, that I were a glove upon that hand, that I might touch that cheek."

"Ray," Mr. Sams said, "Can you tell me what's going on in this scene?"

"Yeah, he's....uh, he's watching her and wishing he could be the glove on her hand because....well, he wants to be closer to her."

He had a pencil behind his ear, which was almost covered up by his curly blond hair, and he was sort of slouched over the book. His hands are big and bony, and his long legs were sprawled out in front of the desk like logs. I wondered what a boy like that might be like, already the size of a man but still the brain of a kid. I had a feeling he wasn't such a jerk as Hank or a big baby like Myron.

"That's precisely right," Mr. Sams said. "Now can you read it with a little *feeling?*"

"Okay ... um, 'See how she leans her cheek upon that hand....O, that I were a glove upon that *hand* that I might *touch* that cheek.'"

"Excellent, Mr. Collins." Ray's face was red, but even if he was embarrassed he still looked fine to me. Something in me kind of shivered. I think Sophie about fell out of her seat.

Much to her disappointment, he always picks up his books and leaves class right after the bell. But she keeps a constant watch on him at school, knows where his classes are and how he gets to them. The other day she came up with a way to start talking to him in the hall—with my help, of course.

This was the plan. I was supposed to walk just ahead of her like I didn't know she was there, then when she saw Ray coming she would call out to me as if to get me to turn around, only I was supposed to act like I didn't hear her. Then, as he got real close, she'd call louder and just as he was about to walk right by her she'd drop all of her stuff right at his feet. He would have no choice but to stop and help her pick it all up and then, of course, talk to her and fall in love.

I guess we should have practiced it, but we didn't have anybody to pretend to be Ray. I agreed to the whole thing since it seemed like all I had to do was keep walking, but I should have known a plan this dumb would go off track.

It was between algebra and home economics. I met Sophie outside the cafeteria after going to my locker and we started out down the C hall, where Ray was known to appear at this time. I was about ten steps in front of her as planned, so her calling out to me would get his attention.

It started out just fine. I was going along like nothing was up, and here he came just like she said he would. I saw him before she did and couldn't help but stare. He's tall, even taller than me, and that light, wavy hair is going every which way around his head, just like I'd pictured what Johnny Dupree might look like. He was walking along with his head down like he was lost in his thoughts, philosophizing maybe, but then suddenly he looked up! He has nice blue eyes, and he smiled right at me. I was so surprised I smiled back, just to be polite, and that was exactly when Sophie called out.

"Angel! ANGEL, wait up!"

I didn't want to look away from him, but I did, and I was about to hurry forward just like I was supposed to do, but before I heard the crash of Sophie dropping all of her stuff right in front of him, I heard Ray.

"Wait a minute. Hey, your friend's calling you!" I *had* to turn around then or else it would seem like I was running away from him, and he was standing there looking straight at me!

"You're Angel, right?"

"How'd you know my name?"

"We're in the same language arts class."

"Oh….yeah, that's right!" It was deceitful, but I was trapped.

"Besides, you look like one." Then he laughed.

Was this a compliment? It seemed impossible that a boy would say something nice about me out loud. Maybe I was being teased. I thought my cheeks were going to burn right off my face, bust into flames, or maybe my heart was going to jump right out of my chest. I couldn't decide if I just wanted to die right there out of sheer embarrassment or if the whole thing was sort of wonderful, although dying would have been a lot easier than thinking of what to say next.

Sophie saved me.

"AAAAAN-GELL!" she pleaded in her very best nasal whine. She was standing with her books and papers scattered all around her.

"Uh, gotta go," I said and hurried towards her. Her three-ring biology binder had come apart and diagrams of a frog's reproductive system were splayed out for all to see. Then I heard some other guy call out, "Hey, Ray!" and they must've gone off in the other direction because he never did walk past Sophie. She was fit to be tied.

"That's not the way it was supposed to go!"

Her face was red and her hair was kind of messed up. One piece was flopping over to the wrong side so her part wasn't perfect as usual. It was almost funny to see her so rattled, but I wasn't so happy either.

"I did exactly what you told me to," I said.

"Yeah, but you didn't have to *talk* to him!"

"Sophie! He's the one that talked to ME! So what was I supposed to do back there, act like a mute or something?"

I felt like walking off and leaving her there. I wish I had. That would have been sort of dramatic and powerful, which wasn't like me at all, but maybe the way I wish I could be sometimes. Instead I helped her pick up her stuff. She didn't even thank me.

"You just don't get it, do you, Angel? When it comes to stuff like this, you are a complete zero."

She might as well have punched me in the belly. I wanted a comeback, but I had to catch my breath and I couldn't think of anything fast enough.

"Oh, forget it!" She started walking off. I couldn't take it anymore.

"No, YOU forget it!"

She stopped in her tracks with her back to me and turned around real slow.

"What's *that* supposed to mean?" she said.

"It means you can just shut up because I'm sick and tired of you and everybody else! That's what!"

I turned away and walked all the way to the girls' bathroom on the seventh grade hallway, as far away as I could, barely making it in time to get in a stall so nobody would see me crying.

I didn't know what in the world I was going to find when I got back over to Crestview Wednesday afternoon, but I was surprised to see Patsy sitting up in a chair and smiling when I came in, the fall sunshine lighting up her face as she looked out her window.

"Why, look at you!" I said. "Something's agreeing with you today."

"I always like to see the leaves change colors," she said.

"It'll be Thanksgiving before too long." She nodded, still smiling. "And you know Daddy says he'll be here for it this year!"

A cloud passed over the room, the sunshine and Patsy's happy mood gone all at the same time. *Not again!* I thought, thinking she was just going to go all inside herself and shut down, but then she turned her head my way like a startled bird and her little dark eyes went into me like nails.

"He ain't coming here!" Her voice was much louder than usual.

"Yes, he is," I said. "Remember, Patsy? I told you he called a while back and said he'd be here for Thanksgiving. Naomi talked to him."

She sat up real straight and her arms were holding so tight to the arms of the chair they started shaking.

"No!" she shouted. "No!"

"Aunt Patsy, what on earth—"

"*Rita! RITA!*" she screamed. Then she started crying and shouting Rita's name over and over until the door opened and she came in.

"Angel, what's this?" she said. "Why, I never!" She went over to Patsy and put her arms around her. "Settle down," she says softly, like a mother to her child. "Just settle down now."

I didn't know what to do except look on while Rita calmed Patsy down and helped her over to her bed. Patsy crawled in and rolled over to the window with her back to us, her shoulders hunched over like some old shriveled person. It made my heart hurt.

"Come on with me for a minute," Rita said and so I followed her down to the little room with the medicine cups and the green vinyl chair. Rita sat me down and stood in front of me with her hands on her hips.

"So what's going on now? What was it set Miss Patsy off? She was having a good day."

"I just told her about my daddy," I said. "He's coming home after all this time, after years and years even, and she *already knew*—I was just bringing it up again! I don't know what's wrong with her."

"Would his name be Cal?" Rita asked. I nodded. "Oh, she knows all right. She been talking about this."

"What's she said?"

"Nothing I can make any sense of, but one thing I know, she sure don't cotton to him too much and don't want to hear about him coming around here."

"But why not?"

"Lordy, I wish I knew."

Then a light bulb came on in my head. "You know what, Rita? I bet he's the one that made them put her in here in the first place! I bet after my Grandpa Joe died, Daddy convinced Naomi and Mama this is where she belonged, where they could take care of her better, and she hates him for it." Rita listened and nodded her head.

"But why's he been gone all this time?" she asked.

"It's always been that he worked far away and such, but he barely ever wrote, never called and never, ever came home all this time. Maybe he had to stay away to make enough money to pay the bills."

"So how long's he been gone?"

"Since I was a baby," I said. "That's why sometimes I think it was all my fault."

"*Your* fault? That's nonsense, child."

"Well, how else do you explain it? There was a happy family, two parents, two grandparents and an aunt, all living together just fine, until all of a sudden I come along and in no time flat, one's dead, one's gone crazy, and the other's run off! I know I was just a little baby and didn't *mean* to do anything, but you have to admit, something's spooky about that."

"But it's not your doing, honey. You got to know that."

"You want to hear something kind of crazy, Rita?"

"Honey, you don't even know crazy. But sure thing, go ahead. I'm all ears."

"Sometimes I lie in bed at night, worrying about stuff."

"What, child?"

"Well, you know how in the Bible there are those bad angels? You know, like the ones God used to kill those babies and stuff?"

"Uh huh."

"I used to worry on account of my name, that I was like one of them, and wherever I went bad things would happen even if I didn't mean it."

"No, baby, no. You *know* that ain't it. God wouldn't use a child for harm, and you know it. You're too big to be thinking such a thing."

Rita was right, of course, but I'd been so used to this way of thinking I wasn't sure I knew how to be without it. Sort of like all my longing for Daddy my whole life. Now that he was coming back, I didn't need it anymore, this way of seeing myself. But these things, it was like they had carved little rivers in my heart and it wasn't so easy to just stop the flow.

"I'm going to go back in and talk to Patsy," I said. "Maybe she's calmer now. Somehow I've got to get her used to the idea of Daddy coming home...in case he really does."

I can see right away that's not going to happen today. Patsy's still hunched over just like we left her, and I might think she'd fallen asleep if it weren't for her face in her hands and her shoulders shaking. I snatch a Kleenex out of the box by her bedside and wipe her cheeks, just like you would do for a little kid. Then I take another one and put it in her hand. I see it's the last one and look around for some more. There's usually a fresh box on the window sill, but I don't see one so I decide to check in her chest of drawers.

She hasn't got that much stuff, so by the time I get past the second drawer they're mostly empty until I get down to the last one, which is stuffed with knick-knacks, things like soap and toilet water and what-not she's gotten for birthdays and Christmas. I don't see any tissues, but I do notice a stack of letters towards the back. Of course I have to take them out and have a look. Just as I'm about to slip the first one out of the envelope Rita comes back in the room, so I put them back quick.

"She needs some more tissues and I can't find any."

"They're on the closet shelf," she says. I go get it and take it over to the bed where Rita's busy rubbing something oily all over Patsy's arms and legs.

"What's that?" I ask, putting the box down where she can reach it.

"Helps keep the skeeters off of her," she says. "She likes to sit there with the window open sometimes and lets 'em in. They like to eat her alive."

I think of the creatures Patsy says come in at night, saying terrible things in her ear.

"She'll be all right," Rita says. "Go on and meet your granny now."

Chapter Thirteen

I decided to go back to Old Susan. Something was pulling me there and wouldn't let go until I could see her again and tell her about all the craziness that was going on in my life. I decided I wouldn't walk in the creek this time. Maybe it was just a part of becoming a woman that made cold creek water and muddy sneakers less appealing to me. This time I'd stay clear out of the water and up on the bank.

It was getting on into October now and mostly chilly, but this one Saturday was so nice and sparkly that when the sun was shining it felt like soaking in a warm bubble bath. On days like this I can't even make myself stay inside. The leaves are turning all colors, and the light is so clear it makes everything seem sharper, the blue sky and the white clouds, the ridges in the tree bark and the veins on the leaves. Even the sounds are sharper, like the sound of the river as I cross over the bridge and the sweet breeze, and those fall crickets or locusts or whatever they are, so loud they make me almost dizzy.

I passed all the landmarks, the same old trash, the tires, that same pair of jeans hanging on a branch. Funny how I never saw anybody else down here, even though you could tell by looking around that plenty of people came and went through this place. Where were all the people that left all these things? I wondered about them, what reasons they had to be tromping by this old creek. Where were they going? It didn't seem likely they were all headed to the Sunshine Bakery, or to see Old Susan.

When I got to the fort I decided to take a break, so I went and sat down in my very own rock chair. It reminded me so much of those fall afternoons all those years ago and made me wonder about all the autumn days even way before that, since before all the car places and stores, before Honey Buns and car tires were even invented.

I'm thinking about what kind of people might have lived way back when, probably right down here in the valley, close to the creek where they could come get their water and do their wash and look for food. I'm picturing what they might have looked like, wearing deerskin clothes, moccasins on their feet, beads around their neck and their wrists and woven into their hair in long black braids.

Suddenly they aren't just in my thoughts. They are there, standing on the other side of the creek, looking right at me. Now, this is the part that's hardest to describe. I don't actually see them there with my eyes. I *feel* them there and I see them in my mind. But it's all the same. I can see their faces so clearly, I can even see into their eyes. I can understand them. They're looking at me but they're also looking out for me. They know I'm a girl from another time, accidentally crossing over into their world, even if she doesn't know how, and it seems strange to them but they don't doubt it and they want no harm to come to me.

I keep sitting there as still as stone and don't dare make too sudden a move or look in another direction. I wanted them to stay. But too soon the moment passed, and as surely as I had felt them there the feeling disappeared and they were gone.

"Don't go away," I said out loud, even though I knew they hadn't left *me*. Somehow I had left that mysterious place where I could see *them*. I knew they were still there, my creek people, but I wished for something I could hold onto, to take with me and help me remember, maybe something to show Old Susan. I remembered the last time I was here with the snake. Brightly colored leaves lay all around and it was sunnier than before, now that the trees were half bare.

I got down on my knees and crawled over to the spot where it had been. It didn't take much to find what I was looking for, almost perfectly preserved under the top layer of leaves, a beautiful long, thin and papery skin, but so light and fragile that when I picked it up the breeze caught it and blew most of it out of my hand.

I tucked the small piece that was left between my thumb and forefinger into my shirt pocket. Then I looked around at where I was, surely a sacred spot, and this was my remembrance. *Pay attention.*

Old Susan was working outside in her yard when I walked up.

"Adawehi!"

It was the same word she said the first time she saw me. She dropped what she was doing and came over to give me a big hug, smelling like smoke and dirt and ashes and something sweet and flowery. The cheek she pressed against mine was damp and warm, her peppery hair sleek and pulled back, smooth and hot in the sun.

"So what brings you up this way?"

"Oh, I don't know," I said. "Nothing in particular." I looked down at the dirt and couldn't think why I'd come and wished for a second that I hadn't, until she piped up again.

"Well, I know why," she said. "You come to have a cup of tea with me, now, didn't you?"

"I reckon." I shrugged my shoulders and smiled, feeling better.

We walked around to the back of the house. The pot of water was already going over the fire.

"You just set yourself right down there now and take a rest," she said. "You looking about like something the cat drug in." I knew it wasn't a compliment but I didn't care. She was right. She came back with a cup of tea in each hand and a small bowl of apples balanced on her forearms.

"Gonna make a pie." She set everything down and took her pocketknife out of her jacket.

"Sometimes it just seems like everything's going on all at once, don't it?" she said. "I mean, I got stuff a-comin' and a-goin'. Been trying to winter down all these beds here and then one of the goats got sick and I had to go all the way over to North Carolina to get something for her from one of my cousins. Then old man Sorrell died up there yesterday so I was up at the place helping out."

"You mean Martha's husband, Clyde?" I asked.

"Yep, that'd be him," she said. "Funeral's tomorrow. Have an apple."

"You going?" I took one out of the bowl and started twirling the stem.

"I reckon not," she said. I wanted to know why, wondering if she didn't feel welcomed.

"What's she going to do about the leg?" I asked.

"Now how do you know about that?"

"Dottie Ames." I took a bite of the apple. It was sharp and sweet.

"Well, now, that figures," she said.

"She told us how upset he was about them having to cut it off and all, and that Martha went and had them dig it out of the incinerator before it was too late."

"Well, the leg's been waiting for him over at the funeral home and they're going to stick it right there in the casket with him, that's what."

"I guess that'll work," I said. We sat quietly in the warm October sun. A big old, fat bumblebee rumbled by, heavy and slow. The air was crisp, smelling like ripe fruit and burning leaves.

"So my daddy should be coming next month," I said. "And I have an idea about why nobody would ever talk to me about him."

"You do?" she said, her tongue poking slightly out of the side of her mouth while taking her knife to the apple in her hand, the long unbroken peel spiraling onto the table.

"Yeah, it was right under my nose the whole time, but I just now put it together after Patsy went bonkers again when I reminded her he was coming back."

"What'd you figure out?"

"That he's the one made her go into Crestview and now she hates him for it. And then he had to go away so he could make enough money to keep his family, because it cost so much for her to live there."

"I see." She looked at me long and hard. "And does that help you some?"

"It's better than thinking I caused the whole thing, by being born and making things harder," I said.

"Look here at me," she said. So I did. Her eyes were fixed on mine, and I mean *fixed*. If they were laser beams they'd have gone right out the back of my skull.

"You ain't responsible for none of this, Angel. Y'hear?"

"Well, I know not *really* but—"

"I said none of it!" She wasn't smiling anymore.

"Okay," I said, wanting to mean it. I looked away and changed the subject. "You ever go walking down by Murray Creek?"

"Not so often anymore," she said. I looked back up at her. Her eyes had changed again, now all sparkly and smiling like when you share a secret. "Why? D'you see 'em?"

"How'd you know? Who are they?"

"It's just the creek folks. They lived there a long time ago. They's some that can still see them if they got the eyes."

"The creek people! Patsy told me about them once! I wonder if she saw them when she was a girl."

"You can ask her about that next time you see her." She smiled real big, handing me a long, curly ribbon of unbroken apple peel.

"So you're a woman now?" she said. I practically choked on the apple piece.

"So how'd you know *that*?"

"Just guessing." She smiled again. "Guessed right, now didn't I?"

"It was that same day, the day of the snake."

"Told you it was a sign, didn't I?"

"Yep, you did."

"So how did you celebrate?"

"Celebrate what?" I asked. "Getting the curse?"

"Why, everything! Especially that! In the days when we was living by the old ways," she said, "some of the native people had a tradition for a girl's first moon time." I liked hearing it called that. *Moon time.* "She would go off and be by herself somewhere for a while. Other women, usually her mother and grandmother, or maybe older sisters, would come see her and bring her food."

"Why was she supposed to be by herself?" I asked.

"Because they believed it was a powerful thing. They was afraid of it. The menfolk wouldn't even look at a girl during that time, or have nothing to do with it. That's why she had to go off somewhere. But then when it was over there'd be a big celebration in honor of her becoming a woman, ready to be a wife and mother."

"Not me!" I said. Old Susan laughed and shook her head.

"Naw, these traditions belong to another world long gone," she said. "But it ain't all just hocus pocus. There's wisdom in the old ways. Don't it make sense that if the moon herself sees fit to hide her face for a few days a month, why shouldn't we?"

"I wish I lived way back when," I said. "I wish I could live that way."

"Well, it wasn't all a bed a'roses! Believe me, we wouldn't want all they had to put up with, but there's some things worth hanging on to, that's for sure. Hold on a minute. I got something for you." She went into her house and came back out with what looked like a necklace with a small brown leather pouch on the end shaped like a little envelope, about two inches wide and long, decorated with different colored beads and leather tassels

"What's this?"

"It's your medicine bag," she said.

"My what?"

"Your medicine bag. It holds things that have special meaning to you." I held it in my palm and stroked it with my fingers.

"What kind of special meaning?" I asked, opening up the little coin-size flap. She laughed.

"Well, you might run across something that strikes you as important in some way. It's not something you can explain, like there's rules to it or anything. It's just something you know."

"—Oh! I already have something to put in it!" I hung it around my neck and reached into my pocket to take out the piece of snake skin.

"Wait," she said. "Don't let nobody else know what's in there. 'Hit takes away from the medicine."

"What medicine?"

"A thing'll have power if you let it, that is if you listen to it."

"How do you know what it's supposed to do? What if it's something bad?"

"If you've got good in your heart, you can trust that whatever's speakin' to you is also for the good. But its message is for you, not nobody else. That's why you keep your medicine bag and what's in it to yourself."

I thought about this, about what the snakeskin was saying to me and about what Old Susan had been telling me. I wanted to know more.

"Do you go away every month?" I ask.

"I do," she said. "I take just a few things with me and go away to be quiet. I'm long past my moon times, but there's always so much to be done here and I get to feeling like a spinning top, so every once in a while I go to a place where there ain't a thing to do but prepare my food and sleep and pray."

"Where do you go?"

She lowered her eyes, and I was ashamed I'd asked something so personal.

"I'll tell you—if you'll help me with a little idea I have," she said.

"Anything you want!" I said. "I mean, if I can do it. Just ask."

"Has to do with them two boys was bothering you not too long ago. You know who I'm talking about?"

"You bet I do," I said. "And I'm happy to oblige! What is it?"

"Well then, listen up!" she said, and I was all ears after that.

Chapter Fourteen

So here's how I found out Sophie really is my best friend. First of all, she called me and said she was sorry for going off on me like that at school. Then she came over to my house on Friday night and it seemed like nothing had ever happened, which I think is a true test. We tried to study Shakespeare.

"Okay, you first," I said. "I'll give you an easy one. *When the hurly-burly's done, when the battle's lost and won.*"

"Is that all I get?" Sophie asked.

"Yes, because it's so *easy*," I said.

"No fair! We get a hint in the bee if we need it."

"Yeah, but you shouldn't need it on this one, but okay, it's at the very beginning of one of the plays."

"Oh, right! It's in *Romeo and Juliet* when they're talking about their family feud."

"NO, it's *not*. Try again. Here's another hint. Who would use a word like 'hurlyburly'?"

"Shakespeare?" she said. She was honestly serious. I let out a big sigh.

"It's the witches, Sophie. The witches in the opening scene of *Macbeth!* You have to know that!"

"Oh, I knew that!" she said. "I did, Angel, really I did. I'm just not in the mood for this. Do we have to study right now?"

So we did other stuff. We turned on Johnny Dupree, of course, and played Mystery Date twice, but had to stop when Marvel kept sitting on the game board. She'd gotten The Bum for the second time and wanted to quit after that anyway. We painted our nails (she used Passion Pink, I used Berry Burst) and hot-curled our hair. Hers turned out with these perfect waves bouncing off her shoulders while mine just got bushy.

"Oh! I love this song!" It was "Tie a Yellow Ribbon Round the Old Oak Tree," which I think is the dumbest one, but I didn't say so. She was playing with her hair, putting it up and putting ribbons in it and such.

"Do you like 'Midnight Train to Georgia'?" I asked, running a brush through mine.

"Oh, I don't know, it's sort of …bluesy or something. I like snappy!" She clicked her thumbs and forefingers together when she said this and I laughed. "You know, Angel," she went on, "the problem with you and me is that we never cuss."

"Cuss?"

"You know." She lowered her voice. "Like 'dammit to hell' and stuff like that."

"Sophie, I know what cussing is, for Pete's sake."

"See, right then you could have said 'for Christ's sake' and you would have come off way more sophisticated."

"Well, that's fine if I want to end up with a mouth full of Ivory soap suds. I know because it's happened before." Sophie stared at me, bug-eyed.

"No! When was that?"

"Naomi heard me call Hank a turd when he was cheating at Kick the Can last summer. It wasn't worth it, believe you me."

"Turd? That's not even a real cuss word!"

"You think that's bad," I went on. "Naomi says I'm not supposed to say someone's pregnant. I should say they're 'waiting on a blessing.'" Sophie thought this was hilarious.

"So what's wrong with 'pregnant'?" she said when we stopped laughing.

"Because if you're pregnant, then you obviously did *it*. But if you're waiting for a blessing, then it's all God's doing, it's not your fault." Of course this set us off again. When we calmed down, Sophie got back on track.

"Well, dammit to hell, Angel, you'll just have to learn to swear when Naomi's not around to hear you. I mean, we're going to be *fourteen* years old before too long and we walk around acting like third graders."

"But what's so great about cussing?"

"Oh, well…you know," she said. "It just adds a little pizzazz to your character. Boys like it."

"Right," I said. "I'll try to remember that." I figured now that I was finally a legitimate woman, Sophie could concentrate on helping me become more refined.

"So Angel, about people doing it. Why's it supposed to be so bad? I mean, it *is* where babies come from, you know."

"It's only bad if you aren't married," I said. "I guess."

"So why can't you use the word 'pregnant' for people that are married?"

"Well…maybe because everybody knows you're naked when you do it and it's embarrassing to think about?"

"It doesn't embarrass me." Sophie closed her eyes and leaned her head back. "I like thinking about it!"

"Well, Naomi doesn't." I said.

"And you don't have to be naked, either. I wonder if you can still get pregnant if you leave your clothes on."

"Sophie! Don't be stupid—you had health class!"

"I know, I'm just kidding!" she said, flapping her hand in my direction. "Naomi doesn't like thinking about it probably because she's never done it."

"She had to," I said. "She had my daddy."

"Okay, maybe once, then. She probably closed her eyes and prayed for it to be over quick."

"Sophie, I don't want to talk about my grandmother doing it."

"Okay, then let's talk about *us* doing it! Sometimes I think I'll never be able to wait until I'm married, when you can just flop around whenever you want."

"Flop around?" I asked, thinking of fish.

"Yeah, that's what it's like."

"How do you know?"

"Well," she said, "contrary to what you might think, I do have an intellectual curiosity about certain things. I've researched this. My parents have a book."

"Oh. Can I see it?" Sophie took too long to answer.

"Well, you see, Angel, I just don't know if you're ready for it or not." This was typical Sophie, asking me all sorts of dumb questions then in one breath turning into Miss Know-It-All.

"Dammit, Sophie, I want to see it!"

"That was good, Angel. Real good!" She was grinning. "Okay, next time you're at my house." It was time to change the subject before she made me mad again.

"Want to see the new panties I got at Parks Belk?" I said. "They have these little butterfly patches sewn on the front and they were on sale, buy one pack of six get the other free." I reached in the drawer to get them and saw the Girl Scout thin mints I had saved from the spring. I'd had to hide them from Naomi because she has a wicked sweet tooth and I like to spread out the Girl Scout cookie season.

"Look what I have! You hungry?"

"Of course I'm hungry," Sophie said. "Even if I wasn't we'd have to sit here and eat them just to celebrate. Imagine, thin mints in October!"

We broke them out. She took one whole cellophane roll and I took the other. I put my Burt Bacharach album back on and we just sat there eating and talking.

"I've still been thinking a lot about Ray," she said. I moaned and rolled my eyes, but she just kept on. "I just can't quit it."

"Well, I guess not."

"Did you know his mother works in the guidance office at school?" she said.

"You mean Mrs. Collins? That's his mom?"

"Yeah, she's a counselor. They always say you can go to one of them if you need somebody to talk to."

"I know. I had to go see Mrs. Rothbottom last year."

"*Mrs. Rothbottom*? If I had that name I think I would kill myself! So anyway, you know what I did?"

"There's no telling," I said, in between licking the mint chocolate off my fingers.

"I went to talk to her, to tell her all about my psychological problems."

"Your *psychological* problems?" I said.

"Well, you know, I have lots of pressures at home. The teachers at school need to be aware of those things."

"Okay, Sophie. So did you go see Mrs. Collins for help or did you go because she's Ray's mother?"

"What difference does it make? I just wanted to see what she was like."

"Did you think she was going to help you get Ray's attention or something?"

"Not really." She shrugged. "But you never know."

"True," I said.

"I just have this feeling he's going to ask me to that party the band has every year in November. Kathy Bledsoe told me about it."

"What gives you that feeling?"

"He came up to me in the lunchroom the other day," she said. "I figure that's him just working up the nerve, you know. I mean, I think he's going to ask me, I hope. I asked Kathy if he liked anybody else and she said she didn't know, so if *she* doesn't know I figure that's a sure sign he doesn't, because she's onto all that stuff."

This was true. Kathy was onto everything, knowing everything, winning everything. Even before she got to be majorette instead of me she beat me out for patrol captain at Andrew Jackson Elementary and got more Girl Scout badges than anybody else in our troop. No surprise there—Kathy is one of those people that get to own the world just by acting like they already do.

"He's in the band? What does he play?" I said.

"Trumpet. He's one of the best junior high school trumpet players in the state. He goes off to all these competitions and stuff on the weekends. That's probably why he hasn't called."

"So what kind of a party is it?" I asked, trying to sound more interested that I was.

"It's a barbecue over at the Cloverdale barn, with—get this!—*square dancing.* Can you imagine me doing all of that 'swing your partner' stuff? I just know I'm going to look soooo retarded…. Angel, why is your cat looking at me like that?"

Marvel was sitting right in front of her on the floor with his feet up under him, looking like a big orange loaf of bread with eyes. He was staring and purring and every now and then he'd open and close his eyes, real slow. Sophie has never been a cat lover.

"He's reading your mind," I said.

"Oh stop it, Angel! You're giving me the creeps."

"But he is! That's what cats do. They know exactly what's going on in your head and if you've got a problem and you're stuck with something, they can tell you what to do."

"Oh, right! So how in the world can a cat tell you what to do, smarty pants?"

"Well, it's not like he *tells* you exactly. You have to be real quiet and just sort of sit and listen. After a while, you might find that an answer comes to you, just like that."

"That's not the cat telling you!" Sophie said. "That's just you thinking it up yourself."

"No, it's not. I know it. I think it has something to do with the purring. He also knows whether or not someone's telling the truth."

"I don't believe you." She took a strand of hair and twirled it around her finger. Then the phone rang in the hallway.

"Hold on a sec." I ran out to catch it. "Hello?"

"May I please speak to Angel?" I was caught way off guard. Number one, I rarely get a call from anybody but Sophie and she was here and number two, I never EVER got a call from a boy, and this was for sure a boy, in fact a boy with a shaking voice.

"This is Angel," I said, very carefully, as if walking into what I knew deep down must be some kind of trap.

"This is Ray, from school."

"Ray?"

"Yes…um, I was wondering if you wanted to go to the band party with me. It's in, um… a few weeks and, um…my mom could drive us and she could bring us home, too." I didn't know what to say, but I heard myself answer anyway.

"Okay."

"Um… that's great. Okay. So, I guess I'll see you."

"Okay …bye," I hung up the phone, practically shocked out of my socks. I had to take several deep breaths. I couldn't believe what had just happened and what in the world was I going to tell Sophie? No, *how* was I going to tell her I'd just flat out double-crossed her without meaning to or planning it or even knowing how I did it? It was just answer the phone and *bam!* You've stabbed your best friend in the back.

I walked back into the room hoping she'd be distracted by a pimple or split ends or something before I had to answer her, but no such luck.

"Well, who was it?" she asked. I was as stuck as could be, caught with my hand in the cookie jar and I hadn't even wanted a cookie. I'm not a good liar, but the thought did cross my mind to try it until I realized it was too late for that. She could already see on my face I was hiding something from her.

"Are you going to tell me who that was or am I going to have to leave and stop speaking to you ever again?"

I made it quick, like ripping the Band-Aid off all at once.

"It was Ray."

"Ray who?" she said, picking at a fingernail.

"You know," I said. "Ray... *the* Ray."

"You mean *my* Ray." She was glaring at me with ice pick eyes.

"Yes." I said it looking down at the floor.

"Oh, him," she said, doing her I-don't-care thing, which didn't work at all because whenever she does it her foot twitches and her face gets red and she starts breathing really fast and shallow.

"So what'd he want?"

"He asked me to the band party," I said. Another rip of the Band-Aid.

"And you said?" The ice-pick eyes were on me again.

"I told him I would...I think."

By that time I wasn't sure what I'd said. I expected her to start screaming and crying or yelling at me or something. It caught me off guard when she just looked straight at me and spoke in a normal voice.

"And how's that supposed to make *me* feel, your very best friend?"

I was so confused. A girl's first date is supposed to be a happy thing or exciting or something, and here I was wishing it wasn't happening. So then it was me that started crying, and I turned to leave the room again

"Angel, wait a minute," she said before I got out the door. "Hold on." She sure sounded calm, but I turned back and saw her looking at me with the saddest eyes I ever saw.

"I'm so *sorry*," I said. "I really didn't mean to betray you. I was so rattled I didn't know what to say! I thought maybe if I went with him this time it could help you out, you know, maybe I could talk about you or something…but that's stupid. Listen, I'll just tell him I can't go—because I don't care. I really don't care at all. I guess you think I'm a terrible friend now."

She was looking away from me out the window, then down, shaking her head. She reached out her hand and started petting Marvel. I'd never seen her do *that* before and I realized she was crying, too. All of a sudden she put her hands in front of her face and just plain started bawling.

"It's no use," she said between sobs. "I'm such a loser!"

"Oh, Sophie, stop it!"

"No, it's true, Angel. I mean it. I'm the one that's done the terrible thing."

"*What* are you talking about?" I sat back down on the floor. Sophie wiped her nose with the heel of her hand and sniffed.

"You know when I said he talked to me in the lunchroom the other day?" she said.

"Uh huh," I said while digging around under my bed for a box of Kleenex. It was a mess under there, but I found it and handed her one. She took her time blowing her nose.

"Well..." she said finally, "he asked me if I would give him your phone number."

"He *did*?"I was downright shocked and amazed that a boy would go to such trouble to talk to me. "So what'd you do?"

"I told him I didn't know it! I lied, Angel! I lied because I was jealous and I didn't want him to call you! And what's worse, I didn't tell you that he likes you instead of me, because I thought I could still get him to like me better! Oh, Angel, I'm the one that's a terrible friend. I'm so sorry!"

For a split second, I agreed with her completely and was so mad I didn't know what to think. Here I hadn't even been able to tell her a fib—and she'd done that to me?

"I can't believe you did that!" I said, wanting her to suffer for it, but she was being all dramatic and sorry and stuff and looked so miserable I couldn't keep it up. So, I forgave her.

"Oh, forget it," I said. "Wonder how he got my number?"

Sophie let out a big breath and let her shoulders fall about a mile. Then she wiped her nose, dabbed her eyes, and gave Marvel a look.

"Now YOU can stop staring at me like that!" she said. He sniffed and started licking his paw, then we both laughed so hard we about wet our pants.

"Hey, know what? Remember our fort in the woods?"

"Yeah—"

"Well, I went to see it. It's still there—even parts of the roof!"

"What does that have to do with anything, Angel?"

It might have hurt my feelings that she didn't get it, but to tell you the truth I didn't mind keeping the whole thing to myself anyway. Besides, Sophie can't help being Sophie.

Chapter Fifteen

It was Halloween. The plan was to go trick-or-treating just like we always did, even though we're a little bit old for it. I don't think people care as long as you wear a costume, which we most certainly did.

We went as bums. Sophie came over after school with two old shirts of her dad's and we went outside and put dirt and stuff all over them. Then we teased up our hair real messy and made our lips real big with red lipstick (we were lady bums) and put on mismatched socks and shoes. Then we rolled up our jeans, and voila!! We were out the door.

We didn't figure out our costumes ahead of time like we used to. Oh boy, back then you knew what you were going to be for Halloween way back in the summer, but somewhere about the fourth or fifth grade we figured out the costume wasn't all that important to the goal of getting as much candy as possible. We had to move fast and light because it usually took a good three hours door to door to half fill a pillowcase. Not that we ever ate that much. It was fun to see how long we could make it last. I was impressed one time after a Fourth of July picnic, when Sophie hauled that pillowcase out from under her bed and handed me a snack pack of Milk Duds! It was kind of an unofficial contest, and that year she won.

"Don't you want something to eat before you go out?" Naomi called after us.

"We're going to get a sackful!" I shouted back, getting on out so as not to have to hear her lecture. I heard it anyway.

"You'uns too big to be doing that!"

We scooted. There was lots of ground to cover and I had to think of a way to get Sophie to go along with what I had to do.

"You want to do something different this year, something really fun?" I said. Usually we would cover our neighborhood first, then go over to Jericho Hills where all the big houses were—and the best candy. There was one that always gave you a whole Pay Day, and it wasn't just the snack size, either.

"What?" She stopped to turn and look at me.

"It has to do with Hank and Myron," I said. "I have to get back at them for something,"

"Well, *what*?" she said, this time with a little laugh. She'd known them a long time too, but not as long as me, and I knew she could have a crush on Hank if he'd just stop acting so stupid all the time. Anyway, I told her what happened that day in the ravine—well, most of it, and I didn't let on how really awful it still made me feel.

"Angel, that's…that's so gross! They're such jerks! I can't believe you haven't you told me before now!"

"There's more," I said and told her about going to see Old Susan, and how she and I were friends now.

"You went to *see* her? By *yourself*? "

"Well, why not?" I said. "She's just a person, like everybody else."

"Well, yeah…But ever since we were kids we were afraid of her, and then you just go and hang out with like she was one of your girlfriends or something? Boy, there's a *lot* you haven't been telling me!"

"I tried," I said, "But you acted like she had some kind of disease because she's an Indian. Shoot, I might have invited you to come too if I'd thought you were the least bit interested." *If you hadn't been so wrapped up in yourself* is what I didn't say.

"So what's she like? What's her place like?"

"Can't go into all that now," I said. "We'll talk about it later, but in the meantime, you just need to listen to what's going to happen, do what I say, and *do not* ask questions. I don't want to hear any what, why, or how come. It'll be worth it. Are you in?"

"Yeah, I guess so….Yeah, okay. I'm in."

It took us awhile to track down Hank and Myron, but we knew we'd run into them eventually. In the meantime we were making our way from door to door, trying to ignore comments like "What grade are you girls in now?" or "Tell me about your costumes!" We saw right through it. One lady came right out and said, "Good gracious! I'd of thought y'all would be embarrassed to be out running around here with all the little ones!" All she gave us was a few lousy sourballs.

We found the boys shortly after that. I had an idea they might be hanging around the school somewhere, so I suggested we cut across the field on the way over to Highlands. Sure enough, there they were, sitting along the back fence smoking.

"Hey, you two!" I called out.

"Who is it?" they yelled. It was dark, but we could see them putting their hands down to their sides trying to hide their cigarettes and straining to see us.

"It's me, Angel!"

"And Sophie!" she shouted. In a minute we were right up on them and we could see each other eye to eye. I had avoided them pretty much all fall, so they were surprised to see me being so friendly, I could tell. This put me at an advantage. As for the cigarettes, I acted like I hadn't noticed yet.

"We've been looking for you guys," I said.

"You have?" Hank had kind of a swagger in his voice I knew was meant for Sophie. "Well, what for?"

"I'm ready to see the cave."

"You…right now?"

"Yep," I said.

"But it's dark!" Myron said.

"Wait a minute," Hank said. "The deal was that you was going to go over to old Susan Blackfoot's place. I ain't going to show you no cave until you been there, and that's that."

"I have."

"Prove it," he snipped as he looked up at me. They were still sitting against the fence with Sophie and me standing there sort of over them.

He thought he had me. I had, of course, anticipated this. I showed them the little leather purse that hung around my neck underneath the bum shirt.

"It's a medicine bag," I said.

"What? She give it to you?" Hank said.

"Yep," I said. "I took her something and she gave me this in return."

"Well, what's in it?" Myron said.

"It's personal…things that contain my own spirit medicine."

"*Spirit* medicine? What in the heck is that?" Hank laughed. "Show it to me. Let me see what's in there!" He made a move to get up but I looked long and hard at the cigarette in his hand. They were caught and they knew it. If I decided to, I could rat them out to Hank's mother in no time flat and they'd be grounded for weeks.

"My medicine bag is magic," I said, "and it's only for me to know what's in it." He backed off and took another puff of his cigarette, trying to be cool. Then he blew the smoke out between his lips, taking a long time as if he was thinking.

"So, you want to see the cave…on Halloween night," Hank said, looking back up at us with his blinking eyes.

"It's okay if you're scared," Sophie said.

"Who said I was scared?"

"Nobody has to say it. We can just tell," I said. I have to admit, we were good.

"I ain't scared!"

Sophie and I laughed.

"Well, come on then," he said, acting as if it'd been his idea all along. He was up and running when Myron piped in.

"But it's dark!"

"Well, it's Halloween!" I said. Sophie looked at me as if she might chicken out or was maybe thinking about it, but I grabbed her elbow and we took off after him. Myron was still bellyaching behind us.

"How we gonna see anything?" he yelled.

"I got a flashlight!" Hank reached down in his pillowcase. "My mama made me bring it."

I wasn't sure what we were in for, but I had a feeling it was going to be good. We took the road to the river bridge instead of going through the ravine, the boys going on and on about race car driving and Tennessee football and what have you. They were walking ahead of us slightly so we couldn't hear exactly everything they were saying, but they sure were getting a kick out of themselves. Every now and then they'd get so tickled they'd grab themselves around their bellies and stumble around laughing. Then the flashlight beam would go all crazy and we couldn't see where we were going, so I had to take it away from Hank and carry it myself. Now they were behind us so we could hear everything, including all the jokes about farts and stuff.

When we crossed over the bridge, they pointed us in the opposite direction from Old Susan's house, which made me nervous since I didn't know where we were going. It seemed like we walked a long way. I was getting cold and was glad when we cut up into the woods at least out of the wind. Something moved in the woods, which made me jump so I started singing the line that popped into my head.

"The water is wide ... I can't get o'er..." It was comforting to me but Sophie was getting impatient.

"Where are we going?" she muttered, sounding like she might be about to cry.

"Shhhhh! We can't stop now," I said, tight-jawed in the cold.

"So build me a boat ... that will carry two..." I sang, wishing I was at Old Susan's house having a cup of tea and talking about everything there was to talk about. I wished it was daytime. I wished it was summer.

We came to this flat place that looked like an old river bottom, and rising up out of it, from what I could see in the dark, was a wall of rock that flanked a steep hillside.

"There's the entrance," Myron said.

He took the flashlight and pointed it towards what looked like a clump of bushes, but as we got closer I could see a small open space. Hardly seemed big enough for a dog to crawl through, much less us. It was mostly covered with brush and looked so dark inside, dark as the end of the world and cold as outer space. An endless hole—again! Was I awake or asleep, and was I *really* going to go in there? It reminded me of another episode on *The Twilight Zone* where these kids are swimming and they see a hole in the bottom of the pool. You're watching and thinking "Don't go in there! Don't go in!" But of course they do anyway, just like we were about to, and they come out in some terrible place on the other side. I couldn't even remember whether or not they ever got back home, but that show's not exactly known for happy endings, so it was best not to think about it.

"You're really doing this?" Sophie said. I felt the same thing I heard in her voice and was about half a hair from turning hide with her, but I took a deep breath and got ahold of myself quick.

"Remember what I told you," I whispered, so the boys couldn't hear. "Stick with me. We're almost done."

"If you want to see in the cave, well, there it is," Hank announced. "And this is the only way in. You gotta get down on your knees and crawl."

I could tell he was just waiting for us to whine or complain or something. I held my breath and put my hand on Sophie's shoulder. She got the point and didn't let me down.

"Well, what are you waiting for?" she said. "I'm not standing out here freezing all night!" Hank went first with the light. He got down on his belly and slithered through like a snake, leaving us out in the pitch black. Myron had more trouble, being a little more hefty, but he wriggled himself in next and hollered after us.

"You comin'?"

"You first," I said. Sophie slid through quick as a lizard, leaving me alone out there, wondering what in the world. I looked at the darkness around me, and dove.

I stood up in what felt like a large space, a room with rock walls. Sophie grabbed onto my arm and about pulled it off. She was sniffing some, I think she'd started to cry. We could hear the echo of our steps, and even our breathing seemed loud.

"Well, this is it," Myron said. "Ain't it something?" His voice boomed into the space.

Hank was jerking his flashlight around so much at first we couldn't tell what it was we were supposed to be looking at, or for. Then he began to point things out.

"Look over there," he said. "See all those things, them stones and bowls? Look, there's a spoon—"

"And it's all ours because we found it!" Myron said.

"That there looks like some kind of animal hide," Hank continued, shining his light over into a corner, "maybe used for a rug or something."

"Well, so what if it is a rug!" Sophie wailed. "Who cares? Y'all are so stupid! I'm cold! This is awful and I hate it! Let's just get outta here!" She had snapped. I jabbed her with my elbow to try and get her to shut up. This was the crucial moment. If it was going to happen it had to happen now, this very minute…And it did!

"What's that?" Hank said. He stopped moving around. We were hearing a low moan, and it sounded close. I couldn't see his face in the darkness but I knew he was scared out of his wits.

"It's nothing," Myron said. "You'll hear all kinda noises in a cave, probably bats or something."

"BATS?" Sophie shrieked.

"SShhhhh!" Hank said. "It's getting louder!" He was right. The moaning got more distinct and sounded closer. Then we heard something moving. I grabbed the flashlight out of Hank's hand and pointed it in the direction of the noise. The beam landed several yards away to light up a figure in dark clothing, all hunched over. The sound rose then from a moan to a wail and the figure lifted its arms up and made like it was reaching towards us and coming in our direction. I don't care if I did know what it was, I about peed on myself anyway.

I didn't have to think of what to say or do next, because by that time all three of them had squirted out of that cave fast enough to break the speed of light. It was all I could do not to run out after them, but just in time I heard a friendly and familiar laugh.

"Perfect!" Old Susan said. "Couldn't have been better!"

"It sure worked," I said as I made my way over to her with the flashlight. "God, you about spooked me, too. If I hadn't known it was you I guess I'd about died."

"What happened to your girlfriend?" she asked.

"Well, I *told* her!" I said. "I told her not to panic when she heard something in the cave, that it'd just be you and not to have a cow. But I guess you were too good."

"Well, they can't be going home in the dark like this without a light," she said. "Let's go find 'em. We'll take my car."

We left the cave and walked the distance back to Old Susan's place, which was much shorter than it had seemed coming, and got into her old Volkswagon van. It had lasted forever since she'd never had to drive very much, so it still ran fine even if the rusty old doors were about to fall off the hinges. Not too long after pulling out onto the road we spotted the Terrified Trio, running towards the river bridge.

"Call to 'em," she said. "So they'll know who it is." I rolled down the window and stuck my head out.

"Hey, you!" I yelled. "Thanks for leaving me behind!" We pulled up to them as they slowed down enough to look around. Sophie stopped to catch her breath, but the boys kept going.

"Get in!" I hollered to her, so she did. She was breathing too hard to speak. "Now, don't go and have an asthma attack on us, Sophie. Not now. We're done!"

Old Susan drove forward to catch up with the boys again.

"Y'all scared or something?" I called out. "You want a ride home?" By this time they had to be worn out, but they wouldn't look up or speak to us.

"Aw, come on!" I said. "Get in the car, let us take you home. Hank, your mama'll be calling the police on you if you don't show up soon."

They got into the van and slumped down in their seats, sulking.

"I'd like y'all to meet my friend Old Susan," I said. "I think y'all might know her, even if you haven't ever met officially." Old Susan gave a big whooping laugh as her van lurched forward across that rickety old river bridge towards home, but they just sat there, shivering and silent.

She dropped us off at the school crosswalk, just a couple of blocks from our houses. All the little ghosts and vampires and cowboys and princesses had long gone by now and the streets were quiet. The boys literally jumped out of the van and fled.

"Trick or treat!" Old Susan yelled after them, and laughed again before she turned and gave me a big wink. "And thank you."

"Any time," I said, then I asked her, "Old Susan? What's that word you say whenever you see me?"

"Adawehi?" she said.

"Yeah, that one."

"That's Cherokee, for Angel."

"Oh…okay," I said and got out. Sophie was waiting for me on the corner. She waved and called back to Old Susan.

"Thank you for the ride!"

"Sure thing, darlin'!" Then she was off with a lurch and a puff of exhaust.

"Angel, that was the neatest Halloween I ever had!" Sophie threw her arms around me in a big hug.

"Glad you liked it," I said. Then we ran home as fast as we could, both still holding our pillowcases, not nearly as full as usual.

Chapter Sixteen

I know that there's an autumn spirit, and she lives as much inside me as around me in these hills, and the trees and crisp smoke and appley scent of chilly afternoons. She's like a beautiful woman wearing an outrageous dress of red, orange, and gold. Come November, she leans her head into the wind as her wild skirts are stripped away, leaving her branches bare like bony limbs reaching out for something. Then she wraps herself in a gray mist and settles herself into some kind of deep sleep, just waiting out the cold.

Winter seemed like a long way off in those bright blue days of October and so did Daddy's homecoming, but now the jack o'lanterns are all gone, pilgrim hats are everywhere and it's dark by suppertime. I know the day is getting close. I try not to think too much or I'll go crazy going back and forth between not believing it and wishing the whole thing would just go away. The craziest thing is feeling afraid that he's not going to show up, then in the next breath hoping he doesn't. Crestview here I come!

Here's the honest to God truth of it. There's this wide place in my heart that wants to be filled with something, excitement or hope or even just the plain old jitters. But what I'm feeling in there is mostly just a chilly wind, and sometimes I'm wishing that I could go to sleep like the trees and not wake up until spring.

There's also this whole thing with Ray. I've never been asked on a date before so I don't know what's supposed to happen. He hasn't called back to tell me anything about it and I keep trying to remember. Did he tell me on the phone when it was and what time and all of that, and I was just too flabbergasted to hear him, or is he going to tell me all that at the last minute, or what?

I see him in language arts class every day. He used to leave right after the bell rang, but now I notice that he takes a little longer to get his stuff together and Sophie tells me to hurry up ahead of her, so sometimes we get to the door at the same time.

"Hi," he says.

"Hi," I say back, and then there's this moment when I think for sure he's going to walk down the hall with me, but always, *always* some guy comes up and slaps him on the back, or calls him from behind, or the crowd comes between us and it's over until the next time.

Sophie's been pestering me about it, saying the party's coming up and all and do I know what I'm wearing and am I going to let him kiss me and all kind of nonsense, and my stomach does a little flip with excitement right before it goes heavy with fear and dread.

"You have to be more pushy," says Sophie. "Think of a question to ask him."

"Like what?"

"Like 'Where'd you get that sweater?' or 'What'd you think of that scene in *Macbeth*?'"

"That sounds so fake!" I said. "I'm not good at that."

"All right then, be an old maid," she says.

So then I hope he doesn't call and I never see him again, and *then* I catch myself longing to hear the phone ring just for the tiny thrill of hope that it might be him. It's messed up.

It helps me to think about what's familiar, and I've been looking forward to doing everything we usually do for the holiday. Ever since I can remember, this is how Thanksgiving Day would go. First thing is to get up and go to church. This isn't too bad as the service is usually short, on account of all the women with turkeys in the oven at home, and there's no sermon. Instead, the reverend does a Big Giant Prayer of Thanks, which is, I believe, the longest prayer of the whole year.

He goes on and on with thanking God for everything under the sun that you can think of and all in-between, from our food, clothing, and shelter to family, friends, and extended relatives…to our president and our vice president, the good old USA, the flag, all of our war heroes, our town of Riley, Tennessee, and our mayor and board of aldermen, our public library, the earth below and the sky above…the Church, our deacons, ushers, the secretary and the women's auxiliary… Jesus, his disciples, the Bible, being saved from sin, life ever after, and so on and so on….A-MEN! Now, I'm all for having a grateful heart, but this is just about enough to do you in. At least it's not as long as a sermon. I've noticed that he never says anything about the Pope.

After that, it's just singing and taking up the collection. I like the Thanksgiving Day hymns. They're fun to sing real loud, even if I'm not sure what it means "to hasten and chasten," and everybody's in a good mood because they know it's almost over and there's turkey at home.

Then we go over to Crestview to check out Patsy for the day. Since she hardly ever leaves the place, it takes a while for us to get in there and get her all packed up. She doesn't stay overnight, but she still brings a little day bag with a comb and a brush, her medications with instructions, her toothbrush, slippers, and the latest issue of the *Ladies Home Journal.* That way if she wants to lie down in my room and take a little nap after dinner, I can read to her and make her feel right at home.

Naomi has to sign a bunch of papers saying we'll be responsible for her medicines that day and we won't blame them if she gets hurt while she's gone. After all of this, we begin the long journey down the hall, with Patsy walking instead of being wheeled out because it's better for her than sitting all the time. By the time we get her to the car, drive her home, and get her into the house, Naomi is chomping at the bit to get the dinner going, Mama starts setting up the table, and I take care of Patsy. I'll set her up in front of the TV to watch the Macy's parade and fetch her sparkly juice and chips or whatever else she wants. I love having her at the house.

I assumed the day would go more or less the same as always, even if Daddy was around. We'd work him in as best we could, but nothing much would have to change. This is what I'd been thinking anyway, but I got to wondering about it. Would Daddy be going to church with us? Then would he be going over to Crestview and helping us get Patsy packed up and all? It seemed strange to think of him being a part of this thing that had been just the four of us females all those years. I was a little worried about how she would feel, seeing as how upset she was about him coming home in the first place. I thought I'd better ask Naomi how she thought all this was going to go.

"Patsy won't be coming over for Thanksgiving this year," she said the minute I brought it up.

"*What?*" I felt punched in the stomach. "What do you mean she's not coming over? Daddy's going to be here and it's the first time our whole family's going to be together in forever! We can go get her like we always have, or just Mama and me could go!"

"It's not going to work. She's not coming over at all, and that's it."

"I'll take care of her!" I'm just about crying now. "She won't be any trouble, I promise! I'll do everything, just let her come!"

This just beats anything I've ever heard of. This is the end-all, beat-all of Naomi's not telling me stuff.

"Can you at least tell me *why*?"

"It's not a good idea, Angel. Trust me on this one."

She's scraping her lip with her top teeth, which means she's worked up. I am dumbstruck, but only for a second. Then it comes out.

"Trust you? You! You are the most hateful, most meanest old…. old BIDDY I ever saw in my life, who has never told me the truth about a single thing, and I don't care what you say, Patsy's not going to sit over there in that old stink hole by herself on Thanksgiving! I'll go over there and sit with her by myself if I have to! I'd rather be there than be here watching you fawn all over your good-for-nothing son, who by the way is worthless as a father and just because he's coming home does *not* mean he all of a sudden earns a halo or something!"

Now I'm shaking and scared because in talking to her like that I am standing on new ground and it doesn't feel so solid. I don't know what Naomi's going to do to me, probably send me away to a home for troubled teens or something. I look at her white face and I know I've gotten myself into a hole so deep I may never be able to get out of it, but I don't care.

She's glaring at me like I'm the devil himself and appears to be in some combination of rage, shock, and hurt. That's the worst of it, the hurt on her face. I want to take it back, at least part of it, such as her son being good for nothing, because I don't really know if he is or not. But I can see it's too late, and the part about him being worthless as a father, well that's the rock-solid, gosh-darned truth as far as I can see, and even if I might wish I hadn't said it, I couldn't ever say I didn't mean it. So I keep looking back at her.

All this staring makes for a long silence, but finally Naomi takes a big breath and thrusts her jaw out to say something. I'm ready for the ax to fall, hear that I'm kicked out forever or at least that I'm getting the whipping of my life.

"Ruth!" she calls out, still not taking her eyes off me. "Ruth! Come on down here right now, this instant!"

"Well, can you wait a minute, for crying out loud!" Mama says.

I hear her starting down the stairs.

"What in the world's going on?" she says when she finally gets to the kitchen, putting her hands on her hips. She looks first at me, then my grandmother.

"You need to do something about your daughter," Naomi says, *still* glaring at me. "She's getting to be more like you every day. May the Lord help you both, because you're going to need it come that Judgment Day!"

"Seems like that's just about *every* day around here," Mama says, and I'm thinking that I might have just been saved, if not from eternal damnation at least from what Naomi might have done to me in the here and now.

"All right, then. Get your own supper!" And she stomps up to her room.

"Come on," Mama says. "I'll take you over to Bright's."

If she was trying to distract me from my rage over this, it almost worked. I love Bright's Family Cafeteria. This time I got coconut cream pie (the desserts come first), chicken fried steak, Waldorf salad, a baked potato, macaroni and cheese, sweet tea, and a yeast roll. Mama was behind me in the line and said get something green, so I took the lime Jell-O. She didn't say anything about it, so I knew there was more bad news to come. When we sat down and started eating, I found out what it was. *She* was in on the whole thing too!

"Honey, Naomi knows what's best here. It's all right, really—Thanksgiving will work out just fine. After we have our dinner, you and me can go over and sit with Patsy while she has hers in the dining room. Even if we're not hungry we'll be with her and help her celebrate."

"What I just want to know," I said, "is *why*? What is the big problem? *Why* does it have to be any different than it's always been?" I was raising my voice, and she started looking around like I was making a scene.

"There are some things you don't know," she said, lowering her voice and her eyelids.

"Oh, *really*?" I said, my arms crossed.

"You don't need to get smart with me, Angel. We have our reasons."

"What reasons?"

"Honey, Patsy's not well, and—"

"That's not it and you know it!" I said, looking straight at Mama. "Stop treating me like I'm stupid! Patsy's just as able to come over this year as she was last year and the year before! Nothing's any different, except that *maybe* Daddy's going to be there. This is SO UNFAIR and you won't even tell me WHY!"

"There are some things that have to be between the adults in this family."

"The adults in this family make me sick!" I said, slamming my spoon into the macaroni and cheese. I looked away from her and watched a mom and dad with four pasty-faced kids at the next table. They were all chubby.

"I'll bet *they* don't lie to *their* children," I said, loud enough for them to hear. One of the little girls turned and looked at me. She had red Jell-O on her face and her mother stuck a spoonful of creamed corn in front of her and made her take a bite. Mama just went right on eating and didn't say anything about my sass.

"So what about Daddy?" I went on. "After dinner, are we just going to go off and leave him at home while we go over there?"

"Naomi will stay at the house. It'll give him time with his mama."

"It's a god-awful crummy plan," I said, "and you'd better not be thinking I'm going to settle for it without you telling me what's going on! You can't just go on giving me all these pitiful little pieces of lies like when I was little. I'm grown up now and I know more than you think!"

Mama looked startled. At first I thought I might be in trouble, but she just stared at me hard, like she was trying to figure out what to say, like maybe she really didn't know what to do. The longer she took to speak the more I was convinced I'd finally gotten through to her and she was going to tell me something, or at least ask me what I knew, but it was wishful thinking. She finally sighed and shook her head.

"I'm sorry, honey, but this is just the way it has to be, at least for now."

Short of an all out bawling fit, I had no response, so I kept my mouth shut and my face down. The coconut cream pie was staring up at me, but my appetite had vanished. What a waste! Those kids at the next table would gobble it right up if they had the chance.

It was clear that I needed a new strategy. I sat and watched Mama eat her baked chicken and biscuit. She seemed hungrier than usual, or excited, or something. Whatever it was, it was puzzling. She didn't seem at all concerned by how I'd just gone off on her. Obviously she had other things on her mind.

"Tell you what," she said. "I'm cooking us up an adventure. Interested?"

Was I interested? Is the sky blue? Is there water in the sea? I couldn't remember anything like this coming from her, ever. And now? She knew it put me in a bind, which made me boil.

"What *kind* of adventure?" I said, dying to know, but making sure I had just enough of a sneer in my voice to let her know I was still mad at her. I don't think she noticed.

"Well, we're going to take a little ride." She spread butter on her biscuit and took another bite as she looked at me, but I didn't say anything. Then her eyebrows lifted up.

"Well?" she said. I sniffed.

"Where to?"

"I'm not telling just yet," she said, "but I think you'll like it."

"You talking about right now?"

"No, next Saturday. It'll take most of the day. Want to come?"

Yes, yes, yes!

"I guess," I said.

Chapter Seventeen

That night I lay wide awake in my bed staring up at the ceiling, watching the light move gently as the tree branches outside my window swayed with the wind. Johnny Dupree was playing, "I'm being followed by a moon shadow, moooon shadow, moon shadow…" and Marvel was sitting square on my belly, purring like crazy. I was having some mixed feelings, mostly good because I had made a decision, but some not so good because I had decided to do something I'd never done before. I was going to flat out defy Naomi by getting Patsy over here on Thanksgiving, no matter what she or Mama said.

"I'm sure I can arrange it somehow," I told Marvel. "The getting her here isn't the problem. It's keeping Naomi from being mad and just plain ugly and ruining the whole day, probably by making her go back to Crestview. That's what's worrying me more than anything. She can punish me for going behind her back if she wants to. I don't even care."

Marvel kept purring and seemed to consider what I was saying. Then it all came clear to me. It wouldn't be just Patsy I'd get over here. It would be lots of people, friends and neighbors like Dottie and Doc and Sophie and her parents, Martha and maybe even some of the folks at Crestview like Opal and Grace. Why I'd even invite Jenkins! Naomi would never, ever in a million years make a scene if he was here. They could all bring food so there'd be plenty to eat, and we'd just set it all up on the kitchen table and let everybody go at it with paper plates and all.

Then there was the problem of her hearing about it before-hand. Somebody was sure to tell her that I was cooking up this whole thing…. unless, of course, they were told it was a surprise. That was it! Naomi was turning sixty-five in early December and this could be her surprise birthday party, so no one could mention it to her! That way she'd be the center of attention and she couldn't get mad at me for doing something so special, just for her.

As for Mama, I'd obviously have to leave her out of it for now, seeing as how it didn't look like she was playing on my team. Since she mostly worked, especially lately, I'd just have to chance it that she wasn't going to run into somebody who might tell her. If that happened, hope-fully it'd be too late for her to stop it. This thing could work.

"Thank you, Mr. Marvelous!"

I sat up and cuddled with him for a minute, then hopped out of bed, got out construction paper and markers, and spent half the night working on invitations. By the time I finally went to sleep that night I was feeling mighty fine.

Mama wasn't going to church any more, but Naomi was still making me go.

"I'll not be raising a heathen in my own house!" she said. I had begged Mama to get me out of it, but it did no good. The feud between her and Naomi was bad enough and she wasn't going to make it worse.

I'd been complaining about this in recent weeks but I didn't say a word about it that next Sunday, because I knew it was the chance to get one of my invitations to the reverend. Sure enough, all I had to do was make sure I was well behind Naomi as we were moving out the door and pull it out of my coat pocket while I was shaking his hand.

"Don't let anybody see this," I said. "It's a surprise." He glanced at it quickly but obliged me by slipping it straight into his pocket and giving me a wink.

"Sure thing," he whispered, making me feel almost friendly towards him for the first time ever. Naomi didn't catch a thing because she was out on the front walk having a private conversation with Dottie. She was leaning in towards her and talking with her head low like it was something she didn't want me or anybody else to hear.

As for the invitations, there were still lots of deliveries to make. I couldn't do Crestview until I was over there by myself, but later that afternoon I tucked a few in my jacket pocket and headed out. I told Mama I was going over to Sophie's to practice Shakespeare, which was true, but only after I'd taken a walk around to drop several off.

When I got over to her house, it took a long time for anybody to answer the door, and when she finally did I saw she'd been crying.

"What's the matter?" I asked.

"Mama's in the hospital and Daddy's gone over there to be with her."

"So how come you're not over there too?"

"Be*cause*," she said, "I am tired and I have homework and I don't *want* to go sit over there all day! He's going to come back and get me later."

She let me in and we went into the kitchen to grab a snack, then headed up to her room like we always do. I wondered if her mom was dying while we were up there eating Little Debbies and drinking Coke, sprawled out on the floor like a couple of cats. Sophie must've been reading my mind.

"If my mom was real bad Daddy would make me go over there sooner, and my grandmother and my aunts would come from New York, and everything would get even more weird than it already is ... I guess."

"Do you feel like practicing for the bee?" I said.

"I couldn't care less," she said. "I hate Shakespeare."

"Yeah, I know." I swallowed hard. Smith's Steakhouse was slipping away, I could feel it.

"Here," I said. "I've got something to give you." Sophie looked at the invitation and laughed.

"Angel, I swear something's come over you. It used to be me that always had some big plan. Now what are you doing all this for? A *party*? For your *grandmother*?"

"Well, there are some reasons...." And I told her the whole story about Patsy and all.

"Let me make sure I've got this straight," she said. "You're going to get Patsy home for Thanksgiving and make it so that Naomi can't make a big fuss, even though she's already told you no."

"That's the idea."

"What d'you suppose old Naomi's got against that poor old girl?" Sophie said, now getting out her box of stuff and setting up to paint her toes. "You reckon she doesn't like her just because she's not her real daughter?" She picked out a bottle and started shaking it.

"It's more than that. All of this is just a bunch of dumb excuses to cover up whatever it is they aren't telling me about Daddy. They must

think I'm really stupid to expect me to fall for all of it. I'm sick of it."
I looked over the colors myself and considered Cherry Splash for my
fingernails, but then I remembered that I'd been thinking about going
for more of a hippie look and decided to braid my hair instead.

"So what are you going to do if she gets ugly about Patsy being
there and starts to make a scene in front of all these people? I've
seen your grandmother mad and it's not nice to be around when it
happens."

"She won't," I said, trying to convince myself, "especially not if
Jenkins is there. She's always trying to impress him, like she wants his
attention real bad, but he never pays her any more mind than he does
all the other church ladies that fall all over him."

"Wouldn't that be hilarious if Naomi and old Jenkins were *dating*?" Sophie said as she went about her toe job, moving slowly and
neatly from one to the next.

"Hilarious?" I said. "I think *weird* would be a better word. Anyway,
I've never even heard of a preacher dating."

"Angel..." she said, changing the subject without even looking
up, "are you still going to be my best friend after your daddy comes
home?"

"What does that have to do with us being friends?" I'll swear I
never know what Sophie's going to come up with next. "Got a rubber
band?" I was down to the end of my braid and needed to tie it.

"Don't use rubber bands, they'll tear up your hair!" She fished
around in her box and tossed me a blue pony tail holder.

"So what do you mean will I still be your best friend? I'll still be
me and you're *you*."

"Yeah, but..."

"But what?"

"You're kind of my inspiration for having only one parent. I
mean, you've not had a daddy all these years and you're okay, you're
smart and normal. I figure if you're okay, then maybe I could be okay

too. But now you're going to have a mother and a father, and before long I won't. You'll probably be real busy now that you'll be a whole family…and I won't."

"Sophie, what in the world makes you think a dad would replace a best girlfriend? It doesn't make any sense!"

"Maybe…but there's something else."

"What?"

"Well, before I heard about your daddy coming back, I'd sort of been thinking…"

I waited. And waited.

"Thinking what?"

"That maybe your mom and my dad … I mean, just *maybe*—oh, wouldn't that be the neatest? We could be sisters!"

Poor Sophie! It made me realize how much she kept quiet about her the real stuff of her life. She made it easy for me not to think about it, but that didn't mean it wasn't on her mind all the time. I tried to smile.

"Sophie, my mom and your dad don't have to get together for us to be like sisters. We already are! Besides, if we had to share a bathroom and hot curlers, we might fight more than we already do."

She laughed, kind of, and I was relieved.

"Things will work out okay," I said. "And who knows, maybe your mom will get better. She told me herself that she's never given up on a miracle. Why, maybe there's a miracle happening right now this very minute!"

"Oh, I don't know," she said. She sniffed and wiped her nose on the back of her hand. "But I sure do like this color polish."

"What is it?"

"Autumn… Flush." She said it slow, as if tasting the words.

"Do you like my braid?" I asked. I was pleased with the way it was falling down my left shoulder, making me look like a folk singer. She glanced up and gave it a quick shrug.

"Yeah, it's okay." Sophie's not big on compliments.

"Hey!" I said. "You never showed me that book you were talking about. You know, the one your parents have about....about *doing* it?"

Sophie perked right up.

"Oh, yeah!" she said. "Come on with me."

I followed her back into a hallway at the top of the back steps that was lined with a bookshelf. She knew right where the book was but had to stretch on her tiptoes to reach it. As she pulled it out she lost her grip and it fell down smack at my feet. *Everything You Always Wanted to Know about Sex But Were Afraid to Ask*. Sophie dove for it and opened it up to show me a full-page illustration. I gasped. Right there in front of me was the most outrageous picture I had ever seen in my life! It was a pencil drawing of a man and a woman—buck naked, with the hair sketched in between their legs and everything, and his...well, and she was...I felt like I ought to close it right away but instead I grabbed it from her and sat right down on the floor and started looking through it.

"Can you believe it?" Sophie said. Page after page of these drawings, these two people with funny smiles on their faces doing all sorts of things that I'd never imagined anybody could do or would ever want to. It was the awfulest thing, honestly, but the more I looked the more I got this sort of warm feeling that started between my legs and rose up, making me feel sort of melty.

"Oh, God, there's one in here you've got to see." She took the book away from me and flipped the pages looking for it. Then we heard the front door open. "Quick!" She sprang up and slid the book back into its place. "Back to my room!"

"Is that you, Sophie?"

"Yeah, Dad. Me and Angel are up here."

We went to the top of the stairs just like two little girls who'd been in their room playing with Barbie, as sweet as pie. Then we scrambled down and Sophie fell into her daddy's hug. He kissed the top of her head and looked back up at me with the eyes of a sad, tired man.

"Hello, Angel," he said.

"Hey, Mr. Steiner. Is Miss Genevieve better?"

"She's sleeping," he said. "She's a little more comfortable now."

"I came to see if y'all can come over Thanksgiving," I said.

"Oh, my goodness! Why, thank you, Angel, but we'll have to see, you know. Is that all right?"

"That's fine," I said. "But it's a surprise party—for Naomi's birthday, so don't tell anybody but me."

"Sure thing," he said and smiled, even if he did look worn out.

"Who else are you asking?" Sophie said as she walked me out.

"Oh, neighbors, friends, whoever I think might want to come."

"You asking Hank and them?"

"Well, yeah, I thought I would, them living on the same street and all," I said. "Why? You don't like *him*, do you?"

"Why not? Don't you think he's cute?"

"Not after what he did to me in the ravine!" I said.

"Oh, he's not *that* bad," she said. "Besides, he'll grow up." She laughed. "Hey! You oughta ask Ray!"

"Now why in the world would Ray want to come to my grandmother's birthday party?"

"Because he likes you and if I'm there and Hank and Myron too, then he'll know some people and have a good time. You don't want this to be just an old person's party, do you? Come on—this is your chance!"

"Well, if he likes me so much why doesn't he call and tell me about this party we're supposedly going to? He hasn't called back once since he asked me and I don't ever talk to him at school."

"Boys are such idiots," Sophie said. "They don't have any idea what girls expect or think about. Why don't you stick a note in his locker telling him about the Thanksgiving Day thing, then he'll be reminded to call you about the other."

I thought it was a dumb idea. I'd wait and see what happened.

Something did happen! I was in Greer's a couple of days later and was in the back, sitting on the floor reading an article in *Seventeen* magazine about Caroline Kennedy's sixteenth birthday, when out of the corner of my eye I saw somebody coming up close. I looked up and there he was, standing there looking at me and drinking something out of a straw.

"Hey, Angel! What are you doing?"

I shut the magazine and jumped to my feet, finding myself closer to Ray than I'd ever been. He was about half a head taller than me, which had me looking straight at his mouth at first. I saw that he had very nice, white, straight teeth before I got the nerve to look up into his eyes. They were the color of a spring sky.

"Aw, nothing. Just sitting here reading."

"Well, what are you reading?"

"Um, just some dumb old magazine."

I jammed it back on the rack but then I didn't know what to do or say. My heart was pounding in my chest and it was hard to get a good breath and no matter how hard I tried my eyes just wouldn't go back to his. He reached in front of me to grab the magazine and scanned the front cover.

"Umuhh, let's see. Caroline Kennedy's sweet sixteen...Very interesting reading, Angel. I didn't know you were such an intellectual!" I tried to snatch it back, but he jerked it away. I went for it again but this time he stepped back and bumped into the display of all the Trojans and personal lubricants and stuff and knocked a whole bunch of them off. The old lady behind the prescription counter looked up from what she was doing.

"Y'all don't be carrying on like that in here! Go on, now git!"

I was horrified. I'd seen her for years while I sat back here and read the magazines, felt like I knew her even though I really didn't, and here I was being scolded by her like a little kid. She probably thought we were shopping for rubbers! I was so embarrassed my face was on fire and I honestly felt like dying right then and there.

"Come on, let's go!" Ray said.

There was nothing to do but follow him straight up the toothpaste and shampoo aisle, right past the soda fountain where the guy in the white hat was dishing up an ice cream cone for a little boy, and out the front door. Ray turned and grabbed my arm as if to hurry me along the sidewalk and didn't let go. All of a sudden I was having fun.

"Did you *see* her? *Go on, now git!*" he said, trying to imitate her voice. "Gaw, what an old hag!" He was laughing.

"*Don't be carryin' on,*" I said, sounding a lot like her, which set us both giggling like naughty little kids. I'm sure people thought we were looney tunes. And while I'm giggling, I'm trying hard not to show the thrill I'm feeling with him touching my arm, even through my car coat. The embarrassment in the drug store had been worth it.

When we got a ways up the street he took his hand off and we slowed down.

"I was gonna offer to buy you a shake," he said, "that is, before we got kicked out of there."

"That's okay," I said. "It's kind of cold for a milkshake, but they do have the very best anywhere. My mama used to always get me one whenever I had to get a shot at the doctor's."

"Yeah, I hated shots too. I guess every kid does. Well here, have some of mine. It's chocolate." He held out the cup to me while we walked along.

"That's my favorite."

I took a sip through the straw and handed the shake back, feeling nervous that we were through with this subject. We needed another one quick. The only sound between us was the crunching of leaves on the sidewalk and our breathing into the chilly fall air as we walked, headed in the direction of my house. I was shivering slightly and thinking it might be a real good time for him to say something about the party.

"So where'd you get your red hair?" he said instead.

"It's orange," I said. "A stop sign's red and so is a tomato, but my hair is orange."

He surprised me, first by laughing a real laugh, like he thought I'd said something genuinely funny. Then he looked at my hair, and it was a real look, like he was paying serious attention to it.

"I guess you're right. So, where'd you get your *orange* hair?"

I shrugged. "Same place you got your blonde, I guess. My mom has it, and my dad...well, his is sort of lighter, I think."

"What do you mean, you think? You don't know what color hair your daddy has?"

"Well, I can't look at it because he's not around. I haven't seen him in a long time."

"Oh," Ray said. "I haven't seen mine, either."

"Where's he?" I asked.

"He lives in New York. He works there." We were close enough together on the sidewalk that sometimes our arms brushed as we walked. This made it really hard to concentrate on the conversation.

"How come?"

"That's where his job is."

"I mean, how come you don't live with him in New York?" I asked.

"Because my parents are divorced and my mother wants to be here near my grandparents, but I go up there every summer. It's pretty cool."

"Neat! You're lucky to get to go there."

"Yeah. So when was the last time you saw your dad?"

"When I was a baby," I said, wondering if he thought this conversation was at all interesting.

"Wow, that's a long time."

"Yeah. He's supposed to come home, though, next week in fact."

"You're kidding me! You haven't seen your father in practically your whole life and you're gonna see him next week!" he said, turning his head towards me like he considered this a serious topic. It made me feel like maybe he would want to come over, like Sophie'd suggested.

"Yeah," I said. "And I'm planning something for Thanksgiving Day, kind of a celebration of his coming home and my grandmother's birthday... and I was going to ask you if you wanted to come, but it's a surprise and you can't tell anybody or else she might find out. There'll be some other people there from school, I hope, like Sophie and Hank and Myron."

"Well, sure," he said. "If it's okay if I can come over later, like after we have our dinner with all my cousins and stuff."

"Yeah, that'd be good." There was another pause in the talking, more crunching of leaves, frosty breath. I saw my chance to ask.

"So have you been studying much for the Shakespeare Bee?"

"Yeah, some," he said. "I have band practice every afternoon after school, so Maureen's been coming over to my house on Saturday sometimes."

I felt my heart race and my face flush.

"So how's it going?" I said.

"Well, I'm nervous that I'll lose it for both of us. She's really smart."

"She *is*?"

I didn't mean it to sound like it did, but I was surprised. Who would have thought she was smart? Most of the brainy kids liked to show it off, or they got treated special by the teachers, like the kid in first grade who got to go to the library every day while the rest of us were learning to read because he'd been reading since he was four years old. But all this time and I'd never heard a single peep about Maureen being smart in school.

"Yeah, she reads tons of books and remembers everything. I think she has one of those photographic memories."

"Wow." I was pretty much speechless.

"Okay," he said. "I've got one for you, but it's really hard. I need to test out my competition. You ready?"

"Go ahead," I said.

"Here it is… *Out, damned spot!*"

"Oh…*you!*" I said and whacked him on the shoulder. "Gee, that's a hard one all right!" We both laughed and I saw that we'd gotten all the way to my house. "Well, this is where I live. I'd better get on inside, it's nearly dark and they'll be wondering about me."

I wished I lived further away.

"Okay, but I almost forgot. You know that party you said you'd go to with me?"

"Oh, that's right. I remember," I said, grabbing my hair and giving it a flip back over my shoulder. Then I saw a Marvel hair on my sweater and calmly picked it off.

"Well, it's on Saturday. Can you still go?"

He looked kind of worried. I was so excited I had to work hard to keep my voice normal.

"I guess so," I said. I was cool as could be, Miss *Cool* Cucumber. Sophie would have been impressed.

"All right, then." I saw his shoulders relax. "I'll call you on Friday night and tell you what time we'll be picking you up and all that."

"Okay," I said, barely getting the word out before he leaned over and gave me the quickest little kiss on the cheek. I about fell over.

"And here, you can have the rest of this," he said, handing me his cup. I had to catch my breath to speak.

"Oh. Thanks… Bye!"

I ran to the house, stopping to turn and wave back before I went in. The whole world was perfect right then, absolutely everything about it. The milkshake had melted down to a liquid, so cool and silky smooth against my warm and quivery insides. I drank it down every drop, all the way to the very last slurp. It was the sweetest, softest, most deliciously rich thing I had ever tasted in my whole life.

Chapter Eighteen

"He KISSED you? Angel, you haven't even been on a date with him yet! Oh my God! Bet he ends up giving you a pre-engagement ring!"

It was a moment that had been a long time coming. After all these years of being Sophie's plain and boring sidekick, I finally got to be the one with something to tell *her*. This was historic.

"What was it like? Was it long and wet?" The truth was that no, it was actually very quick and dry, but I wasn't about to miss this opportunity to play it up.

"It was just so…so *nice*," I said slowly. "He's very sweet, so gentle." I could feel her being jealous for about one second, even over the phone, but good old Sophie wasn't going to let that get in the way.

"I'll bet y'all end up getting married!"

"But we haven't even—"

"Angel Collins…Angel *Collins*…Sounds nice!"

"Keep it up and you'll be picking out names for our grandchildren!"

"I like Destiny and Jeremiah."

"Sophie, I have to tell you... there's more."

"What?"

"I asked him about Maureen. They have been studying together—at his *house!*"

"Oh, no!" She paused long enough consider the weight of this news. "Well, don't worry, Angel. She's certainly not pretty, and she's just so...so *unpleasant.*"

"Well, maybe, but he says she's really, really smart... like a genius. I bet they win it. Ray is kind of Mr. Sam's favorite in the class anyway."

"Well, like I said, Angel, don't you fret. He isn't asking her out on dates or giving her his milkshakes. Maybe she's a vegetarian and doesn't even want to go to Smith's, and then he'll ask you to go in her place."

"Oh yeah—sure!"

"But never mind all that. Tell me all the good stuff again, every single bit of it!"

So I told her again, the whole thing, for her sake making it more than it really was. But for me the simple story was enough, it was just right, and I wanted to remember it just like it happened. That's why I'd snipped off the end of the milkshake straw and added it to my medicine bag, a symbol of my first romance.

My visits with Patsy had been mostly quiet, ever since her big outburst, that is. I'd been keeping it that way as best I could, not a mention of Daddy, or Thanksgiving or anything that might set her set off again. That afternoon we were playing cards. She likes Go Fish, which I'd been playing with her ever since I could remember, but lately she'd been acting like she didn't even know the rules. So we were both sitting there holding our cards with the deck sitting there in front of us. It was my turn.

"Got any sevens?" I ask her.

"Go fish!" she says, even though I know she has two sevens because she won't hold her cards up and I can see them. She just likes to say it.

"Aunt Patsy, you've got two sevens and you have to give them to me because it's my turn and I asked for them." I pull her hand down to show her the cards.

"Go FISH!" she says again and pulls her cards back towards her chest.

"Well all right," I say, and I go fishing just to keep her quiet. I surely didn't want to get her all agitated right then.

"Give me all of your fish!" she said, real loud.

"Aunt Patsy, I don't have any fish. Nobody in this game has any *fish*."

"Then what are you fishin' for?" she asked.

"You're just trying to draw matches to the cards you got. Remember?"

"That's STUPID!!" she said. "I HATE this game and I don't want to play anymore! What are all these things anyway, these little pieces of paper with all these numbers and pictures and stuff? I DON'T WANT THIS!" Then she threw all the cards down on the table, scraped the whole batch to the floor with her arm and turned away from me to stare out over the parking lot.

"Well, what do you want to do, then?" I asked her as I went down on my hands and knees to collect the cards. I knew it was best just to stay calm and act like I hadn't even noticed the tantrum. She'd forget it in a second anyway.

"My daddy will take me fishing," she said, not quite so loud but still breathing hard from her upset.

I went back and forth on whether or not to try and make her talk sense, as if that could somehow slow down what was happening to her. I decided to let it go, seeing that her mind was already off somewhere else anyway. She was looking out the window and humming to herself when Rita came into the room with her afternoon pills.

"Why, there's that Angel!" she said real loud, like she always does. "What are y'all doin' this afternoon?"

"We were playing cards," I said, "but she got mad at me for trying to make her follow the rules." Rita let out one of those roof-raising laughs of hers.

"Honey, you should know by now that any rules Miss Patsy follows are hers and hers alone. Don't be wasting your time trying to tell her what the rest of the world does. She's done gone and made her own world." Rita walked over to her. "Here you go," she said, and handed Patsy a pill and a little white cup of water. Then she lowered her voice and said to me, almost in a whisper, "Course it don't help none, all this medication they've added on to her."

"They're giving her *more*? Why'd they do that?"

"She'd been acting out, saying all kind of crazy things and going into fits, especially after y'all come. I heard 'em saying they was going to have to talk to your grandmother about it, and next thing I know she's got all this shit they want me to give her every day, got her so gorked out most of the time she don't care who's been here or not."

I let this sink in a minute. Patsy was still over by the window humming, and I could tell it was that old folk tune "Barbara Allen."

"Hey Rita," I asked, "you need an extra hand down the hall? Can I help you do something?" She turned and gave me the look I needed.

"Why sure, baby. You just get Patsy settled in here and come on down."

I gave Patsy her magazine. "I'll be back in just a few minutes," I said.

"All right, honey." She started flipping through the pages, so I scooted out and in no time found myself back in the green vinyl chair, waiting for Rita to have a second to come talk to me. The nurse's station was just a tiny room, hardly more than a closet. It smelled awful, like ammonia or something, but at the same time didn't seem very clean. Soon I heard a door close down the hall and here she came.

"Okay, Angel, what is it?"

"Well, it's like this—Aunt Patsy always comes home for Thanksgiving Day…"

"Is that right?"

"Yes—*always!* She's never missed it, ever! And now Naomi's telling me that this year she can't come."

"Why, I never!" Rita said. "Is she saying why?" She was fussing with all her little white cups and not really looking up at me.

"Naomi never says why. She just *says*, period. But I'm sure it has something to do with my daddy supposed to be coming."

"Oh, right," she said. "Maybe Patsy don't need to be spending much time with your daddy." She gave me one of her great eyebrow lifts.

"Well, I don't care. If he's going to be here for Thanksgiving I want her to come home like she always does and for us to have the whole family together for once!"

"Why do I get the feeling I'm about to be a part of this?"

"I need your help," I said.

"So, girl, what is it you asking *me* to do? It's not like I can make your grandmother change her mind."

"Help her get home for the day," I said. "I don't know how you'd do it, but according to Patsy you're an expert at sneaking people out of here."

Rita shook her head and laughed, then stopped what she was doing to turn and look at me.

"You want this?" she said. "You want this so bad as all that?"

"Yes, I want it! It's about all I've ever thought about my entire life, having a whole, real family, even if it's just for one crummy day, I *want* it!"

"What about how anything to do with your daddy sets Miss Patsy off something terrible?"

"I need you to help me with that, too. Convince her somehow that it'll be okay. You're always so good at calming her down, you can talk her into going along with it. I just know that once we get her there it'll be fine"

"Hmmmm. Guess it's worth a try, especially since you ain't going to have it any other way, looks like."

"So do you have any ideas about getting her there?"

"Well, let me think," she said. "I don't have a car right now because my cousin's got it and he's been dropping me off at work. I couldn't take her anywhere."

"What if I found somebody else to come get her? Could you get her all packed up and checked out and stuff and help them get her out? Can you somehow get her past the front desk?"

"Well, are you thinking somebody's just going to bring Patsy over there against your grandmother's wishes? What's going to happen when she sees her standing at the door? What's she going to say?"

"Here's something that might help." I reached into my coat pocket and pulled out three envelopes. "One for you and the others for Opal and Grace," I said. "But please save them until Naomi's already left on Sunday. I'm afraid they won't be able to keep the secret." Rita opened the envelope and looked at her invitation. Then she looked up at me with a smile and a nod.

"I reckon I'll think of something," she said, then glanced around the room as if looking for ideas. Her eyes landed on the tray of pills. "Sure would help if she wasn't so drugged up all the time."

"What if....what if she skipped it, just for a couple of days. Would that help?"

"This is next week you talking about, right?"

"Yes, one week from tomorrow!" I knew it well.

Rita looked at me and grinned the biggest, widest grin I'd seen yet. "Lemme just see what I can do," she said.

I guess I've been studying too much Shakespeare because the first thing that popped into my head was that line from *Macbeth*, from the part where he felt like his plan might be getting a little out of hand.

I am in blood stepped in so far/ Returning would be as tedious as going o'er... Like me, Macbeth knew there was no turning back, but I wasn't planning a murder, just a little surprise.

When I went back down to Patsy's room I found her asleep in her chair. This was just fine, because I'd been wanting to look at that stack of letters I saw the other week and hadn't gotten the chance. This was it.

I tiptoed over to the chest of drawers, opened the bottom one as quietly as I could and slipped them out. They all had the same handwriting on the outside of the envelopes, so I just randomly picked one and opened it up.

> *Dear Patsy, I hope you're feeling alright these days and that the food is good over there. It's been hot this summer but we've had some rain. I've had some fine tomatoes. Will write again soon. Your friend, Awia.*

My mouth about dropped open to the floor. Awia was real! I sat for a minute just to let this sink in. Here we'd heard about her all this time, always figuring she was nothing but Patsy's imagination. Who *was* she? What all else had she jabbered about over the years that nobody believed? Rita was coming back down the hall. I didn't want her to think I was snooping, so I put the letter back in its envelope and stuck them all back in the drawer real quick.

"How's our Patsy doing?" she said as she came through the door. I looked up at her, wondering what all she could tell me.

"Asleep," I said. She gave me a knowing look.

"Don't worry hon, it's all gonna work out!" she said, and was almost out the door before she turned back. "Oh, and I have to tell you about Miss Ida…"

Her door was standing wide open and there was a strong antiseptic smell coming all the way out into the hall. I stepped inside, just for a second. Sure enough, the bed was empty, stripped of its sheets and pushed over against the wall. The floor had been mopped and the furniture had all been dusted and polished. I looked around, struck by the feeling of nothingness in that room where Miss Ida had so recently been sucking at those tanks, begging to die.

Grace was pushing her cleaning cart down the hall and stopped just outside the door.

"She went peaceful," she said.

"I'm glad."

Grace smiled at me, and with a sigh went on. Rita was coming the other way. She paused at the door long enough to give me a kind look, like she understood everything.

"Your granny's outside," she said.

"Coming," I said, glancing around, but just before I turned to leave my eye caught something on the floor almost under the radiator. Lo and behold, yes it was—the acorn, swept aside by some careless broom. I picked it up and put it back in my pocket for some reason. I don't know why, any more than I know why I pressed it into Miss Ida's hand in the first place, not so very long ago.

So we're in the girls' bathroom right after language arts and before lunch as usual, and I'm trying to use every spare second to quiz Sophie on Shakespeare. She's cranky and impatient with the whole thing, but I don't care if she pitches a screaming fit before it's over; there's less than a week left and we're going for it. I'm thinking we still have a chance.

"Okay Sophie, try this one—*O Serpent heart, hid with a flowering face! Did ever dragon keep so fair a cave?*' She let out a big sigh while working on her face at the mirror.

"Hint?"

"Okay. It's a girl talking." A toilet flushes and it's so loud she waits a second to answer, but I can tell she thinks she's got it.

"I know! It's Lady Macbeth after she finds out he's murdered the king!" Just then Maureen walks out of one of the stalls.

"WRONG!" she says. "It's Juliet in Act III, Scene 2, when she finds out Romeo has killed Tybalt.

"O serpent heart, hid with a flowering face! Did ever dragon keep so fair a cave? Beautiful tyrant! fiend angelical! Dove-feather'd raven! wolvish-ravening lamb!"

I was flabbergasted. I'd hardly ever heard her say anything, barely a word, much less string so many of them together at once.

"Oh...Hi, Maureen," I said. She waited a second while she looked at me, as if wondering if she'd really heard me say it.

"Hi," she finally said, and looked down like there was something important on the floor. I'd never seen her that close up before. Her hair was oily and her face was shiny, the pores showing with little black specks in them. She didn't smell so fresh.

"So how's it going?" I asked. I could see in the mirror Sophie's eyes cutting sideways to me, like *what are you doing?*

"Okay, I guess."

I wanted to say something else to her, something that was real. I had some kind of new feeling about her, now knowing what I knew. After all, here was a person who'd actually been inside Ray's house,

sat on his furniture and breathed his air, maybe even had a snack or
something.

"You're good at Shakespeare," I said.

"Oh, gee... *thanks.*" She sort of smirked when she said it and shot
me a smile that was obviously meant to be fake. It hurt my feelings.
I didn't see why she had to be sarcastic. She moved past and started
to go out the door when I heard Sophie suck in a breath like she was
going to say something.

"Hey, Maureen?"

"What?" she said in a flat voice. She turned and gave Sophie a look
that made me wonder if she was going to spit on her or something.

"Are you by any chance a vegetarian?"

"Hell, no!" she said and walked out. I was genuinely mortified.

Chapter Nineteen

I got the call from Ray. It was Friday night, just like he'd said, and we had just sat down to supper. I wasn't hungry, even though the tuna noodle casserole was usually one of my favorites. Tonight it just wasn't tasting good to me and I was picking around at it when the phone rang.

"Catch that, will you, hon?" Mama said, so I got up and went into the hall to pick it up.

"Hello?"

"Could I speak to Angel, please?" said a voice I'd been hearing in my head a lot lately. My heart started doing its cartwheels in my chest and taking away my breath so I could barely talk. I hate that.

"This is...um...Angel," I said. It was times like this I can never remember, are you supposed to say this is *she*, or this is *me*, or this is *her*? I hoped I hadn't messed up already, so early in the relationship, that is if it was a relationship, which it might not be, because he might not really like me. This is what all I was thinking.

"This is Ray." He sounded sort of hoarse.

"Oh, hi," I said, sounding calm and collected, except for just a little bitty shake in my voice.

"I'm real sorry, but I can't go to the party this weekend. I've got the flu."

Now I know it for sure, he really doesn't like me. After seeing me the other day, he realizes I'm completely weird and not legitimate girlfriend material. He can't believe he kissed me. What a mistake! For days he's been trying to come up with a decent excuse to get out of the party, so he's using the oldest trick in the book—getting sick. *Can't you do any better than that, Ray?* I wondered how he had made his voice sound hoarse to make it more convincing.

Well, my heart had stopped its flipping and sunk down into my stomach like a rock, lying right down there with the few bites of casserole I'd unfortunately just eaten. Not that I was surprised about this. It figured. This was everything I had expected. The thought of me having a real date, of being asked out by a boy and actually *going* somewhere with one was not something that was ever going to happen in this life, on this planet. I tried to take a breath so I could say something, but I was feeling a little dizzy.

"Are you there?" he asked.

"Oh...yeah," I said. "Yeah, I'm here. Gosh, sorry you're sick. I hope you get better soon." I wondered who it was that was making those words come out of my mouth.

"Well, I wish we could go to the party."

"That's okay," I said. I was lying. It wasn't okay.

"Well... Bye, then," he said.

"Yeah, see you. Bye." We hung up. So that was it. I walked back into the kitchen.

"Was that Ray?" Mama asked, trying to sound real casual. I sat down hard in my chair at the table and put my head down. I felt awful, even more awful than I thought I would feel when I predicted something like this was going to happen.

"Who's this Ray?" Naomi said.

"He asked her to a party," said Mama. "He's a real nice boy." I knew she didn't know Ray from Adam's house cat, she was just heading off Naomi's protests.

"She ain't got no business going out with no boy!" Then she got up to clear the table, making a lot of noise banging the plates around and splashing them in the sink.

"He can't go," I said. "He's sick." Then I started crying, which was a stupid thing to do. I almost never used to cry, and here I was blubbering all over myself again.

Mama looked over at me. "Oh, honey…don't worry about it! It'll work out next time, you'll see."

I sat up straight and dried my eyes. Honestly, I could've used a hug, or at least a shred of girlfriend-like sympathy or something, but her attention had shifted to cleaning up. Naomi wouldn't let it go.

"They ain't going to be any next time before she's seventeen, not in my book!" she said. I groaned and my head went down again.

"Why don't you go on to bed?" Mama said, then came over and spoke so low Naomi wouldn't hear. "Remember, we've got plans for tomorrow. Still interested?"

I nodded, even though I really wasn't so sure, but I thought the going to bed part was an especially good idea. So I did.

The first thing I knew the next morning was Mama shaking me awake.

"Angel" she said. "Wake up. I need your help."

"What is it?"

"I need you to go into Naomi's room and look for something. I'll make sure she stays downstairs so you can get in and out of there without her knowing." This was so completely unlike anything Mama had ever asked me to do and it was hard to grasp, especially having just woken up.

"Please?" she said. I sat up. It was starting to sink in, even though I had a dull, thudding headache.

"I can't go in there and go through her things! That's so… creepy!"

"I know, I know…but I'm telling you it's okay this time. It's very necessary."

"What're you looking for that's such a big deal?"

"It's a gold key on a little chain that says 'Granny's House' on it."

"Granny's house?" I asked. "Your granny?"

"Yeah, you've heard me talk about her little house up in Virginia. You and I are going up there today. I haven't been there in years and years and I'm looking for something."

I didn't know much about Mama's growing up, but I'd heard a lot about Granny Belle.

"So what's over there?" I said.

"Her loom. I want that loom and it's got to be there. Nowhere else it could be, unless they sold it when she died. But something tells me it's there. Nothing to do about it anyway except go look."

"So why are we looking for the key in Naomi's room?"

"Because it's not where I always kept it," she said. "And I've got a hunch that somewhere along the line it ended up in all her stuff. If she's got it, shouldn't be too hard to put your hands on it. It'd be in her top drawer or her bedside table, most likely."

"I don't see how in the world you're going to keep her downstairs while I'm breaking and entering, seeing as you're barely speaking to her. Why don't you just ask her if she's seen it?"

"Because I don't want her to know what I'm doing, that's why.

She'll be asking me all these questions and wanting to tell me this and that, and I don't want to mess with any of that. So are you in, or not?"

Of course she knew what I'd say.

"Yeah, I'm in," I said, though in for what, I wasn't so sure.

Sneaking around Naomi's room was the strangest thing ever. Mama had somehow convinced her to make a batch of bread. That meant she had to mix the batter, then knead the dough for a good ten minutes. I knew there was no chance of her coming upstairs as long as she had flour up to her elbows.

I was almost afraid of what I would find. Here are some things I hoped I would not see: granny panties, dirty magazines, love letters. Some things I *would* like to find: any pictures, clues to my past, answers to the mysteries of my life.

I spent a good bit of the time going through the top drawer of her bureau. It smelled funny. There was an old yellowed sachet that had probably been in there fifty years at least, a dried up crumbling corsage that looked like it used to be a rose, some loose papers and letters and stuff, old tubes of Ben-Gay and Linocaine, an old library card, a small jar full of coins, paper clips and bobby pins all dusted over with powdered rouge from a broken compact that was in there too and various bottles of pills. There was a letter that had my childish handwriting on the outside and I opened it up.

Der Santa, it said in my giant first-grade letters. *Plese brng me a chaty cathy.*

Another one from when I was at camp one summer said, *Dear Mama and Naomi, How are you. I am fine. There's a girl here who cries in her bunk every night and another girl wets her pants. Don't worry, I am not vomiting anymore. When do I get to come home? Love, your Angel*

Then something else caught my eye. Ah! It was an old photo-graph, faded and torn, but I could see that it was a picture of a young girl about my age in a beautiful white dress, sitting with her arm around a little girl there beside her. Why, the older girl was Naomi! I could see it in her face! I couldn't tell about the other one. She'd never talked about her childhood at all, so I didn't have any idea who it might be, but I considered this a great find. Why hadn't I ever thought to snoop in here before? I hurried on, making a mental note to come back in here some time when it wasn't so risky and look some more.

No key in the drawer. I closed it and went quickly over to the bedside table. This felt especially weird, but seeing as I was on a mis-sion for Mama, I kept right on it. All I found there were her reading glasses, safety pins, a nail clipper, several religious tracts, a menu from Joe Gong's Chinese take-out, her small Bible (as opposed to her big leather one), and a jar of Pond's cold cream.

I knew I didn't have much more time, so I had to think quick. Where might there be a key that she never used? I thought to look down in the basket she keeps by her rocker. That's where she sits and does her Bible study in the mornings. Maybe it was dropped in there way back and she doesn't even know it. I started rummaging through and sure enough came across an envelope that had something in it. I looked inside. There was the key, enclosed with a single piece of sta-tionary that just said, "Thank you!"

Now who in the world would have been using the key to Granny Belle's house? But there was no time to dither, so I just stuck the enve-lope back between all the notebooks and stuff where I'd found it and left. As I slipped out of the room I met Mama coming up the stairs and handed the key to her. She let out the tiniest little squeak of excite-ment and bolted to her room without giving me a chance to tell her about the note. I went on downstairs to make sure Naomi was still in the kitchen, which she was.

"Ain't hardly gonna rise in this weather," she muttered.

We left later on in the afternoon, after washing up the lunch dishes. Since Mama and Naomi were supposed to still be mad at each other, I could tell Naomi was caught off guard by Mama's change in mood and was having a hard time keeping up the standoff all by herself, especially with the bread smelling so good in the oven. She wasn't giving it up entirely, though, on account of her loyalty to Jenkins. She had sworn she wouldn't forgive Mama until she officially apologized to him for her insulting behavior.

This was okay, though, because it made it all the easier for us to head off without her for the afternoon. We said we were going to the mall, and Mama took a big risk in asking her to go along, but not too big because Naomi doesn't like the mall and generally sticks around home. Still, the whole thing could have been ruined if she'd decided to join us. The mall part wasn't a lie, either, because we did go there. We went and got us each a Karmel Korn and a cup of hot chocolate before hopping back in the green Mercury and heading north into the hills of Virginia, up to the home of my long dead great-grandmother.

I liked being on a road trip with Mama again. It'd been a long time. We used to drive over to Memphis occasionally to visit her family there, just her and me. We'd leave after supper and drive halfway, stopping at a motel somewhere between Knoxville and Nashville, sleep in the next morning and get there by afternoon the next day. Mama said she liked the night part, the quiet on the dark road and not having to think much, it being a straight shot from one end of the state to another. I liked the day part, sitting beside Mama all that long way watching the sky get bigger and the land flatten out as we went west, leaving the closeness of the hills behind us. I liked seeing how it opens up and breathes over there, the sun touching everything, the shadows of home forgotten for the time being.

I learned all kinds of things about Mama on those road trips, the long hours being good for talking. She and her sister Reyna grew up right here in Riley, but their daddy died when she was eighteen. Mama hadn't ever gotten along too well with her mother, even worse after she got mixed up with Cal, mainly because he was so much older, I'm told. So when they got married, my grandmother just up and moved to Memphis to live with Aunt Reyna and Uncle Bain and is still there to this day.

It's my mother's Granny Belle that I heard about the most. She lived out in the country in the very house where she grew up. Mama loved to go over there and spend time with her when she was a little girl. There was a swing hanging from a tree out back beside the big garden and a chicken house. Mama loved to get the fresh eggs for breakfast and her granny showed her how to put up beans and berries and other stuff from the garden. But that was back before she got so old they had to move her into a nursing home where she died way later. I wondered how it was that we had a place like that and it had just been sitting there all this time.

"Do you remember how to get there?" I asked.

"It's easy," she said. "Route 43 about forty miles to Lynch Cove, go right for about three miles then left at Mt. Gilead Pentecostal Church until you come to a little wooden house on the right. There's a well in the front yard."

The higher up in the mountains we went, the more the colorful trees had gone bare, the blazing yellow, red, and orange now gray and silver. I felt happy, being on a secret mission with Mama, sipping that sweet chocolate and watching the countryside roll by.

"Mama, if Daddy's really coming home, why haven't we heard something from him? Seems we would have if it's for real." I knew she heard me but it took her a few seconds to answer back.

"I honestly don't know what to expect," she said. "Or what to think. I'm just trying to wait and see how things are going to be."

"What about Dennis?"

"What about him?" She glanced over at me.

"Have you been seeing him?"

"Naomi doesn't need to know that," she said.

"So what are you going to do if Daddy does come? And if he stays?" So when did I get the nerve to ask her questions like this? Something about being in the car, looking straight ahead and not at each other made me bold. She answered me straight.

"I don't know anything right now, Angel. Don't know what it means if your daddy comes home, or if he's even coming home in the first place, or if he's staying if he does. It's a confounded situation is what it is, and it's something I need to handle my own way, without your grandmother and the rest of them waving the Bible in my face over it. I'm sorry for you, honey. I know it's worst for you, but there's nothing to do right now but ride it out."

So I guess that's what we were doing, riding it out and up into the hills on a cold, gray November day, not knowing what was coming next or what we'd do about it either.

We turned left at the church and bumped along for the longest time, it seemed, past dozens of mobile homes perched on grassy plots coming right up to the rocky banks along the road. It all looked so drab now, but many a spring Sunday as a child when we'd go riding out in the country, I'd seen such hillsides go crazy with the pink and purple phlox and the Easter bunnies and plastic eggs that dotted the yards.

At long last Mama pointed.

"See that post? That marks it, the beginning of Granny's land— our land. Won't be too much longer to the house, but it might be hard to spot if it's all grown over."

We'd gotten a late start, and the drive had taken much longer than we'd thought. It was already getting dark.

"Days are getting shorter," Mama said. There were no streetlights, no other cars, just me and Mama bumping along in the old car. My excitement had worn off. I was beginning to feel sort of shaky and hoping this wouldn't take too long. After a while she pulled off into a driveway and her headlights shone onto a fine little house, not the least bit overgrown like she had said.

"Why, look at this!" she said. "Everything's all cleared out...and look at those two rockers on the porch. Those aren't ours. Look at the flowers in front!" She was looking at the yellow chrysanthemums blooming on each side of the steps. It had been a dry fall, and I knew they wouldn't look like that if they hadn't been watered. "Somebody's living here," she said in a hushed voice.

"Um, I forgot to tell you... Naomi must've lent the key to somebody," I said. "I found it with a note."

Mama took in a quick breath and turned to face me.

"What did it say? Do you know who it was from?"

"No, it just said, 'Thank you,' but it wasn't signed."

"She had no right! Well, I've got a thing or two to discuss with her!"

I shivered. "So what're we going to do now?"

"Well, nobody's here, it's too dark. Let's leave the headlights on and go look inside."

I didn't say it, but it was the last thing I wanted to do. I wasn't feeling too good. My legs felt like lead weights as I got out of the car and walked up onto the porch. My whole body was starting to ache. We looked in the windows. It was too dark to see anything, so Mama got out her key and opened the door just enough to peek in.

"What do you see?" I asked.

"Can't tell much. I can see a table with a lamp on it. You keep watch out here and I'll go turn it on.

As soon as she flipped the switch the little cabin room glowed with a cozy light. There were two nice armchairs and a small coffee table with books and magazines. It sure didn't look like an old granny house to me.

"Why, look here," Mama said as I stepped in. We walked through and into the next room and flipped on the wall light. It was a small kitchen, clean and cute with blue gingham curtains in the windows and matching dish towels hanging beside the sink. "This is nice," she said, "...considering it was just about empty the last time I was here. Who on God's earth has done this?"

I followed her into another room, a small bedroom. Looked like something out of one of those catalogs full of nice cabin furniture. A queen size bed took up almost the whole space, with a headboard made out of tree limbs. Then there was this little bitty bathroom.

"Well!" Mama said. "Looks like somebody knew we weren't using this house and didn't expect us around anytime soon."

"Wonder where they are tonight?"

"I don't know, but let's go see if we can find what I'm looking for." I followed her back through the little living room and up a tight little staircase with a door at the top. She shoved it open and we peeked in. It was pitch black up there and we didn't have a flashlight, but we crawled up in there anyway and tried to look around a little bit while our eyes adjusted. We could make out boxes and various pieces of furniture, but without more light it was useless to be looking for anything in particular.

"We have to come back in the daytime," she said, "or at least with a flashlight. How'd we get such a late start? I'm just *itching* to figure out what's going on here and get to the bottom of this with Naomi!" We made our way back down the skinny steps, switched off all the lights in the house, and stepped outside into a deep darkness.

"Uh oh," Mama said.

"Didn't you leave the headlights on when we went in?" I asked.

"Yep."

"But we weren't in there that long!"

"I guess long enough," she said. "Dammit! Sam was supposed to put a new battery in this thing last time he worked on it. Now what are we going to do?"

"Maybe it'll start," I said.

We got in and she tried to crank it. Nothing. Dead as a doorknob. We sat there a minute while I felt like my whole body was sinking down a hole.

"As long as we're stuck here," I said, "…can we go in and fix us some tea or something? I'm not feeling so great."

"What's wrong?" Mama asked.

"Just tired and achy is all."

"Well, I don't see why not. It's my house." So we went back inside and turned on every light we could find. I opened the pantry cupboard and found all the fixings. Mama filled up a shiny black kettle and put it on the heat. We found some bright blue pottery mugs and when the water got hot we fixed our tea and made ourselves at home in the big easy chairs by the fireplace.

"Not bad," Mama said. "But whoever's been pulling this off owes me a lot more than a cup of tea."

"We've got to figure out how we're going to get home tonight." The tea had revived me a little bit.

"We're going to walk down that road out to 43 and get a ride back, that's what we're going to do," she said.

"Oh, *no!*" I said. "Couldn't we just stay here? There's a bed and everything…. I'm really beat."

"Well, it *is* awful dark," Mama said. "But tell you what. It's not that late. Let's just get on out to the road and see if we can't wave somebody down in the next half-hour or so. Then we'll see."

"I guess," I said, wishing I could just lie down anywhere and go to sleep.

"If we don't go back tonight, Naomi's going to be calling the police anyway," Mama said, then she let out a little laugh. "Too bad whoever it is didn't put in a phone up here."

"Well *then* what would we tell her?"

"Why, I'd tell her we were stuck up at Granny's house with a dead car battery, that's what I would tell her."

"Somebody around here's gotta have a phone," I said.

"We'll figure out something." Mama took the last sip of her tea. Then we washed out our mugs and put everything back just exactly like we found it. I thought of Goldilocks, how she left her trail of destruction and was caught sleeping. But not us. We were caught like deer in the headlights when we stepped outside on the porch and a car pulled in.

"Somebody's home," I said.

Mama didn't waste a second walking around to see who was in that car. He probably would have backed right out of there and left had she not walked up to the window and knocked. I had to move away from the glare of the high beams before I could tell who it was that climbed out. Then someone got out of the passenger side. The four of us looked at each other like we were waiting for somebody to tell us what was next. Mama was the first to speak.

"Reverend Jenkins!"

"Miss Ruth…"

"And L.B.!" Mama looked back and forth between the two of them, like she was putting it all together. "Well, I must say I'm surprised! I came up here hoping to find my granny's loom, but look what I found instead!"

I never thought I could feel sorry for the reverend, but honestly, I did right then.

"Miss Ruth, I know this isn't exactly right, but your mother-in-law has given me permission to store some of my things here and…"

"Looks to me like you're doing a little more than storing things here, Jenkins. You, or somebody, has gone and set up housekeeping in there! What d'you know about this, L.B.?"

"Aw, now Miss Ruth...." His head shook back and forth, but his hands stayed in his pockets.

Jenkins rescued the poor guy. "I take full responsibility for this."

"So's that your mother's stuff in there?" Mama said, putting her hands on her hips. "Doesn't look like any old lady's furniture if you ask me."

It was getting really cold. I was standing on the porch, shivering and watching and listening to all of this, feeling like I might fall down any minute.

The reverend crossed his arms like he was cold, and when he spoke it wasn't like the man in the pulpit on Sunday but like a regular person trying to give his side of the story.

"I sold my mother's stuff, then L.B. needed a place to stay. Miss Naomi was so generous with letting me use the house, and she said y'all didn't have any use for it, and one thing led to another. I honestly didn't think there was any harm in—"

"So she gave you a key."

"Yes ma'am, she did."

"I see." Mama's arms were crossed over her chest. "Did she know you were using the place like this? I doubt it."

I wondered what was she getting at, then thought of the one bed in there. *Surely not!* There was an awful pause. LB kicked some gravel with the top of his shoe and Jenkins cleared his throat. It was so dark I couldn't see much of anybody's face, but I could hear the uneasy breathing into the chilly night.

"Are you afraid of being judged for what you are, for who you are?" Mama asked. Another pause. "I can understand that. I've had that experience, rather recently, too, I might add. You may remember coming around to my house to warn me about sin and Satan and such, all while you were carrying on with this little charade."

"Oh, dear Lord...." the reverend moaned, then he dropped his head.

"Don't worry. It would have mattered before, but it doesn't now."

"I'd be forever grateful to you, Miss Ruth, if—"

"But this is my place and you're going to have to take your stuff and get out of it, both of you, or I'm going to have to call the police."

"Don't worry, we'll be gone....and I'll make it up to you, Miss Ruth," he said, "I promise. But please, have mercy on us and don't repeat this. What can I do to persuade you to keep this to yourself?"

"You can start by apologizing for telling me how I've sinned," she said. "Seems to me that's the pot calling the kettle black. Then you can write me a check for the rent it looks like you owe me."

"How about you just keep all the furniture," L.B. chimed in, sounding jittery. "It's nice stuff, the best."

"Maybe I'll think about it," she said. "But please go in and get your personal belongings out of there. Oh, and Reverend—do you happen to have any jumper cables?"

"You bet I do, Miss Ruth. Anything you need, anything at all."

Chapter Twenty

You could tell Naomi was all agitated about us being gone so long, but she didn't say much.

"I don't know where you'uns have been," she said, "but y'all ain't got no business prowling around after dark."

"Battery died," was all Mama said.

If only she knew, was what I was thinking.

"Your supper's on the stove," Naomi said, and went on in the living room to watch her show, *Marcus Welby, M.D.* "By the way..." she called from the other room. "In case you're interested, Calvin called. Said he'd be here on Wednesday."

"Well, what else did he say? How long is he staying?" Mama walked in there to get more information. I sat down at the kitchen table and realized I could barely sit up. I heard Naomi being ornery.

"Didn't say nothing else," she said. "He don't have to say nothing but that he's coming home far as I'm concerned. And you being his wife and having waited for him all these years shouldn't be a-wonderin' when he's leavin' again!"

Mama ignored her and walked back into the kitchen.

"And Angel," Naomi added, "Sophie says for you to call her right away, it's urgent."

"You are NOT going to believe this," she said when I got her on the phone. "You just are NOT!"

"Well, what is it?" I was thinking this had better be good because I felt too awful to talk for the sake of talking.

"It's about Maureen. She's left school!"

"What do you mean, she's left school. You can't just *leave* school."

"You can if they take you out!"

"Who's they? Sophie, *what* are you talking about?"

"Okay, this is what I heard. Some people from the county came to her house yesterday and took her to some foster home up in Virginia."

"Why? Why would they ever do that? They can't just come take you away! I never heard of that happening to anybody!"

"Well, apparently something really horrible was happening to her at her house, something *really* awful."

"So do you know what it was?" I could hear her breathing real loud on the line.

"You can't tell anyone."

"Well, somebody told *you!*"

"Yeah, that's because this lady from Social Services comes to see me every couple of weeks to see how I'm doing, you know, what with my mom's cancer and stuff. Do you remember when I told you I went to see Ray's mother in the guidance office to tell her about my problems?"

"Uh huh."

"Well, after that they sent this lady and now I'm supposed to talk about my feelings and everything like that, and I heard her talking to my mother when I was in the kitchen and they thought I had gone to my room, so I'm not supposed to know any of this but I'm telling you because you're my best friend, but you can't tell anybody else!"

"Okay, so *tell* me!" I said.

"Well, all I know is she was saying something about *abuse.*"

"What kind of abuse? Did they hit her or something?"

"I'm not sure, but if they were hitting her wouldn't she have bruises?"

"You'd think," I said, "but maybe she does, where nobody can see them."

"She's got all those brothers," Sophie said. "Kinda gives me the creeps to think about it."

I knew Sophie was talking about something else then, something besides hitting, and it just about took all the breath right out of me. I'd heard of this terrible thing. There was talk going around school about whatever happened to Gloria James, this real big girl with bad teeth that talked about her daddy all the time. She didn't come back to school this year and I heard some people say it was because she was having her father's baby. I didn't believe it. I didn't even see how that could be possible and I figured they'll say anything, whoever it is that starts that kind of rumor, and besides, it's not even a thing you can bear to think about, much less believe.

"How would they know?" I asked, barely able to suck in air enough to talk.

"I think Ray's mother knows something because Maureen's been going over to their house, like you said, you know? I wonder if she got her talking, or maybe she could just tell it, her being a counselor and all."

"Maybe they lock her up in her room and don't give her enough to eat, like they did to the lady in that book *Rebecca*," I said, thinking if it had to be abuse then anything would be better than that other. It made me think of what Hank and Myron did to me that day except times a thousand. I wanted to push it out of my mind because it was the worst thing I could ever imagine and it made me feel sick and I *was* sick, felt like my head was going to come all to pieces right then and there.

"I have to go," I said.

"Okay. I just knew you'd want to know. Call me tomorrow!"

I could barely get myself back to the kitchen. It had been quite a day, and I had learned way too much for my own good.

"Well, what in the world!" Mama said after taking just one look at me. But I didn't have to say a thing because she came over and put her hand to my forehead.

"Good gracious, Angel, you are hot as a firecracker."

I don't remember much about those next days. There was a long, fitful sleep, full of tossing and aching and shivering and sweating. There was Doc Ames, standing over me and poking around, somebody walking me to the bathroom and back, Mama trying to get water down me, fluffing pillows, straightening the covers, the door opening and closing, whispering—the lights going on and off, the day coming and going, then coming and going again. I felt trapped in my weakness and not for all of my trying could I break free and join the world that was humming all around me.

Then there I was again, looking down at myself curled up dead, fighting to get back into my body and wake up, fighting to breathe into my own lungs and move my limbs, to get up and run away from all the lies and confusion, the disappointment and heartache. I saw others too, their faces coming and going in front of me like ghosts. There was Patsy, trying hard to tell me something but I couldn't understand her. The words were all garbled and made no sense. And Naomi—she was crying. Her eyes spilling over like a faucet, so full of tears she couldn't even see anything. I tried to reach my hand out to her but it wouldn't move and she went away, then Mama's face came to me but she was looking off somewhere and I called out to her, but she didn't answer. *Mama, why can't you hear me? Why won't you answer me? Why can't you see me, Mama? Why? WHY?* Then the hole opened up and I was in a whirling black storm, like a tornado, with the wind going wild all around me and I felt myself falling, falling again, falling so fast into the awful blackness, it was more than I could stand. Suddenly there was Ida, crying for the Angel of Death to come take her away—begging *me*. Was *I* the Angel of Death? I sat up in my bed.

"NO!"

And there was Dottie, sitting there with a bowl of something steaming hot.

"What? What *is* it child? You were dreaming!"

"Where…am I?" I couldn't get my breath. My mind felt full of cobwebs. It was night.

"Bless your heart! Calm down now, you're right here in your room. Come on, you've got to sit up and eat and drink something or my Martin's going to make you go up to the hospital so they can put it in you. Wake on up now and eat a little."

"What happened to me?" I asked. Whatever she had there smelled good and I realized I was really hungry.

"Something got a hold of you," she said. "Some kind of flu. Lots of people have had it, but you got it bad."

I thought about Ray and wanted to laugh, but my body felt frail like a bird and almost anything was too much. I looked around a little.

"What day is it?"

"It's Tuesday. You've been like this for days."

I tried to think. I couldn't remember anything clearly after coming home with Mama on Saturday night. Dottie helped me sit up and propped me on a pillow.

"Here's some chicken corn soup." She offered me a spoonful.

It tasted wonderful, those sweet crunchy kernels in the salty broth. I could feel my head begin to clear. The pain was less now, not so much pounding as an ache. I took a few more sips.

"If it's Tuesday," I said, "then Thanksgiving is the day after tomorrow?"

"That'd be right," she said.

Then it hit me, the whole thing coming back to me at once. It was like I'd had amnesia or something and got the whack on the head that suddenly brought me out of it, but it was a blow in more ways than one. Sunday had been the day I was going to go see Old Susan and get her help in getting Patsy home for Thanksgiving! Now Daddy was supposedly coming tomorrow and I was sick and no way was I going to get back over to Crestview. On top of that, a whole bunch of people were going to show up over here the day after tomorrow and from the looks of things I'd be lucky to be out of bed by then, forget trying to get ready for this thing in secret. Then I remembered something else.

"Oh, no—the Shakespeare Bee! I've missed it!"

"The *what?*" Dottie said.

"The Shakespeare Bee! It was today and I slept through the whole thing! Oh…I can't believe this!" I put my head back down into my pillow and cried.

"Well, honey, I don't know what that is, but whatever it was, you have an excused absence." She patted my shoulder. "Shhhh, shhhh now, don't get overheated. My Marvin will write you a big old note that says how sick you've been, so don't you worry about it one bit." She put her hand on my forehead and held it there a second. "Now, what did you say it was that you missed today?"

"The Shakespeare BEE!" I said, annoyed with her for not under-standing, for not knowing what it was or how important it had been to me. Seemed like everything that had been such a big part of me the last few months, all the excitement and hope I'd had about things, about

Daddy, Ray, Thanksgiving with Patsy, and now this, had all fallen apart right here, right now, sucked down that big black hole of nothingness.

"That must be what Sophie's been calling you about every day. We had to tell her you were sick and couldn't come to the phone."

I'd suddenly had enough soup and turned my head away thinking what a mess I'd made of things and feeling too weak to know what to do. I knew I needed to speak to Sophie, but I couldn't do it just yet.

"Keep eating," she said, "or you're going to end up with a needle in your arm for your Thanksgiving dinner."

"Don't want any more," I said, trying to keep the quiver out of my voice. I rolled over facing the window now, with my back to her.

Here's what I was thinking. It was a prayer, and though I had no idea whether or not he'd be listening, I was saying it in my mind anyway.

Dear God, I know that most of the time I don't live up to my name and you must be so exasperated with me for all the planning, scheming, and defying I've been doing lately and I might as well be talking to a tree stump as to expect that you'd want to help me out here....but I am wanting something real bad and if it wouldn't be too much trouble, even if I know I don't deserve the favor, I sure would like a miracle right now. Not a big one, like bread falling from the sky or the parting of the sea or anything, just a little one, just this chance for me to know what it feels like to have a real family around.

"All right then, honey," Dottie said, "but I'll leave it right here in case you can take a few bites a little later. Can I do anything for you now?" She leaned over to help me put my pillows back down and switch off the light. It was late afternoon, a cold twilight, and as I settled myself back down I remembered something. I gave it just a few seconds' thought before I answered her.

"Yes ma'am, you can."

"Well, what is it, honey?" She sat herself back in the chair. I turned around in the bed to face her, even though I was lying down.

"How's your arthritis?" I asked. At first she looked taken aback, as if I was being too forward in asking. It's not something a child would normally ask an adult, so I gave her another hint. "Have you been over to Old Susan lately?"

Then she caught my drift, and we talked. I told her the situation about Patsy, the party, the half-laid plans, the whole pickle.

"Well now, don't you fret one more minute about it," she said, leaning over to put her hand on my forehead. "Just get some more rest and I'll call you later. Will that be all right?"

So I nodded and went back to sleep, finally a real sleep, thinking at least there might be a chance. If there was anybody that could save the day, it'd be Dottie.

Chapter Twenty-One

The first thing I noticed waking up the next morning was the stiff November wind, sure to send the last leaves swirling. It seemed fitting, like everything was flying around me, all the hope—and fear, dread, and uncertainty, all the ghosts of my life coming alive for *this* day, the day I was finally supposed to see my daddy again.

I stayed in bed a long time before venturing out, not at all sure what to do with myself. As for my sickness, I could tell I was a lot better, but I wasn't too eager to let the others know it yet. Something told me that being a little under the weather might come in handy before it was all over.

So here's how the next few hours went. After getting out of bed by myself for the first time in days, I took a shower and washed my hair, then put on my old green Camp Windy Pines sweatshirt and jeans, which hadn't been hanging quite so loose on me when I last wore them Saturday. The one thing I had to do before anything else was telephone Sophie, even though I dreaded it.

"I've been calling your house every day!" she said. "They kept saying you were sick. What's the matter with you?"

"Some flu," I said. "I've been in bed about a hundred years."

"Hey," she said. "Did you go to the band party?"

"Oh," I said, not so happy to be reminded about that. "No."

"*What!* What happened?"

"Ray called the day before. He said *he* was sick." I heard her gasp. She was speechless, for about a half-second, that is. I felt like I should do some more explaining but was afraid I might start to cry. Then she laughed out loud.

"Angel! You caught the flu from him! I know it's true because he was out of school too. It must've been the kiss! He kissed you and gave you his germs. Awww, that's soooo sweet!"

I hadn't thought of it that way. Even if he hadn't kissed me on the mouth, there was the milkshake.

"Did you ask him over tomorrow?" she said.

"Yeah, but I'll bet he doesn't come."

"I'll bet he *du-uz*," she said in her sing-songy voice. I was tired of the topic.

"So what happened with the Shakespeare Bee?" I asked, anxious to know even though it hurt so much that I'd missed it.

"Well… we did *not* win," she said, her tone very matter of fact. I let out a big breath.

"Who's *we*?" I asked.

"Me and Ray."

"Thought you said he was out of school."

"He got back just in time. Maureen's gone and you were sick, so that left both of us without a partner. It was the logical thing." She was right, of course, but it took a couple of seconds for me to decide it was *okay*.

"We did pretty good, though. You each had to answer one question per round, without consulting your partner! But your team didn't get kicked out unless both people missed their question. We made it to round four, when Ray and I both missed ours."

"You didn't get to talk to each other about the correct answer? That's awful!"

"Yeah, it was hard, and I was so nervous, Angel…but I actually got the first two right."

"Oh! What were they?"

"*But, soft! what light through yellow window breaks?* I got that one!"

"That's *yonder* window."

"Oh, yeah. Then I got the one about a plague on both houses, or something like that."

"So which one got you out?"

"Well, Ray missed *that which hath made them drunk made me bold.* It was Lady Macbeth and he said it was Macbeth, then I missed *What's done cannot be undone* on the same turn."

"Sophie! You knew that! What did you say it was?"

"I said it was Friar Laurence. OOPS!" I had to laugh.

"All right. So tell me—who won?"

"Kathy Bledsoe and Tammy Tilson, of *course*… those goody two-shoes!"

"Of course!" I said. Kathy would win my life if there was ever a contest for that.

"Thank God it's over is all I can say."

I agreed, and with that my disappointment began to fade, right along with my dream of that happy Smith's steak, baked potato, salad with blue cheese…. I felt a little hungry, so after hanging up I made my way slowly down to the kitchen on wobbly legs.

There was Naomi, rolling out a pie crust. She had her back to me and was singing, "*So build me a boat, that will carry two… and both shall row, my love and I…*"

So there was that song—and that was the voice I remembered singing to me when I was little! It had been so long ago, and why, I wondered, had she never sung it since? She was humming the melody and I let her go on a minute before making myself known. There was something sweet about her standing there, so happy and oblivious to everything else but what I knew was going on in her head. She would see her boy today, and in this moment she was so full of love and joy that she was literally busting with song. When she started singing the other verse I joined in on the last line and we were singing together.

> *"But not as deep, as the love I'm in ...*
> *And on that boat, I'll sink or swim."*

Surprised, she made a sudden half-turn in my direction, her bifocals resting at the end of her nose.

"Angel! Look at you—up with the chickens!" she said when the song was over. I laughed because she used to say that to me a lot and it'd been a long time since I'd heard it. "Why, you've got such a pretty voice. I don't know as I ever heard you sing. Imagine that!"

Imagine that. "Now don't go getting all excited and thinking you're over this thing! You need to save your strength."

"I feel some better," I said.

"You say that now, but you just wait. Something like you just had ain't to be hurried."

"I feel like I could eat something."

"Well, that's a good sign. Tell you what. I'll fix you some eggs and grits if you'll promise to go back to bed right after." I said I would, and after I ate a little I did go back up, but I knocked on Mama's door before going into my room.

I found her sitting on the edge of her bed, dressed in her favorite ankle-length brown corduroy skirt and a big rusty-colored sweater. She was looking out the window but turned her head and looked at me with a blank expression.

"You're up?" she said.

I sat down beside her and let her feel my forehead and my hands. Then she held her palm to my cheek and looked into my eyes.

"No fever!"

"Where're you going?" I asked.

"Just out for awhile,"

"Mama don't..."

"Don't what?" she said.

"Don't leave me here by myself with this, Mama. Okay?"

"What, you think I'm not coming back?" I couldn't read her face.

"I don't know what to think," I said. "Just don't make me wonder?"

"I'm just going for a couple of little errands." She laughed. "Angel, this is going to be okay. You know you're going to be okay, don't you?" I nodded and tried to smile.

"I need to go lie down again," I said, and got up to go.

"You do that and I'll see you later. Y'hear?" It made me feel uneasy, her saying it like that. A few minutes later, I heard her leave.

So what was it like for me, this last day of waiting for my dream to come true? I knew for sure that it *was* the last day, because if he came, of course, then I'd have gotten my wish, and if he didn't come, then I knew it would be over for me anyway, I would never wait again. Whatever happened, it was a red letter day.

I was curious about the plan, but there was nothing I could do about it until the afternoon. Dottie had said she would call, but it was too risky for me to call her. If Naomi caught me she'd know for sure something was up. So what exactly was I going to do with myself, I wondered.

First, I picked up *Wuthering Heights* and read for awhile, dozing off and on. This wasn't the first time, so I knew exactly what was going to happen, but I still wished things would turn out different. How could it have gone so wrong? I got to the part where Cathy went away to the rich person's house party and Heathcliff was so upset, but he didn't know the half of it at that point. It sounded like Wuthering Heights outside, the wind and now the rain pounding the roof. I kept looking at the clock. Only one o'clock! Johnny Dupree didn't come on until three. I got up to open the window and saw that the car wasn't there. Mama was still gone. The air felt heavy.

I tried to catch up on some of the homework I'd missed, just to get my mind off things. That didn't go so well, so next I dumped out my underwear drawer and matched up all the socks. There was another cellophane wrapper of thin mints in there! I ate some of those and it perked me right up. Then I remembered that forever I'd been meaning to pull everything out from under my bed and get it all cleaned out. I found lots of stuff there. Among other things there was my missing gym shoe, my baton from last year, which I don't think I'd touched since that awful tryout, a box of Girl Scout badges that were never sewn onto the sash, miscellaneous hair ties, bobby pins, pencils, and some more unmatched socks. All the while I kept an ear out for Mama's car, hoping she'd come before...well, just hoping she'd come, period. Now that was a twist, on this day of all days, wondering what *she* was up to. I just know I'll have wrinkles way before my time.

So there I was just thinking it sure seemed quiet for a day that was going to change my life forever. Then I heard somebody at the front door and Naomi talking.

"She ain't been well, honey. I don't know if you oughta be over here."

"Please, Miss Naomi? Please? I need to speak to her!" It was Sophie.

"Well, I reckon. But keep it quick."

She was up the stairs in about two seconds and busted in my room all out of breath. Her eyes were red and her face was all mottled, signs of a big crying jag.

"What's going on?" I said, a little alarmed. "You're not upset about the Bee...are you?"

"No, this is *not* about the Bee or boys or anything like that. Angel, I'm scared."

"Of what?" I asked, almost scared to hear it myself.

"My daddy just told me this morning, Aunt Ginny and her daughter Lois are coming down from New York!"

"So, your aunt's coming for a visit," I said, trying to sound calm, but I was afraid to think of what it might mean.

"They *never* just come for a visit," she said. "We always have to go up there. So you know why they're coming. Because they or my daddy or all of them think Mama's gonna die soon."

Then she fell on my bed and buried her face in my pillow and cried like I've never seen a person cry. Her whole body was shaking and my mattress was jiggling. I didn't know what to say. This thing was way past trying to get her to think about something else, or talking about it like it wasn't really as bad as it was. All I could think to do was to lie down on the bed beside her and hold her while she cried it out, maybe help keep her from flying all apart while she cut loose. So that's what I did.

We stayed like that a long time. Her sobbing gradually slowed down, but she kept her face mostly down in the pillow and took a big quivering breath every now and then. I was lying on my side right next to her and had my arm draped across her back, giving her a rub or a pat every once in a while as she wound down. Finally she turned a wet, hot, swollen face towards me.

"If you're going to have an asthma attack," I said, trying to lighten her up a little, "it'd be much better if you waited for Mama to get back."

"I outgrew that," she said, "but how about a nervous break-up?

"That'd be nervous break*down*, Sophie." She sniffled.

"Get me a Kleenex?"

"Whatever you want," I said, reaching over to the nightstand and whipping one out.

"Oh, Angel! What am I going to do? Who's going to take me to buy clothes? It would be so weird with my dad, I couldn't stand it." She had just finished wiping her face up but then she started blinking, like she was about to cry again.

"My mom will take you, don't worry."

"You and your mother aren't exactly the experts on style, Angel."

This hurt me, even if it was true. Once again Sophie beats all I ever saw. And here I'd let her get tears and snot all over my pillow! Leave it to her to take such a tragic moment to point out my imperfections. Mama's, too! It made me feel sad and scared and mixed up, and longing for Mama. I wanted to have a good cry of my own, but I changed the subject instead.

"You all coming tomorrow?" I asked.

"I don't know," she said. "Who knows anything anymore? How'd you get Dottie Ames in on this anyway?"

"She called you?" I was glad to hear that things were happening after all.

"Yeah, at least three times, just to make sure we got it all straight. If we come, we're bringing a pumpkin pie. Hey, isn't this the day your dad's supposed to come?"

"Supposed to," I said. "He's not here yet."

"Are you going to ask him if he's a secret agent?"

"Yeah, right."

Then the front door opened. I held my breath and waited for a minute, just to make sure. It was Mama. I had meant to be nonchalant when she came in, like I'd never worried about where she was or been afraid what she might be thinking, but when she came in I ran to her and about squeezed her to death. I don't think I'd ever been so glad to see her. She looked at me and shook her head.

"I guess we're in this together, whatever it is," she said, then looked over and saw Sophie. "I thought you might be here. I was just at your house, checking on your mom and dad. They said you'd gone looking for Angel."

So was that where'd she'd been? Not all this time, surely, but somehow it made me feel better to know she'd been close by. Sophie sat up and wiped her eyes some more. Mama walked over to my bed and put an arm around her.

"This is hard," she said. "No two ways about it, this is real hard for anybody. But I want you to know, we're going to be right here for you, you hear?" Sophie nodded and looked down. I decided it didn't matter what she had said about the clothes.

"I mean it," Mama said. "You are not alone." Another sniffle.

"When will it happen, Miss Ruth?"

"I wish I could tell you, honey, but these things don't go by anybody's time but their own. We just have to take every day as it comes."

"Thanks for letting me be here," she said.

"You come any time, day or night," Mama said. Sophie let her head fall on her shoulder as she stroked her hair, just like she was a little baby, just like I'd have loved her to do for me sometimes.

It was way later. Sophie had gone on home and I was listening to Johnny Dupree. He played the Carpenters' "Top of the World" and I wanted to feel like them, then I wanted to cry with Marvin Gay and Diana Ross doing "You're a Special Part of Me."

"Neeext up... we'll have Jermaine Jackson... singing... 'Daddy's Home,'" Johnny said.

I turned it off. Mama was helping Naomi in the kitchen. I could hear them down there, fussing around and talking about dinner the next day. A good while went by. Even if things had been rough between them, they could come together when it came to feeding people. It's a woman thing, I reckon. But it was good that they had something to do together, because really what they were doing was holding vigil, sort of like people do when they're waiting on somebody to die but they don't know exactly when it's going to happen. Supper was already late. The evening was stretching into night and there was a lot of wondering going on.

I was back into *Wuthering Heights*, all the way to the part where Cathy's dead and Heathcliff is wandering the moors hollering for her…. Then I heard it, a car pulling up—an unfamiliar car. I was almost too scared to look out, but of course curiosity got the best of me and I went to the window.

Yes! There he was! He walked with his hands in his pockets and his head down, braced against the wind and the cold. He reached a hand to smooth his hair, then zipped his short leather jacket up the rest of the way as he came down the walk. I heard the doorbell ring. Something told me to hold off a minute before I went down. I heard voices, exclamations, nervous laughter, talking. It was enough.

I put on a clean shirt, went into the bathroom and looked into the mirror. Who was this person he was going to look at and see as his daughter? What would he think? I brushed my hair, splashed some cold water onto my face and tried to pinch a little color into my cheeks. Then I stared some more, finally deciding that even if she was rather ordinary, this person was okay for what she had to do next. That was when he called up the stairs for me.

"Hey, Angel! Come on down here and see your daddy!"

Chapter Twenty-Two

So there I was, face to face with my father for the first time in my memory, and I had no words. For somebody who's been told to keep her mouth shut for most of her life this shouldn't have surprised me, but the moment wasn't what I always imagined. All of the hope and wanting that had been filling my heart for so long seemed to be coming up and making a big lump in my throat. My main concern was being able to swallow.

I finally got the nerve to look up at him. Sure enough there he was, Calvin Stone Bishop, without a doubt the man from the picture I had stared at a million times over the years. He was smaller than I'd imagined, especially in the loose-fitting tan work pants and the big, plaid wool shirt he was wearing. His hair was a mixture of strawberry and gray and thinned out, his eyes gray-green. He looked older, of course, but that was the face all right, the reddish cheeks, the fine features, the sharp nose that looked so much like mine. It gave me a jolt. It was like my brain was split into two parts, one saying, "Who are you?" and the other one thinking, "*Daddy!*"

"*There she is!*" That was the first thing he said, making it sound like he'd been looking for me or something. He spread his arms out real wide like I was supposed to run smack into him and bury my face in his shoulder and shed tears of happiness. If my tongue hadn't been frozen solid in my mouth I might've told him—"Well, I've been here my whole life, where've you been?" But I didn't say that, because that's one of those things you think of later, along with how smart you'd have sounded if you *had* said it.

Instead I just stuck my hand out like some dumb fool and said, "Nice to meet you." His mouth opened into a huge grin and he laughed too loud.

"Baby Angel, is that any way to greet your daddy who's come all this way to check up on his little girl?"

I just shrugged and looked down at my feet. I noticed that my Weejuns were awfully worn out and thought maybe I should have gotten a new pair for the homecoming, this being such a special occasion and all.

"I hear you been sick!" He was smiling real big and just about shouting at me. I felt a dull ache returning to my head.

"Yes sir, I reckon," I heard myself saying. I looked down at my shoes again, not wanting to meet his gaze anymore.

"Well, you look like a mighty healthy girl to me!" He patted my left shoulder. "Looks like your mama's been taking good care of you. And your grandmother sure ain't goin' to let you go hungry, now is she?"

"No sir." I sounded like a little weak mouse, even to myself. I didn't want to act this way but I didn't know what else to say, how to be with him. Why, oh *why* couldn't I feel anything!

"Aw, come here and give your old daddy a hug, will you?" I stepped forward and he grabbed me with both arms, pulling me into him. He wasn't that much taller than me. I wrapped my arms loosely around him and let my cheek rest on his shoulder, there catching a scent. I guessed it was a man's smell, a sweaty cotton undershirt shirt mixed with the fragrance of some aftershave or cologne that I imagined was called something like "Maverick" or "Musk for Men." I'd seen them in Greer's. If I caught a whiff of anything even vaguely familiar about him, maybe my cold, unfeeling heart would open up and begin to warm.

But nothing happened, nothing that helped me know deep down inside that yes, finally, *this is my daddy*, nothing that is until I pulled away and saw it. Right there, tucked just out of sight so that almost no one would ever know it was there, was a small, almost heart shaped port wine stain... *just like mine!* There it was in the exact same spot, like a brand.

I dropped my eyes down, not wanting him to see me looking at it, not knowing how to take it all in—everything there was in that moment. Naomi announced we were all going into the living room for a glass of cranberry juice before supper. She and Daddy went on in there talking and laughing while Mama and I got the glasses out to serve everyone. She noticed my hands were trembling.

"Are you all right?" she said.

"Just...just a little headache is all."

"Lord knows it must be more than that." She brushed the hair off my face with her fingers. "Say a prayer, just in case there's someone there to hear it."

When I walked into the room, Daddy looked up at me from the sofa as if measuring my height from my legs up.

"Lord a'mighty, Mama, what *have* you been feeding this gal? She looks about half colt if you ask me!"

"She's grown up so fast," Naomi said. I thought I heard a little wobble in her voice, which I knew for sure was more about seeing her son sitting there than anything about me.

I handed Daddy and Naomi their juice. Mama walked in behind me and sat down on the sofa, but not right next to him.

"Get on over here!" he said like he was teasing.

"Oops! Forgot to get the rolls out!" she said and scooted off into the kitchen again.

"God, it's took me a while to get here, hasn't it?" he said, taking a sip of his juice and looking back and forth between Naomi and me. Mama called from the kitchen.

"So Cal, we've all been dying to know. Are you just passing through or what?" Her voice had just the tiniest edge on it and Naomi's eyes went hard in her direction.

"Oh, I reckon I'll be around awhile," he said, loud enough for her to hear him. The phone rang in the hall and I got up to go get it, grateful as could be for the excuse to leave the room. It was Dottie Ames.

"Angel, is that you?"

"Yes ma'am."

"Are you better?" she asked.

"Yes ma'am, much better. I've been up some today."

"Good, but don't push yourself. Is your daddy there yet?"

"Yes ma'am, he just got here."

"Oh my goodness! Well now, isn't that something, after all these years? Well… well, I'll let you go enjoy your daddy now, but I just wanted to ask you, is anybody else there?"

"Why, no," I said. "Just us and Daddy is all. Why? Is somebody else coming that you know of?"

"Who is that?" Naomi called from the other room.

"It's Dottie!"

"Oh, I want to talk to her!" And she was already headed into the kitchen. "Uh, Naomi's coming to get the phone." I had to say it real quick, before I had a chance to hear what she was going to tell me. Then Naomi whipped the receiver out of my hand.

"Our boy is home!" She was practically singing. "Yes, he's right here in the flesh and blood. Praise the Lord! ... Yes ... why, yes! That would be just wonderful! So if you're dropping by anyway why don't you and Doc just stay and have dinner with us? We won't be eating until about two o'clock... Why, that's wonderful! That'd be just fine! Yes, Praise Jesus! Jesus be praised!" Then she hung up and headed back into the living room, leaving me to wonder what was going on with *the plan*.

"That was Dottie, said she was dropping a casserole by tomorrow for our celebration dinner, so I just invited them to stay and eat with us."

"You mean Dottie Ames?" Daddy said. "Doc and Dottie Ames are coming?"

"That's right," Naomi said. "You'll see they haven't changed a bit. They're so thankful you're back home, too. This whole town will be glad to see you, Cal. You've been missed around here."

"Well, if we're having company tomorrow, then I'd better make another batch of rolls tonight." Mama said, still from the kitchen. "Angel, do you feel like you could come and help me get supper on?"

I got up to follow her without even looking over at Daddy. I wasn't feeling so good anymore and had to sit down a minute.

"Take it easy, honey," Mama said. "The last thing you want is for this bug to get you again. It'd be worse than ever. Here, drink a little cranberry juice and just sit there. I'll get the table set." There was a rumbling overhead.

"What was that?" I asked.

"Sounds like we've got us another storm kicking up. Listen to that wind knocking everything around out there. Be cold tonight." I felt a chill, maybe not so much the weather as uneasiness.

"Supper's ready!" Mama called to the others, and suddenly I saw it, all in an instant like a flash of lightning or a shooting star. I had my daddy home.

"Fixed your favorite tonight, Cal," Naomi said when we were all around the table.

"Chicken fried steak? Thank you, Mama! I never yet had any like yours. Nope, the food out there on the rig isn't what I'd call home cooking. This is real good!" Naomi beamed like the harvest moon and practically sang the blessing of the meal, going on and on about the long-awaited return of the son, husband and father. I wasn't listening too much.

"So Angel, baby, tell me something about school," Daddy said once we got to eating. I had to think a minute since I'd been out for days.

"Well, there was a Shakespeare Bee today, and the winner gets to go to Knoxville to Smith's Steakhouse, and I think me and Sophie maybe could have won it but I was sick and missed it."

"Oh... surely you don't mean it... the Shakespeare Bee!"

"You ever heard of it? I hadn't, not before my teacher told us."

"Have I ever *heard* of it?" he said, and then he started.

"*Come, Antony, and young Octavius, come, Revenge yourselves alone on Cassius, For Cassius is aweary of the world...*"

"That's Shakespeare?" I blurted out. "Where's that from?" Suddenly he stood up, pushed the chair back, and raised his arms up like he was on stage.

"*O, I could weep my spirit from mine eyes! There is my dagger, And here my naked breast,*" he said, placing both hands on his heart and letting his head fall, like he was a real actor. Mr. Sams would have liked it.

Mama had her hand up in front of her mouth and was looking back and forth from his face to mine, kind of swallowing a smile. We were all quiet for a few seconds until he lifted an eyebrow towards us as if to see if we were watching. It was funny and I couldn't help but burst out laughing, Mama too, and Naomi was grinning from ear to ear. Then he took a bow.

"Angel honey, you are looking at the very *winner* of the eighth grade annual Shakespeare Bee at Ralph S. Coleman Junior High, some years ago by now, me and my partner Henry Chase, that is."

"Are you kidding me?"

"I wouldn't kid you about that!" He sat back down. "Didn't your mama ever tell you that you had such a smart daddy?"

"I didn't ever even know you were in a Shakespeare Bee," Mama said.

Naomi put her elbow on the table and flipped her fork around to point with it. "Law, hit's true!" she said. "I had plumb forgot about that, been so long ago! He brought home a certificate, probably still stuck away somewhere around here."

"I can't believe it!" I said. "Mr. Sams told us they used to do it years ago but I didn't know it went back *that* far." The three of them had a good laugh at that.

"So what was that you were quoting?" I asked again.

"You tell me, Shakespeare girl!"

"I don't know. We only read *Romeo and Juliet* and *Macbeth*, and I know it's not from either one of those. That's what I've been studying up on for the bee."

"All right, it's from Julius Caesar, Act IV, Scene 3. Now here's one for you. '*Come what come may, Time and the hour runs through the roughest day.*'"

"That's Macbeth."

"Well, listen to that! Looks like she takes after me!" He winked at Mama.

"What are you saying?" She was looking down at her plate but smiling anyway. You could tell she knew he was teasing.

"Actually, I can't take all the credit for you being smart, Angel. Your mama's the brainy one around here. Did you know she's going to be a doctor someday? No doubt the first woman doctor in this whole gosh-darned county."

"Probably too late for that," Mama was still looking down and pushing her food around with her fork, but you could see that she was pleased.

"Now that just ain't so," Daddy said. "If ever there was somebody could get what they want, it's you, Ruth Ellen, and I mean it."

Mama's eyes darted towards him with a shy smile.

"Angel's always done good in school," Naomi said. "I ain't never had to get after her too much about her homework."

"Glad to hear that," Daddy said. "You get a good education and make something of yourself now, y'hear?"

"Yeah, I hear," I said. There was an awkward silence. Seemed to me the good feeling around the Shakespeare Bee coincidence should have lasted longer than that.

"So you been out there all this time…offshore?" Mama asked.

"For the most part," he said. "But I've been laid off from time to time and would have to go find something else. Why, I've picked lettuce and waited tables, done just about everything except shine shoes 'till they'd be hiring offshore again." *So why didn't you come home? They told me you couldn't ever get off work.* That was what I was thinking. He helped himself to another piece of steak. "Then there was Mexico."

"What was in Mexico?" I asked.

"Oh, I was down there for awhile, working on a special project."

"Don't you want some more potatoes and gravy?" Naomi said.

"I'm fine for now, thank you, Mother." Everybody suddenly seemed so stiff.

"So what's been going on in this old town?" he said. "You think maybe they're hiring over there at the chemical plant?" I knew that's where Dennis worked, and I glanced over at Mama to see her reaction. She kept quiet and didn't move a muscle.

"Only one way to find out," Naomi said. "If not, there's lots of places probably need help during the holidays."

"That reminds me. I need to excuse myself for a minute. Got to get something out of my car."

He got up and went out the door, leaving all of us to look at one another and our food. There didn't seem to be much to say.

We went on and ate without talking while his plate sat there and his chicken fried steak got cold. He was gone several minutes when the door opened and here he came back in holding a paper bag with handles.

"Thought I'd never find it." He sat back down at the table and handed each of us a package wrapped in green tissue paper and tied up with red curling ribbon. Mine was small enough to fit right in the palm of my hand.

"Early Christmas," he said with a laugh. I could smell his breath. It was a strong, sweet smell and vaguely familiar. I could tell Mama noticed it too.

"Do we open them now?" I asked.

"Sure do. You go right ahead!"

"Let's get these dishes cleared first and do it when we're having dessert," Naomi said, "...after you've finished your dinner, of course, Cal."

"Thank you, I believe I've had enough," he said. I thought she'd object and insist he eat more, but she just looked at him and then got up. Mama and I jumped up too, right at the same time.

"While you're doing that I'll go get my bag out of the car," he said and left again.

The three of us gave each other more awkward glances. Mama went to wash up the dinner things in the sink and I set out the dessert plates. Naomi put the apple pie on the table and got her good pie server out of the silver drawer.

"Well, don't just *stand* there," she said to me all of a sudden. "Go out there and help your daddy. He might have a lot to carry in."

I didn't want to do it.

"It's raining," I said.

"Well, you ain't made of sugar! Take the umbrella and git out there!" Slowly, I made my way out the door and headed down the driveway, meeting him halfway as he was already coming back in with a small, worn duffle bag in one hand.

He stopped right in front of me and took a long look, like he was searching my face, for what I don't know—and I looked back. There was something different about him out here in the dark without the others around, like a piece had fallen away. I could hardly see him with only the porch light behind me, but even so, there were those eyes, the very eyes I'd been staring at in the photo my whole life, right there in front of me. They were pale and watery and sad and the rain was spilling down his face.

"Oh...here," I said, holding the umbrella out to him and leaving myself standing there to get drenched. He shook his head so I pulled it back, thinking he'd move under it with me but he didn't. The rain started coming down harder.

"Angel..." he said over the noise. The water was splashing all around us now, and all over him. I could hardly hear but it sounded like maybe he had something caught in his throat, maybe a question, so I waited. I wanted to turn and run back in the house but we were both standing in the pouring rain looking at each other, each of us wanting something, it seemed—but I'm not sure what.

"Well, come on—let's get you back in!" he said finally and grabbed my elbow as we both made our way towards the door. I got a whiff of something sweet and strong—and suddenly the spell, or whatever you'd call it, was broken. It was strange to have him touch me. I could feel his grip on my arm even after we got inside and he let go.

We shook the rain off ourselves and I closed up the umbrella.

"I'll just set this right over here and take it upstairs later," he said as he put his bag over in the corner. We both went back to the table.

"All right, then! Merry Christmas!" he said, loud enough for the neighbors to hear. That's when I could tell, now that we were inside and in the light. He'd been drinking.

I eyed him and rubbed my elbow as we set about opening our packages. Mama was keeping her straight face. She got hers open first. It was Chanel #5, her favorite, the very thing I always gave her for Christmas. Only I gave her toilet water, and this was the real perfume.

"Do you still like it like you used to?" he asked.

"Why, yes," she said, keeping her gaze on the bottle. "Thank you. I can use it."

Naomi had stuck her jaw out, which meant something was eating at her. She didn't seem nearly as eager for chit chat as she had been a little while ago. Her gift was a red checked apron that had "Grandma's Kitchen" printed in big letters on the front. She chuckled.

"Well, I reckon I can use this!" she said. "Thank you, Cal! That's real thoughtful."

I was next, but I didn't want to be doing this. The whole scene was feeling like something out of a bad movie.

"Angel, you're looking a little green around the gills," Mama said. "Maybe you should go lie down for a little while. You can come have some dessert later if you feel like it."

"Aw, let her open up her present, Ruth!" Daddy said. I didn't like the edge in his voice. "Go on, now. I want to see how you like it." I tore into it as quick as I could and opened up the small box that was under the wrapping.

I gasped. It was a tiny silver charm in the shape of an angel, the sweetest, prettiest, most delicate thing anybody ever gave me in my whole entire life.

"Thank you," I said, holding it in my palm, looking at it instead of him.

"That's for *my* Angel," he said. "Now how about a kiss for your old daddy?"

I just sat there, not knowing what to say, what to do. But then things changed. I saw his eyes look behind me and turned around to see Marvel, who'd just come through the kitchen door and was making his way right over to the table. Before I had a chance to do anything about it he'd jumped up and knocked over Daddy's cranberry juice. It was dripping off the table onto his lap.

"Dammit to hell!" he said, pushing his chair back and dabbing himself with the napkin. I thought this was a little dramatic, but then Naomi went off like a house afire.

"ANGEL! You *know* that cat's not supposed to be inside! GIT! GIT!" She grabbed her pie server and waved it at poor Marvel like she was going to take his head off. Mama was sitting there with her hand over her mouth, probably hiding a laugh.

"You never did like cats, did you, Cal?" she said. I was beginning to think it was sort of funny too, until what happened next. Instead of running off like you'd expect with all the commotion, Marvel looked up at Daddy, hissing and showing his fangs and arching his back way up like he'd seen the devil himself. I could tell he was afraid, but when I went to pick him up, he hopped off the table and landed on the floor right next to Daddy, who you'd have thought had just been tossed a rattlesnake or something.

"Get the damn thing away from me!" he yelled, jumping up out of his chair. "Get it out of here!"

I'll never forget what he did then. He kicked Marvel! He swung his foot out and *kicked* him!

"Don't DO that!" I ran to grab Marvel but Daddy got hold of him first.

"Stop!" I screamed. "Let him go!" But he headed straight for the door and tossed him out into that terrible night like a sack of trash. I ran past him but Marvel had scooted off somewhere into the darkness and was nowhere in sight. When I came back inside I was crying.

"Calm down, Angel, he didn't do nothing to your old cat!" Naomi said, moving to clean up the mess. "How'd he get in here anyway?"

"I let him in because it's *horrible out there!*" I said, not even caring that she knew I'd disobeyed her.

"You didn't have to kick him, Cal!" That was Mama. She got up and started clearing the dishes off the table. We hadn't even eaten the pie yet, but supper was as over as anything ever could be.

"You cain't hurt an old tom like that." Daddy was brushing off his pants leg.

"Yes, you can!" I said. "You scared him and now he's out there all cold and wet and alone!"

"Well, I'm sorry, baby," Daddy said. "He just startled me is all. Look, now I've got cranberry juice and fur all over myself. Your mama's right. I've never gotten along with cats. He'll be all right. Let's just forget it.... Now where's that little kiss you promised me?"

I just stared at him hard, the tears still on my face. I think he got the message. I would rather have kissed a porcupine.

"I have to go to bed now."

"Yes, Lordy, you do need to go lie down," Mama said. "Look at you, pale as a ghost!"

Naomi put her two cents in. "I been telling her she was up and about too much today, but she wouldn't listen to me."

"Well, go get some rest and feel better tomorrow," Daddy said.

I didn't say anything to any of them, just fled from the kitchen and up the stairs.

Chapter Twenty-Three

$\mathcal{A}$s soon as I got to my room I flung the window open and gave Marvel the cat call.

"*Yum-Yum! Yum-Yum!* Mr. Marvelous, where are you? You can come in now! Don't be afraid, I won't let anybody hurt you anymore, I promise. Come here, kitty!" My throat was thick with a sob that wouldn't break loose, so I hoped he could hear me.

It was awful cold with the window open, so I wrapped myself in a blanket and stretched out on my bed, heartsick and aching, then realized I still had the angel charm in my hand. Now what in the world was I supposed to think—or feel? What I wanted to do was throw it clear out the window, wishing I'd never met that man downstairs. *He* wasn't the daddy I'd always been waiting for, even if he did win the stupid Shakespeare Bee a hundred years ago! He was some drinking, bad-tempered jerk whose coming had changed everything, and if he thought he was going to come here, trying to make up for ignoring me my whole life then mistreat my cat, he had another think coming!

I pulled the blanket even tighter around me and crawled out on the roof to wait for Marvel. It was wet out there, but I didn't care. The wind was still strong but the rain had stopped for the time being and the cold air felt good on my face. It helped clear my mind. I opened my palm and looked at the charm, knowing I wouldn't toss it. As mad and disappointed as I was, and as much as I told myself there was plenty good reason, I couldn't bring myself to hate Daddy.

I'd gotten a few gifts from him over the years, but he'd never been here to hand me something, saying "I hope you like it" and then watch me open it. For all the strangeness of this whole evening, the surprise of the Shakespeare and the shock of his bad temper and his drinking, at least I could hold onto this one thing as a memory of something a real family would do, sit around and open gifts. And it wasn't just any old gift, either. It was an angel, sort of like he had given me the gift of...*me!* And he had, really, even if he was a disaster as a father, leaving us all like that, staying away, breaking our hearts then coming home and making such a scene—he *had* given me my life, had made me Angel. Whatever else there was about him and our story as a family, he was my daddy. And now I'd even seen the birthmark to prove it.

I heard a distant rumble and felt it starting to rain again, so I crawled back inside, my heart aching for Marvel in the worst way. There was no way I was going to close the window on him, in fact, there was no way I was going to leave him outside all night. I decided that after everybody else had gone to bed I'd sneak out and look for him. He wouldn't be too far on a night like this. So I put on an extra sweatshirt and extra thick socks, piled every blanket I had on the bed, and crawled in to wait.

Nights like this I liked to look at the things in my medicine bag, so I slipped my hand under my pillow, took it out from its hiding place, and emptied it right onto the bed. There was the snake skin, which I think has something to do with becoming a woman, the piece of straw from Ray's milkshake that's a memento of my first love, and the acorn from Ida's room.

I didn't know about this one, since she'd wanted me to help her die. Old Susan had said the things that end up in my medicine bag have a special message, just for me. Was the acorn trying to tell me something about death? The room had really gotten cold and I shivered.

The rain was coming down hard now and the wind was blowing it in, but I didn't care. I was just waiting for all of them to go to bed, waiting and thinking and listening to the wind, but I must've fallen asleep because I can't remember anything after that, until I felt somebody sit down on the end of my bed and shake me by the leg.

"Angel? Angel? Wake up, baby, I need to talk to you. Wake up and talk to your daddy, Angel."

I jerked upright and held my covers to my chest. At first I felt confused, didn't know what time it was or what he was doing there. Then I remembered.

"What are you doing in here?" I said.

"Just wanted to talk to you, sweetie. It's been a long time." I could tell by his voice, he was out and out drunk.

"Uh huh," was all I could say.

"Now, you aren't worried about that old tom cat, are you?" he said, looking toward the window."...'cause they're tough, tough as nails. You know? So don't worry about that, y'hear?"

"Yeah, I hear."

"Now I came back here to tell you something, little girl. I wanted to say I'm sorry I had to go away. I'm sorry I couldn't have been around for you when you was little." His words were slurred and he sounded like he might start to cry. "I know it's been hard, but I want you to know, baby, I have always loved you and thought about you, all this time. You are my girl, my only little girl, and I missed you. Whole time I was gone."

Again, I couldn't speak. There were so many things I had wanted to say to him for so long, but right then I couldn't come up with anything, not one word. I just sat and looked at him in the little bit of light that was coming through the window.

His face was in the shadow so I couldn't see his eyes, but I could make out the outline of his body. I had half an urge to reach out and touch his shoulder, just to know what it felt like. Every little girl should know her father's shoulder. I couldn't ever remember resting my head on it, but even so, maybe just touching it now would be something-not enough, but something. But I didn't do it. I just sat there frozen in the dark, staring at him at the foot of my bed.

"I know it's going to take some time, but I really want to make this up to you," he said. I still said nothing. "I don't expect you to like me right away, but do you think you could be just a little bit friendly?"

That was all I could take. "I've been real sick, Daddy, and I have to go to sleep. Could you... could you just please leave?"

"Aw, Angel, baby, don't be like that. Just give me a little kiss, then I'll leave you be."

I saw his face coming towards me in the shadows—

"NO!" I yelled. "Please *don't!*" That's when my closet door opened and somebody stumbled out.

"LEAVE HER ALONE!" It was a voice I knew, but it was out of place. Even in the dark I could see her come upright and raise both hands up in front of her. I jumped out of bed and switched on the light.

"Aunt Patsy!" She had a gun, and she was pointing it right at Daddy! I about had a heart attack

"Jesus, woman! What are you doing?" Daddy said.

"Remember this, Cal?" She was holding her gaze on him and moving the gun up a little higher. "Remember what you told me?"

"Calm down, sister!" He threw both his hands up, but his eyes were darting back and forth from where Patsy was standing to the door.

"You lied to me!" she said.

"Patsy, for God's sake, that was so long ago...we were kids!"

"When Angel was born I told them what you did to me, Cal, and you said, 'By God, Patsy, if you ever say anything like that again I will use this on you.' Well, I said it again—told all of 'em—but you didn't have to use it on me, did you, because they got me out of the way for you, locked me up real tight. That's what I got for saying what I did and if it wasn't for that little girl right there, I'd be wishing you *had* shot me. But I'm still here and long as I am *you will not lay a hand on her.*" She steadied herself, taking aim.

"Now just hold on, woman," he said, bringing his hands down and hanging them on his hips. "Where'd you get the gun?"

"So you couldn't find it when you left it—could you, Cal? I took it! I knew where you hid it, and I put it behind the loose board, right there in my closet. Lord, how I've prayed for this day, prayed for the chance to turn this on you! Lord a'mercy how I've longed for this very day, you lyin' son of a bitch!"

"I hate to tell you, but that thing was never any good to begin with... I wasn't going to shoot you, Patsy, and you know it, and it's not going to go off after all this time, either. Let's just quit all this now, be done with it once and for all," he said, taking a step towards her. "You might as well just hand it over—"

"Step back!" she yelled, and he did. His hands flew back up and then he pleaded with her.

"Now, Patsy, don't you be doing this!" His voice was tight and high. "This isn't right, it just ain't right! You can't ruin it all over again, you—!"

"I'll ruin *you!*" And she lifted the gun even higher.

"Angel, tell her I wasn't hurting you! I would *never* hurt you! I just came in to say goodnight, I promise! Angel, you're my baby girl and I've missed you all this time, missed seeing you grow up and being around for you, and all because of *her!* She's crazy! Please, sweetie, don't let her do this!"

At first I didn't know what was going on. Don't let her do what? But then I got it. The piece that had always been missing from the puzzle of my life was right there in front of me where I could grab it with my mind and snap it right into place. Now I could see the picture, and it wasn't what I'd hoped to see at all.

Not this. This was pure blackness, the pure blackness I'd been seeing all this time in my dreams. My heart froze. My brain was paralyzed. I couldn't imagine what the next minute would be like, much less the minute after that, or the next day and all the days and months and years to come. How was I supposed to just go on now, knowing what I knew? I thought of Gloria James and Maureen, too. This thing wasn't just something for strangers or too-big families in broken-down houses. It was this dark thing that had shadowed my whole life, this unnamed thing that was finally swallowing me up completely.

"Mama!" I called out.

"No, don't—don't wake them up," Daddy said. "I can handle this," and as I saw him glancing down at Patsy's hands holding the gun and shaking, saw him inch towards her like Marvel when he's about to pounce, I screamed.

"NAOMI! MAMA! Come here! Come here QUICK!"

And then he leapt—not at Patsy but right out the bedroom window into the cold wind and rain, scrambling across the porch roof and somehow scampering down that skinny little hemlock tree, making it halfway to the ground before he let go. I ran to look and saw him land on the carpet of wet leaves and roll over, but then he was up on his feet again in no time and across the yard. Patsy came to the window too, still pointing the gun and yelling after him.

"Don't come back again! You stay away Cal because by God I will kill you the next time you come near her!" I believed it. Then she pointed the gun up at the sky and fired. "How's that for an old gun not going off?" About two seconds later we heard the car screeching away.

That's when Naomi came running in, her belly and breasts all a jiggle, still trying to get one arm through the pink nylon robe that had come in a set with her nightie. Then there was Mama in her big tie-dye nightshirt that came to the top of her knees, her thick hair crazy all over her head. I don't know what was the bigger shock, seeing Patsy there with a gun or hearing Daddy's car roar off into the night.

"What's going on here?" Naomi cried.

"He's gone, that's what!" Mama said. I was sure I heard relief in her voice. Then she ran over and just about broke my neck hugging on me. "Honey, are you all right?" I had to pull myself back.

"You KNEW!" I said.

"Now, Angel..." She sounded afraid. I looked straight into her eyes.

"How did you ever look me in the face all those years! How could you ever look at Patsy? How could you share a house and food with his mother? Why didn't you ever tell me anything, all this time and all these questions, and you *knew*?"

"No, honey—you've got to let me explain. It wasn't like—"

"You must've known! You *had* to!" There was such hurt in Mama's face. She just stood there with her arms out towards me, shaking her head while tears ran down her cheeks. I wanted to fall into those arms and cry an ocean, my heart open and broken all at once, but all I could do was stand like a cold statue and glare.

"Okay," she whispered. She dropped her eyes and turned toward Patsy, who was standing there now with her arms limp by her side, head hanging. The gun dropped to the floor just as she sank into my mother's arms, weak as a kitten. Thank God it didn't go off. Mama eased her over onto on my bed and kept holding her as they both sat down.

Naomi was catching on. She sat down beside them, looking at her stepdaughter and stroking her hair with a pudgy hand.

"Patsy, oh Patsy," she said. "Is it true? Oh, my Lord, is this thing true? I didn't believe you, I *couldn't* believe you. Oh, Lord *Jesus*." She closed her eyes and lowered her head for a few seconds. Maybe she was praying. Then she got hold of herself, took a deep breath and looked back up at Patsy.

"Now how in the world did you get here?" she said. "We have to call over there and find out what's going on and—"

There was something going on in the closet, some thumping around, hangers clanging. Then we saw who else was coming out. I heard Naomi gasp.

"Susan!"

"I think I can help y'all explain some of this," she said as she stepped up to Naomi and looked her square in the face. "But first of all let me say I did not know she had that gun!" She was standing there wearing a leather fringe jacket over her purple mumu, with her long pepper gray hair in two braids and a knitted skull cap pulled over her head. Something else clicked together for me right then, another puzzle piece. With Old Susan and Naomi standing side by side I could see the resemblance. Sisters!

Then Patsy murmured something most of them didn't catch in all the commotion, but I heard it clear as a bell.

"Awia."

My friend looked up at me with her biggest grin. Our eyes met.

"That's Cherokee for Black-Eyed Susan," she said.

Chapter Twenty-Four

It was just all too much. If you had asked me what I was doing after that I wouldn't have been able to say. All I knew was that I was running as fast as I could, past all of them standing there, down the stairs and out the front door into the cold, wet dark. It must have started sleeting by then, because the raindrops felt like little stinging needles on my face, but I didn't care. Nothing stung as bad as that stuff that had come at me all at once back there, all of everything I wanted or thought I wanted crashing down on me like a bolt of lightning, flashing a light— way too bright—on all those things I didn't want to see.

I heard them yelling out after me, Mama, Naomi, Old Susan, maybe even Patsy, a scattering of voices like startled geese.

"ANGEL! Come back here! You can't be running out in all this…"

"Angel, honey…DON'T DO THIS! COME BACK!"

"Gonna catch your death if you don't get back in here!"

Catch my death. Well, fine. There wasn't much to keep me here, especially after all this. Now I knew—Mama was a stone-face liar. She might as well have ripped my heart out and stomped on it. All this pain and confusion my whole life about not having my daddy, all those lame explanations—and she just left me on my own to wonder, not even caring if I went insane because of it. Or was Patsy crazy enough to make it all up, which basically means she ruined our whole family forever if she did? She's nuttier than that horrible fruitcake of Dottie's, and Naomi's all confused between Jesus and the queer preacher. And how could she act so righteous and pious all the time while living with this? Even Old Susan led me on, never telling me that she's Naomi's sister. One thing was for sure—if they never cared enough to tell me the truth, then what did they care whether I lived or died? They could holler all they wanted back there. All I knew is I wanted to get away from the whole conniving, scheming, deceiving, shameful bunch of them. My mind was racing away even faster than my legs.

"Aaannnngelllll! Angel! Where are you?"

I was leaving the voices further behind me, headed for the only place I knew to go that would take me away from everybody. I didn't know why I was going or what I was going to do once I got there, but I knew I wanted to be alone—maybe forever.

As long as I was running I was warm enough, but when I turned off the road down into the ravine and started having to pick my way along the creek path, the cold started seeping in.

It was pitiful slow going at first. Branches were whacking me in the face, sticks and dried leaves were getting in my hair, and I was stumbling all over the slippery rocks and sticks and all. I practically had to get down on my hands and knees to feel my way along, but after a few minutes my eyes began to adjust to the dark and I could see just enough to keep moving. My face, hands, and feet were wet and muddy.

When I got to the fort I was glad to find that the old roof had kept most of the rain out. It was still awful damp, but when I took off the top layer of wet leaves it wasn't so bad. I lay down and curled myself up into a tight little ball, thinking only to get warmer, but there was something eerie and familiar about it, something that sent a shudder way down into my bones, into the deepest, innermost part of me.

Then I knew. This was it, this was how I'd seen myself so many times, looking down at my body coiled up all cold and wet and lifeless, just like that poor little pig whose life had ended before it even started, chopped up in some dumb science lab. So I wasn't dead yet, but it looked like I sure was going to be soon, my shivering the only sign of life.

Once I'd stopped moving a mighty weakness set in and I couldn't move at all. I lay there a long time in perfect stillness, surrounded by the pungent, musky smell of wet leaves, feeling the cold on my cheeks, the taste of salty tears on my lips, the night so dark, blacker than black except for the faint shapes of the trees around me. My senses were still alive, but maybe this was my last smell and taste ever. Maybe my last feeling was cold, my last sight pure blackness. What a strange thing— to be witnessing my very own passing.

I wasn't afraid—it was probably all for the best and not so bad, really. I was even starting to feel separate from that shivering girl lying there with her arms all tucked close to her body, and I already felt myself beginning to leave, to float away. It almost seemed like something was pulling me, like it was okay to go, like I *wanted* to go. Why not? I was curious, like a little kid, wanting to see what was waiting on the other side. How long would it take? I thought how nice it would be just to go to sleep and let it all be over, to not have to wait anymore.

To this day I'll never know for sure if it was a dream or what-in-the-world, but the next thing was I started feeling something warm.

When I opened my eyes, I still couldn't see, yet it felt like something was moving towards me, something so big and overpowering I was frightened at first. But then I felt it hovering, like a tender presence, and I wasn't afraid anymore.

The next thing is the most amazing of all. I saw hands—*hands*—reach down out of the night and come so close I thought they were going to touch me, but they didn't. They were reaching for something—something *on* me, something I hadn't even known was there. I looked down and saw a beautiful golden string wrapped around me and tied in the front, keeping my arms curled into my body, and the hands were so silent, so gentle, untying this shining string until it disappeared into thin air, and the hands too, and I felt my arms let go and stretch out, only now I saw they were more than my arms, so powerful and wide they were lifting me up off the ground. Wings!

Just as soon as I was certain I'd died and was for sure leaving this earth was when everything changed—I was jolted awake, and suddenly I was cold again, so cold, and on the ground, not above it anymore. As weak as I was I put my hands on the ground and pushed up, taking a deep breath that felt like I was pulling myself back into my body—and then I knew. I didn't want to die! Everything was swirling around my head and it didn't even matter anymore what all of them had said, or not said, or what they'd done or told me or whatever—I wanted to go home! That was when I heard the most night-piercing, earth-shattering wail I could imagine. And it was coming from me.

"SOMEBODY HELP!"

I stopped. There was no sound other than the whisper of falling sleet.

"HELP! IS ANYBODY THERE?"

Did I hear voices? I wasn't sure, but there was a rustling of leaves getting louder and louder, and a flashlight beam bouncing all around me and yes, the one voice I wanted to hear most in the world.

"Aaangel! Angel!"

"Mama? MAMA! Here I am!"

Then I saw them, Mama in her yellow poncho and Sophie in her red rubber rain boots and trench coat.

"I figured this is where you'd be," was all my best friend said.

Mama fell into the pile of leaves, right on top of me, and about cried her eyes out. There were acorns all over the place.

After everything that happened—Sophie and Mama getting me home, Naomi breaking down in some kind of hysterical fit so they had to get Doc Ames over here to check her out and me too, them making me drink hot broth and telling me how I'd taken such a risk after being so sick and all, saying get straight to bed or they were going to take me to the hospital, Doc telling Mama and Naomi they had to get some rest or he was going to take both of *them* to the hospital—the whole thing about Patsy being there was sort of sidelined. It got so late they just decided she'd stay in the guest room, and Susan stayed with her in case she needed anything in the night. Somewhere in all that Sophie's dad came over to take her home. She gave me a big hug before she left.

"You can't fall apart on me, Angel. I need you," she said. Of course, she was right.

Once things had finally quieted down, Mama made her way in to be with me. I'd been expecting her. I knew she wasn't going to let me be by myself.

"Can I come lie down next to you?" she asked.

"I guess." She crawled over me and grabbed a pillow, squeezing it into her like it was a life raft. I turned onto my back to stare up at the dark ceiling.

"Angel, why in the world do you still have the window open?"

"He's not back yet—Marvel, I mean." I heard her sigh in the dark.

She pulled the blanket up over herself and I knew that was the end of that.

"You scared me, Angel. You scared me bad." I didn't say anything. I'd scared myself, too—and still didn't know what to think.

"If there is a God," she said, "then I sure do need to be asking him for forgiveness, but even before I do that I'm coming to ask you for yours."

"Mama…"

"I know what you must be thinking about all this," she said, "what it must look like to you."

"You lied to me!"

"It's true, I didn't tell you everything."

"Saying Daddy couldn't be with us because he had some big important job he couldn't leave when all the time he was *running*? You don't call that a *lie*?"

"So what do you think I should have told you? It's not something a little girl needs to hear, especially about a father she needs to love, even if he's not around." I didn't know what to say to that, so I kept my mouth shut.

"I'd be mad too if I was in your shoes," she said. "But I'm asking you to hear me out, let me try and explain what it was like being in mine. Can you do that, Angel?"

"Oh, so *now* you'll talk," I said. She gave a big sigh.

"I was so young, and Patsy was…well, as long as I'd known her she was living in her own world, saying all kinds of strange things, and when she started with all of that, it was just so easy not to believe her."

"What *was* she saying?" I asked. Then Mama turned onto her back and we were both looking up at the ceiling. There were dim shadows from the hemlock dancing around like a weird movie.

"I guess I should go back to where this all started, about the time you were born." she said.

My worst fears confirmed—I was the cause of everything!

"That's when it all broke loose," Mama went on, "but it really goes back much further."

"It does?" Maybe I was redeemed after all.

"Yes. I've heard it said many a time that when Naomi married Joe and brought Patsy in, everybody could see that she was an odd little girl. Something about her was just...well, *off*. When I met her she was already a grown woman, but she was different, for sure.

"Then you came along, and Patsy adored you from the first minute she saw you...and not too much time went by before she started speaking out about this... *problem* with Calvin. She started talking about things that had happened when she was young, but she wasn't quite right, you see, never really had been, and it had been such a long time since then, and she'd always said strange things and been so... well, *peculiar*, so nobody paid any attention to her at first—and that includes me, I'm sorry to say."

"So what happened? Did Patsy just keep talking about it?"

"Lord, yes, she kept on and on, saying she wasn't going to let him hurt her baby girl like he'd hurt her. She'd tell it everywhere she went, whenever she could catch somebody's ear, and Calvin all the time trying to deny it. Can you imagine? It was just horrible, and the more we tried to get her to stop, the worse it got. She got to where she'd go into outright screaming fits and get herself so exhausted she'd just about pass out.

"We took her to Doc Ames and he tried to help, but it just got worse and worse, her crying and going on and on about it until we had to take her to a specialist over in Knoxville. That's when they gave her this diagnosis, said there was nothing they could do about it and the best thing was to just put her somewhere she could be watched all the time."

"So you let them shut her away," I said. My heart sank with the heaviness of it, with the sorrow of knowing my part in such a sad, sad story.

"I thought it was the right thing to do at the time. I honestly did, Angel. I hope you can find some way to understand that—but it didn't change anything for us, the damage had been done. Patsy had said it out loud enough that people were talking, and your daddy was feeling the pressure—so after so much of it, he went away. The well was poisoned, so to speak."

"So if he said he didn't do it, why did he leave, Mama? If none of it was true and Patsy was shut away, the talk would have died down. Didn't he even want us to try being a family? What about... well, what about *me*?"

"He was crazy about you! You were his pride and joy. You need to understand that, Angel. Whatever he did—or didn't—he loved you every bit as much as any daddy on this earth. But with all the talk and such we felt we needed another chance. We were going to try and start over somewhere. His leaving wasn't supposed to be for long. He was going to go find something, some place. You and me, we'd stay here in the meantime and go to wherever, when the time came—but it just never did."

"So in all that while—didn't you ever think, not even for one minute, that Patsy might have been telling the truth?"

I heard Mama turn her head towards me. I sat up to face her, even in the dark, wanting to hear every word of what she had to say. My heart was pounding inside my chest so hard it's a wonder my body wasn't bouncing off of the bed. I was finally—*finally* getting answers.

"At first I hoped and waited, wanting to believe none of it was true and we could just go on and start somewhere else, but time just went by and went by, and he drifted further and further off, never hardly getting in touch, always making excuses and such—that's when I really started to think maybe he was running away from the truth. But I didn't want to face it—I was too young and didn't know what to do. All I knew was to stay right here where at least you had your home and your grandmother. With him gone, it was too easy to leave things as they were. But then..." Her arms fell away from the pillow and she put both hands on her forehead, like it was hurting her to think.

"Then what?"

"When that phone call came, when he decided to show up again, it all came back...and after all this time, I suddenly had to ask myself again—*what if he did it?* I hadn't really confronted it in years, hadn't really taken that old rotten thing out of the basement and given it a look."

"But why would you be thinking anything different now than you were all those years ago?"

"Because he stayed away," she said. "The longer he was gone, the more likely the story seemed. But when he left, we didn't have that same need to know what really happened—or not. Life took over and we could just go along and never have to deal with it."

"So what did you think? I mean after the call."

Now Mama was sitting up and facing me. All I could see was her shadow moving while she talked, her hair all messed up and going crazy around her head. It was almost funny.

"I thought I was in quite a pickle, is what I thought. Either way, my life was about to change in a big way, and how was I going to know? Were you getting your daddy back, or were we getting a mighty big problem?"

"Mama, what did you *know*?"

"Angel, I didn't *know* anything—and I still don't. Wondering isn't knowing, not enough to sound the alarm, not enough to jeopardize the family you wanted so bad, or to bring back all that pain of twelve years ago. Patsy is ill, and what if it is all in her mind. Can you see it? Can you see how, with this being what it is, there's no *knowing*?"

I pulled myself up more and sat cross-legged on the bed, the pillow in my lap now. Maybe a little piece of me was beginning to understand.

"But if it was all in her mind, then Daddy's been gone all this time for nothing!"

"If it was all for nothing, then why has he been gone all this time?" There was a long pause.

"Naomi told me something else, years ago," Mama said.

"What?"

"She says Patsy got real jealous when Cal married the first time, that that's when her mind started going really bad."

I looked long and hard at her, thinking and thinking about that little bit of information, what it could have meant if a person wanted to believe it.

"Honestly, Angel, when you look at the whole thing, what else could we have done, and what else can we do now? Besides just go on?"

I didn't know. And I didn't have anything else to say.

Even with all the crazy things I'd learned in the last few hours, even with the questions still unanswered, I now knew the one thing that was going to make the real difference in my life, put an end to an aching deep inside me—I knew Mama wasn't hiding anything from me anymore. We lay there awhile, listening to each other breathe and the sounds of the night all around us, the sleet now a gentle rain, a light wind, an occasional car driving over the wet leaves in the road out front.

I thought about what she said, how if I could have chosen another way through this for her, Naomi, and Patsy, what would it have been? What could they have done differently for me, as a child? I guess Dottie was wise when she said I would learn everything I needed to know when the time was right. What if they'd all just done the best they could?

What if the biggest mystery of my childhood wasn't as much about my daddy as it was about what had been holding Mama and me at arm's length—and now I could see it? Maybe I had some of my own forgiving to do. I felt turned loose, set free by those hands from heaven, a lifetime of wondering let go. Now I could fly.

Chapter Twenty-Five

I woke up in the early light. Mama wasn't in the bed anymore, but there was Marvel pummeling fast and hard on my chest and purring to beat the band.

"You came back!" I said. "Oh, thank goodness you're back!"

I wrapped him up in my arms. His fur was still wet and cold from the outside, and he smelled like the smoky autumn air and moist leaves and dark earth. I tried to get him to go under the covers with me to cuddle but he was too busy rubbing his cheek against mine. He'd been out there in the night, like me, but right now that seemed so long ago, like it had never happened. Maybe I would've been thinking about what it had all meant, or if it had even been real, but he was purring so loud and pummeling my chest so hard it just made me laugh.

That was when Dottie came charging into my room, carrying a cup of tea, as always swooping in to the rescue just like she'd done two days ago.

"Well, look at you—so here we are again! I'm so glad to see you awake. Mercy, child, you've been sleeping like it was your last!"

"I think it almost was," I said, but she didn't realize how much I meant it. Even with all the big mess of everything, I was glad not to be dead, and I made a vow right then and there never to wish it again.

"Oh lord, honey, you poor thing. All y'all have just been through so much right here lately. It's just hard to believe everything y'all have had to endure." Then Dottie paused a minute like she was trying to decide whether or not to say something, but of course she went on and said it, as usual.

"Now honey, you're a smart girl, but what in the *world* were you thinking running off in the night like that?"

"Thinking wasn't much a part of it," I said.

"I suppose you're right, honey, of course—I know what you're saying and…and we just thank the Lord you're okay now, but don't you *ever* go off doing anything like that again, you hear?" Her voice wobbled a little and her eyes looked moist. I nodded.

"So what's going on?" I asked. "Where is everybody?"

"Well, I got here a little while ago. I don't think your mama and Naomi have gotten a bit of rest, they're so torn up about this whole thing. It's all such a shock to begin with—even if it wasn't for worrying about you. I told them I'd look in on you and then help get the dinner going."

"What about Patsy? Is she still here?"

Dottie smiled. "Old Susan's in the kitchen right now getting the turkey and the stuffing ready, and Patsy's down there too."

"Naomi's going to let her stay?"

"She said you wanted her to be here so bad she reckoned it was all right, especially since your daddy…well, things have changed."

"How'd she get here last night?"

"That's what I was calling to tell you about when Naomi took the phone from you yesterday, if you can even remember that far back through all this! Once Patsy heard he was coming yesterday afternoon, she pitched a fit, said she had to be here. I don't know what in the world she told them, or why they thought it was any kind of a good idea, but for some reason Rita and Old Susan were in cahoots about the whole thing. I had no idea they were going to sneak in like that and—oh Lord, I hate to think! Oh Lord, the *gun* and all!"

"I wonder how she knew he was coming yesterday, and how in the world they got in without any of us knowing anything—and them right there in my closet all the while I was getting ready for bed!"

"Lord, have mercy, I'll never know. I will *never* know."

"Miss Dottie, why didn't Naomi or anybody else ever tell me Old Susan was her sister? Why didn't you *ever* tell me?"

"Oh, honey," she said, "Naomi didn't want it. She didn't want the relationship. It was always hard, with Susan so determined to live her life by the old ways. It offended Naomi—such a strict Christian, you know, and she was ashamed of all that folk stuff, said it was all heathen."

"So she stopped speaking to her sister because she wasn't a Christian?"

"Well, no—they weren't ever close, but they did used to see each other from time to time, holidays and such—so Susan got to know Patsy and took an interest in her, seeing as how she'd had such a hard time as a little one. Growing up, Patsy spent a lot of time over at her place across the river."

So Patsy had been like me, visiting Old Susan when things got confusing.

"So how'd it get so bad between them?"

"When Patsy started speaking out about her... and Cal, everybody was trying to shush her up. But it was Susan that said not so fast, you just can't assume she's making it all up."

"Did she believe her?" I said. "She would have known if it was true."

"I think you're right, but even if she had believed her, there was nothing in the world she could've done to help Patsy, especially back then. Her living her ways out in the open like that made her no better than a colored person. Nothing she could have said would have helped in the least. What it would have done is kept Patsy from seeing her. You know, Susan had to endure a lot of taunting through the years. It's only been by laying low and keeping to herself all this time that she's been able to stay over there without too much trouble."

I thought of the boys wanting to torment her back in the summer.

"But anyway," Dottie went on, "Naomi felt betrayed by Susan speaking up for Patsy later on, got mad as a hornet and just cut her off, told her she never wanted anything to do with her again, and not to try and have any contact with Patsy ever again either." She shook her head and sighed, her face just full of sadness for Old Susan.

"But she managed to do it anyway," I said. "Old Susan and Patsy had a secret correspondence."

"Apparently," Dottie said.

"I'm glad Patsy had something—*somebody*—all those years."

We sat in silence for a couple of minutes after that. I needed a chance to try and put it all together, but at the same time I knew I'd have the whole rest of my life with this one. All of a sudden I realized how much there was to do for *this* day.

"So, what are we going to do? Thanks to my brilliant planning," I said, "in just a little while a whole bunch of people are going to show up here with a whole lot of food, saying happy birthday to Naomi and welcome home Calvin Stone Bishop. I didn't plan on his nearly getting murdered by Patsy and escaping into the night."

"Well, now," she said, "you are going to stay right where you are for now and save your strength, because in a few hours, it looks like we're going to celebrate."

"Celebrate *what*, I'd like to know."

"Everything," she said. "There is absolutely everything to celebrate, and don't you forget it." She straightened my covers, felt my forehead, and grabbed my teacup.

"This has gone cold," she said. "I'll bring you some more directly."

"Dottie, I need one more favor."

"What's that, darling?"

"Can you make one more phone call?"

"Sure enough, honey. Who to?"

"I want you to call Mama's friend Dennis," I said. "I don't know the number."

"Don't you worry, honey, I've got it covered!"

All of a sudden there was a big crash coming from the kitchen, followed by more than one scream. Both of us jumped up and headed for the stairs—even with me kind of wobbly on my legs and Dottie with her arthritis, I'd say we got down there in record time. It was a sight to behold, Naomi standing there with a big wooden spoon in her hand, Old Susan kneeling on the floor in front of a broken bowl and a big pile of mashed potatoes, and Patsy sitting at the kitchen table, giggling. It was a hoot. Then they all three looked up at us and just started cracking up!

Mama came tearing down the stairs.

"What's so hilarious?" Then she saw, and by that time I was about to bust with joy, not because the mashed potatoes had spilled but because there we all were, laughing together, which I'm telling you was a miracle if I ever saw one.

$\mathcal{E}$pilogue

$\mathcal{S}$peaking of miracles, that was only the first of many that day. For one—despite the whole world being turned upside down—the Thanksgiving plan turned out just fine, even if there were no mashed potatoes. Most everybody came, bringing all kinds of food and gifts and laughter and goodness of every sort. Genevieve had rallied some and gotten out of the hospital, so even Sophie got to come for a little while. Naomi was surprised by all the fuss over her birthday, especially since it wasn't even December yet, and it helped get her mind off the whole thing about Daddy.

So what was the explanation for his not being there? Well, his plans had changed, we said, which was certainly true. Besides, everybody probably knew the whole story by the time they got there, because Dottie had surely been busy on the telephone.

I think the biggest shock of all had to be when Jenkins showed up—with L.B.! He didn't stay since he was driving up to Kentucky for the holiday and L.B. was helping move some stuff up there. He wanted to come say goodbye because he was going to stay a good while this time.

"Things have come up in the family, so I'm taking a leave from the church until further notice. I just had to stop by and tell y'all the news first and especially to pay my respects to Naomi, a fine lady and a great friend."

Naomi sniffed, tugging at the back of her blouse. "So who's going to take over the pulpit while you're gone?"

"I think the elders have got some good ideas," he said. "But I'm sure you'll keep them straight, Miss Naomi. I will certainly miss your companionship after all of these years and will pray for your continued good health and well-being."

Naomi just beamed when he hugged her goodbye, but later on, after he left, I found her sitting at the kitchen table by herself dabbing her eyes with a napkin.

"Hit's a lot for one day, Angel," she said. "I cain't believe how it's all come about like this, all at once, all this with your daddy and all. It don't feel right, but maybe it's all the Lord's will."

"We'll be all right, Naomi," I said. "Something good will come out of all of it, you'll see."

"Reckon it already has," she said, so quietly I could barely hear it. She opened her fist so I could see she'd been clutching something. I recognized the black leather cord, the same as mine, but instead of a medicine bag hanging on it there was a small cross, woven from narrow leather strips.

"It's nice," I said, "and so is your sister." She sniffed a little and nodded.

"I reckon it's time to try and put the family back together as best as we can, what's left of us anyhow. None of us is getting any younger. That's surely the way the Lord wants it." Then I gave her a hug, and she hugged me back, which got her crying again and almost had me going too. I could see that she'd go right on working hard and praising the Lord and loving Jesus, despite losing her son again after having so much hope. But tears could wait. Today was a celebration, just like Dottie had said.

When Dennis showed, Mama's face lit up like the sun, and the wrinkle in her brow that had been there for weeks just vanished. Looking at her you'd have thought he handed her a diamond ring instead of a box of Goo-Goo Clusters. Patsy sat right there in the big chair in the living room through the whole thing, talking up a storm to anybody who'd give her an ear.

"...and he was a'barkin'!" I heard her saying. I was grateful to those listening to her, just so long as she didn't get going about chasing Cal off with a gun the night before.

And then Ray came, after dinner, just like he'd said. He brought a sweet potato pie and said again he was real sorry he couldn't go to the party. I laughed and said I sure could believe him now about the flu! All of us teenagers went out back after dark and built a bonfire. We took the transistor radio out there and listened to Johnny Dupree's special Turkey Day broadcast.

"Here's to each and every one of my listeners out there tonight ...have a wuuunderful Thanksgiving with family and friends... and remember, now... be grateful each and every day, for all the blessings of this life." His voice was as smooth as gravy.

Then there was Jim Croce. "*If I could save time in a bottle, the first thing that I'd like to do...is to save every day till eternity passes away, just to spend them with you....*" This was the best part of the whole night because I was sharing a blanket with Ray and that was when he reached over and grabbed my hand. I shivered and moved even closer to him because it was getting so cold out there. Everybody was telling each other ghost stories and Hank even told one about a haunted cave. We all about died laughing.

All day long, one miracle after another. So what was the miracle around my losing the dream of my daddy? Well, as I see it, I had the chance to grow a love for him all those years. Even if it was mostly full of pain and longing, I did make a place for him in my heart that will never completely shut down. I will never understand him, but at least I can understand why he was running, and that it wasn't me he was running from. I know this is so, and I have the angel charm to help me remember. And what about Patsy? There's a lot we don't know and never will, but whatever happened—however we all left each other— she's the one who's brought us to here. It's what we have.

I'm thinking about God and what I might say to him about all of this, but maybe I don't have to *say* anything. What if God is just there waiting for you to let him in, like a light that's shining all the time, behind everything we think is real—and it's only through the cracks that we start to see him? Surely there's love now coming through the broken places in our family. Maybe that's how it's supposed to be.

Then there's the picture. The one I've been staring at all this time and holding in my mind has kept me from seeing the bigger one. I'm looking at everything with new eyes.

There's a new photograph now, the one we took that day. We're all on the front steps of the house, starting with Patsy in the very middle with Rita and Old Susan on either side of her and the rest of us all around. Doc Ames is on one end because he was the one setting up the picture and messing with the tripod. He would click it and run around to stand up and smile, waiting for it to snap. It took a while to work right. Sophie was on the other end, leaning into Mama. I gave her the job of holding Marvel in her lap, which she wasn't crazy about but she did it anyway.

I knew right where I needed to be in this picture. I wanted to wrap myself around all of them, all of those friends and family, sisters, brothers, mamas, aunts, sons and daughters and grannies and whatever they all were, so I stood up behind everybody, took a deep breath, and just as it clicked, threw my arms open wide. They named me Angel— and my wings are untied.

Acknowledgements

I'm grateful to so many people who helped and guided me through this process: first of all to my family—Ted, John Christian, Cameron and Mary Emma—who, all being creative souls, understood and supported what I was doing and always had words of wisdom when I needed them; to my parents, who gave me such a wonderful foundation in life and who have been my biggest fans from the beginning; to my friend and editor Renni Browne, who was my wise and patient midwife in the writing of this book, and her assistant Shannon Roberts; to Jill Colgan, whose thoughtful reading of the manuscript and assistance with the audios has been enormously helpful; to Beth Jusino, Christopher Fisher, Pete Garceau, Jane Ryder, Ross Browne, and the whole team at The Editorial Department who rallied around me to make this happen; and to many, many friends and family members along the way who have been encouraging me all of these years, believing with all of their hearts that this day would come—and helping me to believe it too! You know who you are. My love and thanks are immeasurable.

About the Author

Mary E. Kingsley was born and raised in northeastern Tennessee, surrounded by the hills of southern Appalachia. She now lives in Washington, D.C., with her husband, two cats and a dog. When not writing she enjoys spending time with friends and family, yoga, gardening, occasional painting, paper making, and photography. *ANGEL* is her first novel.

Angel: A Reader's Guide

Reading Group Questions and Ideas for Discussion

1) What is unique about what Angel brings to the story as the narrator?

2) Consider the actions and reactions of the adults in Angel's life—particularly Ruth, Naomi, and Patsy—as they deal with the family situation. How might Angel's childhood experience have been shaped for better or for worse had they reacted differently?

3) Think about the major factors affecting this family's story. Which are actual events, and which are assumptions? When are the characters led by fear? In what instances does love become the guiding force?

4) Discuss Patsy and Cal, each as both a culprit and a victim.

5) Angel espouses her own brand of theology. How does she see God? Compare and contrast it to both her mother and her grandmother. Where do their spiritual journeys depart

from one another, and what common ground can they claim by the end of the story?

6) Where does Angel's thinking threaten to take her down the wrong path, and where does her innate wisdom keep her on solid ground?

7) Reflect on the character of Old Susan and her place in the community, taking into account the historical and cultural setting of the story.

8) How is Angel a typical teenager, and how is she not typical at all? Think about how she is growing up compared to your own childhood experience, or to that of girls her age today.

9) Despite the fact that Angel and Sophie are quite different in temperament, they are still very close friends. Discuss their relationship.

10) Each of the major characters demonstrates a measure of wisdom at some point or another, some more than others. Discuss this in terms of Angel, Old Susan, Dottie Ames, Patsy, and Ruth—and even in the less obvious cases of Naomi, Calvin, and Sophie.

11) Near the end of the book, Angel considers that perhaps the biggest mystery of her life wasn't where her father was, but what has been "holding Mama and me at arm's length." What does she mean by this? Consider their relationship over the course of the book, and what it might look like going forward.

12) Where do you think Ruth went on the afternoon of Cal's return? Might it have had anything to do with the events of that night?

13) Given some of the content of Patsy's ramblings, what could the reader glean about her emotional life both as a child and as a young adult?

14) Where, if anywhere, do you see symbolism in the novel? Consider elements such as the ravine, Angel's journey across the river, her red hair, the acorn, her experience with the snake.

15) Consider Angel's immediate reaction to learning the "piece that had always been missing from the puzzle of my life." Given the circumstances, how might the adults in her life have better prepared her for that moment?

16) Discuss death as a thread that runs through the novel. How does Angel grow in her awareness and understanding of it?

17) Discuss the ways hope, redemption, and healing are manifest in this story. Explore how these experiences might affect each of the main characters' lives moving into the future.